ROOKIE MOVE

PLAYING FOR KEEPS, BOOK 1

RILEY HART

NEVE WILDER

SYNOPSIS

McRAE:

I've had a crush on my brother's best friend since the moment I laid eyes on him four years ago.

Warner Ramsey is 225 pounds of sex on a stick, a media darling, and one of the best quarterbacks in the NFL.

Hell, he's the reason I figured out I'm bi.

It was easy to keep my crush under control when I was in college. Now, we play for the same team, and every time he talks smack, I want to shut him up. With my mouth.

But I've got other things I should be focusing on, like dominating my rookie year with the Denver Rush and finally stepping out of my brother's shadow.

Besides, Ramsey's straight.

RAMSEY:

I've never tapped into my bisexuality—never told anyone except my best friend that I'm queer. All I want is to play football and not draw media attention like my dad, who got ousted from the league.

Garrett McRae is my biggest temptation. He's gotten under my skin for years.

I'm supposed to be looking out for him, not thinking about getting him naked.

And definitely not about the kiss we shared.

That I somehow instigated.

It was stupid, and not like me, but God, it was hot.

We're teammates, with million-dollar contracts on the line. And yet...is a little experimentation really so bad?

AUTHORS' NOTE

Rookie Move is set in Denver, CO and uses both fictional and real locations and references. Any football mistakes are our own or aspects of the game/league that we've taken liberties with. While we followed the NFL structure fairly closely, we also created our own team names and, again, took liberties as we saw fit.

PROLOGUE
GARRETT

The foyer of Ty Roberts's mansion had a giant fucking compass embedded in the floor.

"Jesus," I breathed out, staring at the ornate tile and stonework that probably cost more than my life. "Is this thing here so we don't get lost? Is that onyx?"

Houston struggled to shut the equally gigantic mahogany door we'd just walked through. It was twice as tall as him, and he'd had to put actual effort into pushing it open—impressive, considering how much he'd bulked up since being drafted to the Denver Rush last year.

"I think it's semiprecious stone, yeah. Something like that. Damn, Ty needs to oil this thing." Houston planted a palm against the door, gave it a hard push, and it finally shut all the way. Even the creaking of the door settling back into the frame sounded expensive. Good luck to the next person trying to enter. "If you get lost, just stand still, and I'll find you eventually." Houston grinned.

"Think there's a rack of lingerie around here?" That had happened once in a department store when I was a kid. My mom and Houston were trying on shoes, and I'd wandered off. Houston had found me underneath a rack of lacy women's panties and garters, playing with the fasteners.

He chuckled and ruffled my hair. "Maybe. Ty does like his women."

I swatted his hand. "Cut it out with the hair-ruffling shit, okay? I'm an adult now."

"On a technicality. You still have the rest of senior year to go, jackass. And I don't care how old you are. You'll always be my sweet wittle baby bro."

I batted his hand away again when he reached out to pinch my cheek, and Houston's laughter echoed in the cavernous space.

To either side of us, staircases swept up to the second floor, but the action seemed to be ahead of us. Houston ticked his chin toward the sound of voices and the *thump* of a heavy bassline coming from beyond the foyer. "C'mon, let's... *Wait.*" He clapped a big paw on my shoulder and spun me to face him before I could take a step. "We need to cover some ground rules."

"No, we don't." I scowled. "I can take care of myself, and you'd better not lead me around introducing me as your 'baby brother.'" I already knew it was inevitable; he'd do it just to fuck with me the way he always did, and I was just encouraging him by mentioning it in the first place.

"Then behave." He cocked a grin that sobered quickly. "This is Ty we're talking about, so there'll be a lot of alcohol here. A bar. Definitely kegs. Do *not* drink too much and get me in trouble with Mom and Dad."

"I promise," I said solemnly.

Houston narrowed his eyes at the twitch of my lips. "Seriously, Garrett. If you do something stupid like spew on Mom's 'nice' couch again, it'll be your funeral, and they'll never let you come out with me again."

Okay, that was better motivation. We weren't even fully in the party yet, and I already wanted to be invited back to all of them. Actually, fuck that. I wanted to be the one *hosting* shindigs like this in a big mansion someday. And, for the record, I'd only spewed on the couch *a little*. It had come right up with some Resolve, even though the vodka had been mixed with Hawaiian Punch. Grandma Ruth's rug had taken the brunt of that bad decision, and Mom had been looking for an excuse to get rid of it anyway. I no longer drank anything mixed with Hawaiian Punch. My gut revolted at the mere thought. Vodka, eh, that was a little different.

"Yeah, yeah, I'll be good. Swear."

Deciding I sounded sincere enough, Houston checked my shoulder and brushed past me. "Onward, then."

The music and cacophony of voices grew louder as we passed through one archway and then another that led to a sunken living room packed with people. French doors were open to a patio and offered a glimpse of a sparkling pool beyond, lit with LED lights that gradually shifted in color from blue to purple. I almost tripped over my own feet as we descended the steps because I was so preoccupied staring at everything and everyone. "This is crazy."

"Huh?" Houston cast a glance over his shoulder at me, then hooked his elbow through mine. "Oh, crazy, yeah. It's weird how fast I've gotten used to it, but it's a lot, right?"

It was a whole hell of a lot. A lot of people, a lot of music, a lot of booze, a lot of stuff on the walls that even I could recognize as nice art.

I spotted Houston's teammates easily—I'd been watching their games like a hawk since the season started. Beautiful women surrounded them, even the less attractive guys on the team, and I watched as Houston's gaze landed briefly on a few of them before moving on.

As far as I knew, I was the only person Houston had come out to. He'd told me at the beginning of last summer and made me swear not to tell anyone, not even Mom and Dad. He had his reasons, I guessed, though I wasn't clued in on those, but he was my brother, and I loved the hell out of him, so I kept it locked down. As for me, I was still trying to figure my own shit out, but a brunette, cheerleader-looking type standing near one of the doors had just caught my attention.

"Think any of the women here are into younger guys?"

Houston cracked up. "Sure thing. Go tell them you'll be graduating from high school in the spring. Bet they'll be all over that."

"Some women like younger guys. We're full of energy." I waggled my brows.

"You, in particular, are full of shit."

I flipped him off just as one of the wide receivers, Jace, called out Houston's name and elbowed his way through the crowd toward us. "Dude, I still can't believe that catch. Killer."

"Got lucky." Houston grinned back, doing his typical modesty thing that annoyed me to no end. He thumbed toward me. "Brought my brother with me to celebrate. Garrett, Jace. Jace, Garrett."

"Right on." Jace up-nodded me, then proceeded to ignore me in favor of doing a play-by-play of the last quarter of yesterday's game. It'd been a huge win for the Rush, putting them one step closer to the playoffs, and Houston had scored the touchdown that had turned the game around after an iffy start. Not bad for a rookie.

My attention wandered, circulating over the crowd and

eventually back to the hot brunette, who was now shim-
mying against either her girlfriend or a friend. I was hoping
for the latter. But if I was gonna approach her, I needed
some liquid courage, so I signaled to Houston that I was
heading out the door.

He fired back with an eyes-on-you gesture I waved off
as I passed through the doors and into the biting
November chill. This was just like any of the high school
parties I'd been to, I told myself at the sudden self-
consciousness that twinged in my gut as I moved through
throngs of strangers. Just twenty times fancier and with
people who collectively earned the GDP of a small country.
No big deal.

Steam rose from the pool, where, despite the tempera-
ture outside, a few brave or incredibly drunk folks took
advantage of it being heated. A line of kegs stood sentinel
near the deep end, and I managed to locate a stack of Solo
cups. As I finished filling one, I glanced up and found
myself staring into the rugged features of Ty Roberts.

I fought not to get flustered all over again, trying for cool
as I dropped the tap. "Awesome party. I dig the compass."
That counted as polite conversation, didn't it? Fuck if I knew.
The party I'd been at last weekend with all my football
teammates had involved a game of Never Have I Ever that
ended up with Darrell Arrowood hurling into a bonfire and
swearing the amount of liquor in his vomit had made the
flames go higher.

Ty's gaze flicked over me impassively. "Thanks. And you
are?"

"Garrett McRae." When Ty's gaze narrowed, I tacked on,
"Houston's little brother."

Fuck me, I'd done that to myself. But the change in Ty's
demeanor was instantaneous. His lips split in a wide,

perfectly aligned white grin. "Aw, hell yeah, man. Welcome. So do you play ball too?"

It was almost always the second question I got asked anytime I introduced myself as Houston's brother. It had trailed me through the last decade, and in a roundabout way was what had gotten me into the game in the first place. Houston had shown promise the second Dad had signed him up for peewee football, while I'd initially preferred track and field. Then I hit puberty, and it became clear that my build was changing. I went out for football freshman year of high school on a total lark, just to see what happened, since people were always asking me anyway. I'd never expected to end up loving the sport as much as I did, or be as good at it.

"I play, yeah. I'll be starting at Silver Ridge U next fall."

"Runs in the family, huh?" Ty blew some foam from his cup. "Make yourself at home. Did Houston explain everything?"

"Everything like...?" Damn, was there something I was supposed to know about partying with pro footballers that Houston hadn't filled me in on?

"I mean the password."

"The—"

Ty broke into a laugh and socked me hard on the shoulder. "I'm fucking with you. No password. I mean, did he tell you there's a shit ton of food in the kitchen? Full bar inside. All that shit. Bedrooms are open if you need them"—he waggled his brows—"and if a door's locked, it's locked for a reason. Don't mess with it. Other than that, have fun, man. Go find some trouble."

As soon as Ty swaggered off, I meandered through the crowd, still more or less invisible. I scoped out the living area for the brunette. She wasn't by the doors anymore, but I thought I caught a glimpse of her head near the stairs. I made my way in that direction, trying to figure out an opening line.

But when I got to the stairs, she wasn't there either. Houston stood surrounded by his teammates and, not wanting to be a clinger attached to his elbow, I decided I'd take Ty's advice and see if I could find some trouble. Or at least do something besides standing around by myself.

I walked down one hallway and found a den, a library, a bathroom, two bedrooms, and a locked door someone hollered at me through when I jiggled the handle.

Retracing my steps, I went down the other hallway and found much the same until I got near the end and discovered a door offset in a small alcove, slightly different than the other ones I'd passed. I listened at the door for signs of anyone getting busy before reaching out and twisting the knob.

"Halt!"

At the stern command, I snatched my hand back from the doorknob and craned a look over my shoulder. Did Ty have in-house security? That wouldn't surprise me.

But it wasn't a security guard.

I recognized him instantly. It was impossible not to, considering how often I saw him on the TV screen. Warner Ramsey was the Rush's quarterback, and an undeniably great one. Also, my brother's best friend. They'd connected during training camp, I gathered, from how often Houston talked about him. So often, in fact, that I'd wondered whether they had something going on. Subsequent stories negated that idea, though. But seeing him in person for the first time got me curious all over again. Because another undeniable thing about him was that he was even hotter in person. Tall, leanly built, with a stubbled square jaw, dark hair, and the kind of blue eyes that could pierce you even from the far end of a hallway. Which they were definitely doing now.

"Bathrooms are the other way," he said as he approached, a Solo cup in one hand and a loose, half-smile on his lips.

My pulse thrummed against the sides of my neck. "I know. I just passed it. I'm not looking for the bathroom."

"I know you." Ramsey's gaze turned appraising, heat moving through me as his eyes tracked over me. "You're Garrett. The baby brother."

The "baby" part rankled and, as if he could tell, Ramsey's eyes took on a mischievous twinkle.

"You're Warner Ramsey, the guy with two last names," I fired back, cocking a brow. I'd only ever heard Houston refer to him as Rams or Ramsey, though.

Ramsey's lips split into a musing grin. "My parents couldn't decide on a first name, so they stuck my mom's maiden name on the front and called it done." He ticked his chin toward the door. "So if you're not looking for the bathroom, you're snooping? That a habit of yours?"

Damn, he was as bad as my brother, except his teasing had a different effect on me. A bolt of awareness shot through my blood and sizzled through my gut as I met the arctic blue of his eyes. The rare sensation put me on edge as much as it intrigued me. Dragging my gaze away, I set my jaw and shrugged. "Ty said I could look around, so that's what I'm doing." I gestured expansively. "Envisioning my future."

"Ambitious of you." Ramsey rested his shoulder against the doorway, so close I could feel his body heat and catch a whiff of his laundry detergent mixed with a tinge of peppermint. He didn't seem to notice the closeness but, once again, it moved through my core like a current, unsettling me. "All right, then, Snoopy, let's see what's behind door number"—he glanced around pointedly—"five hundred and three?"

"Five hundred and five, I think." I ignored the "Snoopy," not wanting to give him any more leverage. "You forgot that linen closet back there."

"Ahh, my bad."

"This one's locked, anyway."

"Is it?" That enigmatic smile ghosted over Ramsey's lips once more. He reached a hand to the top of the doorframe and produced a key, which he handed me. "Go ahead."

"Ty said not to go into any locked rooms."

"Ty told *you* not to go into any locked rooms," Ramsey countered. "He won't care if I show you."

"Show me...?"

Ramsey shrugged lazily. "I dunno. Guess you're gonna have to unlock the door."

Turning the key over in my hand, I chuckled. "Now it's all built up. It's gonna be disappointing, isn't it?" A laundry room? Or else, maybe I was about to walk in on some *Eyes Wide Shut*-style orgy that would blow my mind.

He tilted his head, his smile both infectious and a little annoying, like he saw me as an amusing kid brother. "I doubt that. Open it and see."

I fitted the key in the lock, turned it, and pushed the door open. Ramsey reached around me and flipped the light switches.

"Damn," I exhaled reverently. I was so distracted staring that by the time I registered the goose bumps from the brush of Ramsey's forearm across my chest, he'd already swept past me into what appeared to be a giant shrine to Ty's impressive career.

A wall of flat-screen TVs faced the longest, plushest

couch I'd ever seen. Framed posters and prints of promo pieces the marketing team put together for each player over the years decorated the other walls. A ton of cardboard cutouts of Ty in various poses were scattered around the room, and trophies were displayed on underlit glass shelves along with other memorabilia.

"Way better than an orgy," I muttered.

"Hm?"

"Nothing." I walked along one wall of posters, eyeing them, acutely aware of Ramsey's gaze on me as he sipped his beer. "Guess this is something to look forward to," I joked. "Does every career pro get one, or do you have to win a certain number of Super Bowls first?"

My brother sure didn't have anything like this, but he was only in his rookie season. What he did have was a sweet new pad in downtown Denver, and more disposable income than my parents, that would only grow the longer he played. He'd recently bought them a new SUV to replace the old Highlander my mom had driven since we were kids.

"I think the main requirement is being full of yourself." Ramsey's look was a little too pointed, in my opinion.

I snorted. I wasn't full of myself, but I was ambitious, that was for damn sure. I'd been running around the edges of Houston's shadow for years, and even though we were close, I wanted to stand in my own light, wanted a piece of my own success. I'd known that for a long time. College ball was going to be my gateway.

I twisted around to look at Ramsey, that odd sensation moving through me and speeding up my pulse again. "I'll be in the starting lineup at Silver Ridge U come fall. That's not being full of myself; it's just the way it is. Self-awareness and shit."

Ramsey seesawed his hand. "Houston showed me some

tape of your games. You're decent. College will hone those rough edges, as long as you keep your focus. Word to the wise, though, it's easy to lose focus the first couple of years."

I wondered if he was speaking from experience or basing it on something Houston had said about me. I couldn't deny I got a little wild sometimes. But I knew how to focus. "I know what you're doing."

"Kinda my job to bust your balls and keep you honest when your brother's not around to do it." He winked, and I turned away, sucking in a breath as I stared mindlessly at a team poster. There was Ty, posing with a football and his shit-eating grin, my brother on one end; Ramsey kneeling in the middle, not with a full-on smile like some of the other guys, but with a knowing half-smile, and...why the hell was I creating my own catalog of Ramsey's fucking smiles?

My gaze dropped lower, to the football tights stretched over his well-defined quads, the bulge in his groin, and...*goddammit*. The back of my neck prickled as blood rushed to my cock.

"Hey, space cadet, you done envisioning your future yet?"

I whirled around and rubbed the stubble on my cheeks, still hot beneath my hands. "Yeah, think I've got it firmly cemented in place." And that was where I needed to keep my focus, like Ramsey had said, rather than the firmness in my pants. "I need to grab another drink."

I headed into the hallway, and Ramsey switched the lights off and locked the door behind us. "I think there's some juice in the fridge, Little Man."

"You got a sippy cup I can borrow? I left mine at home." When I flipped him off, Ramsey threw back his head and laughed, the sound rich and warm, and...God, why couldn't I be a pro already instead of some dumbass high schooler?

"There you are!"

We both swiveled at the same time. The hot brunette I'd been eyeing earlier toddled toward us, drink in hand, her expression going all heart-eyed as she got closer, and Ramsey extended his arm to pull her into his side. He brushed a kiss over her forehead before angling the bottom of his cup toward me. "This is Houston's brother, Garrett. He's a starting wide receiver at Silver Ridge U. Garrett, this is Ashley, my girlfriend."

He got points for not using "baby brother," but the hollowness in my chest expanded. Of course they were together. They looked fucking perfect.

"Aww, aren't you a cutie. I'll bet the girls are gonna eat you up. You've got that Chris Evans thing going on." She smiled conspiratorially at me, and even though she was paying me a compliment, with Ramsey standing there, it just made me all the more self-conscious of my age. Me and self-conscious didn't go well together.

"With any luck, we'll see, yeah." I pasted on a grin, ready to get the hell away from their love connection.

"C'mon, more drinks," Ramsey said, draping his other arm around me. If I hadn't been so on edge, I might've liked the familiarity as much as I liked the warm scent of him.

———

HOUSTON FOUND ME IN THE KITCHEN A HALF HOUR LATER, a plate piled high with ribs in my hand. "You ready to head out soon?"

"Already? For real?" I sucked sauce from my fingers. Maybe the socializing part had been a bust, but the food was fucking delicious.

Houston shrugged. "Yeah, I'm beat, and I don't want to keep you out too late anyway."

It was only ten, but the guy did look exhausted. "Yeah, sure. Hey, is it true that Ramsey's parents just mashed two last names together?"

"What?" Houston cracked up. "No. He was just fucking with you."

"Dipshit."

"Nah, he's cool. He's spending Christmas with us, you know?"

Fuck my life. "Great, I can't wait," I deadpanned, ignoring the thrill that spread through my chest and died a quick death as I thought of something else. "Is he bringing his girlfriend?"

Houston shrugged. "I doubt it." He glanced at his phone, then reached out and took the plate from my hands. "Uber's here. Let's jet."

"I'm taking this with me, dammit." I snatched back the plate and followed him out.

I'd learned two things tonight. One: these were my people. Or at least, I *wanted* them to be, and I was hell-bent on spending the next four years getting there. And two: I was most definitely bi.

1

RAMSEY

Four years later

"Come on, man. You got this. Three more," I told Houston, standing in front of him while he worked on the leg-press machine in my home gym. He was still able to exercise at the Rush facility, but it wasn't something he liked to do very often. I was pretty sure it wasn't something he liked to do at all, but sometimes he faked it well. In the beginning, when he was cleared to train after the knee injury that ended his career, I used to ask him to meet me at our training facility, thinking it would be good for him, that he'd like to feel as if he was still part of the team.

In some ways, I figured he wanted that, but in others, I was positive it was the last thing on his mind. That made sense, given the conflicting feelings he must have had swimming around inside him—loving football, but angry at losing it. So I'd stopped asking, but some of the other guys hadn't, and Houston would go because that was the kind of guy he was. The fucker always thought about other people first.

"Goddammit." He grimaced, pushing one more time before slowly letting off. He was still building strength—the weight a quarter of what he could have managed before. Sweat made his brown hair curl slightly against his forehead. Houston's hair was a shade or two lighter than Garrett's, but the way their grins kicked up, a little higher on one side, and the rumbling sound of their laughter, made it clear they were related. They were similar, yet not. Houston was humble while Garrett wanted the whole fucking world to know how great he was. He wasn't wrong either, the little bastard. At least when it came to football. Some people thought he'd eventually be even better than Houston, if only because my best friend's career was cut short.

"You good?" I asked when he picked up a towel and wiped his face.

"You better not be talking about my knee." That was one of their similarities. Neither wanted to appear weak.

I'd gotten to know the family pretty well over the years. Not Garrett quite as much as the rest since he'd been away at college, but he'd spent his summers at home in Denver, and I tended to end up with the McRaes most of the important holidays. The cocky little shit was one step away from making all the dreams he'd told me about the first time we'd met come true. He'd killed it in the combine. The draft started tonight, and Garrett was expected to go in the first round, just like Houston and I had.

"You're the only person I know who'd rather talk about something emotional over physical," I finally replied.

"I wouldn't. I'd rather not talk about any of it, but I know you. You're real good at questions and won't stop until you get answers, but you also don't like to provide many about yourself. It's annoying as shit."

"I'm a complicated man. What can I say?" I winked.

When he sighed, I added, "You know, it's okay to be feeling a whole lot of complex shit right now."

"Tell me more, Dr. Ramsey."

"Wow, this is serious. You're bringing out the sarcasm."

Houston stood. "Ha-ha. I'm always sarcastic. Pay attention, and you might learn something."

I was grateful as hell to have been traded to the Rush my rookie season and become friends with him. Houston and I hit it off right away. Growing up, I'd always wondered what it would be like to have a brother, if for no other reason than to help shoulder some of Dad's drama, but nope, all that motherfucker's shit had been heaped on me. It was better that way, I guessed. I wouldn't wish growing up with Mike Ramsey on my worst enemy. Maybe that was being a little dramatic, but it was true.

"So, are we going to talk about the fact that your little brother has entered the draft and will live out the life you thought was yours?"

Luckily, Houston barked out a laugh like I hoped he would. He wouldn't want to be coddled. "You forgot to add that I'm happy for him, while also being jealous as fuck and scared out of my goddamned mind. He's not like you and me. He's not careful. He doesn't think shit through. He's balls-to-the-wall in everything he does, and I don't want it to get him in trouble."

I understood what he meant. I'd seen it in Garrett's eyes that night at the party when he'd walked around Ty's "shrine." Garrett wanted that. He'd do anything to be the best. While I admired that, I knew that the league would knock him down a few pegs, and he needed it too. It wasn't all a good time. The NFL was hard as shit, and not everyone could deal with it. My father hadn't been able to.

"It doesn't matter how careful you are. This is football, man. You did everything right and—"

"I still ended up with a fucked-up leg?" He chuckled humorlessly.

"Not the words I would have used, but they work."

"That's what makes it even worse with Baby G."

I laughed. "That's maybe the best nickname I've ever heard for him. Did you just come up with it? I haven't heard you use it before. I might have to steal it." I liked getting under Garrett's skin. The problem was, he liked getting under mine too, and he was good as hell at it. I hadn't figured out what to make of him yet, even after four years. He rattled me, and I didn't rattle easily. There was something strangely compelling about him, and I wanted to figure him out even though I didn't typically care to do the same with others. I sure as shit would never tell him that, though.

"He'll kill both you and me."

"Yeah, but it'll be a good way to go, knowing we tortured him until the end." We shared another laugh before Houston sobered.

"I don't want him to get himself in trouble."

And we all knew trouble was easy to find—money, power, sex, people praising the shit out of you. It went to people's heads. It had happened before, and it would happen again. My chest tightened with that thought, but I shoved it away. "He'll be all right," I said because that's just what you did. I wasn't sure Garrett was any more of a loose cannon than a lot of guys that made it to the league. We were football players. Being a bit wild often came with big dreams and bigger egos. But I thought the hunger for greatness burned a little brighter in Baby G—fuck, I was so calling him that.

"Yeah, you're right. I'm just all up in my head." Houston nudged me. "Also, Mom wants you to come over for the draft. She said family, and for the last few years, that includes your dumb ass."

I grinned, not just because of what he'd said about family, but because being there would give me a chance to bust Garrett's balls. After my two favorite *F*'s—fucking and football—there was almost nothing I liked more.

"Bet. I don't have anything else going on tonight."

"What about Alyssa?" Houston asked.

"Oh fuck. Don't remind me. I need to stay away from women whose names start with *A*. They always end up going a little crazy on me."

Ashley had been first. I'd thought she was great—sexy as fuck, loved football, and was a good time, but she'd literally stalked my ass. When I'd stayed at her place one night, I'd gotten something from the fridge, and when I closed it, an envelope had slid off from on top of it. Photos of me fell out —leaving the stadium, getting home, out to lunch with Houston, of me asleep in my goddamned bed. Yes, I'd known she was there when those were taken, but who in the hell took pictures of someone when they were sleeping?

Alyssa was my second *A*, and while she hadn't been as bad as Ashley, we'd only been fucking for a month when she asked me to marry her, ring and all. It was ballsy as hell, and I wasn't the kind of guy to balk at a woman doing her thing like that, but I sure as shit wasn't ready to get put on lockdown by someone I'd only chilled with a handful of times. It had become a bit of a joke. I hadn't had the same issue with other women I'd dated, just the two *A*'s.

"Maybe there's something wrong with you, and *you* drive them that way."

"Nah, it's just because they know they're never gonna get

the *D* as good as they do from The Ramsinator." I grabbed my dick for extra emphasis, making Houston burst out laughing.

"Never use that term in my presence again."

It was what they'd called me in some online article talking about my game on and off the field. "If the shoe fits," I joked. It was ridiculous as hell, and there wasn't a part of me that wanted to be known as The Ramsinator, but it made for a good laugh.

"Shut the hell up," he teased, then asked, "you been with a guy yet?"

Houston was the only person who knew I was bisexual. I mean, I assumed I was since I found men fucking hot. I hadn't actually hooked up with a dude yet. I'd thought about it in college but chickened out. Now time kept going by, and I continued making excuses, but then I thought about all the hoopla that would go with it—the questions, the media, attention away from my game—and that was always when I shoved my desire even deeper into the closet. "Nope."

"You're missing out." Houston waggled his brows at me. "I'd offer, but you're like a brother to me, so that's kinda gross."

"You're kinda gross," I tossed back with the maturity of a twelve-year-old. Houston was my boy. I loved him like crazy, but I could never see him in a sexual way. I agreed with him. It *would* be like fucking around with my brother.

"Anyway, I'm out. I'll see you tonight at my parents' house at six."

My gym was downstairs, in my finished basement. I walked up to the main level with Houston, where we bumped fists. "You know your way out. I need to go shower. I stink."

"Not any worse than you always do," he taunted as he headed through the living room toward the foyer.

This was the nicest place I'd ever lived in, though not completely my style—I didn't really need four bedrooms, six bathrooms, and four thousand square feet of space. But I was good with my money, made responsible decisions and shit like that, so my house was one thing I'd splurged on. In the grand scheme of things, it was nothing compared to some of the other guys'. I wasn't flashy, but I wanted trails, lots of green space, and to be a little out of the city. Cedar Grove was the perfect neighborhood for that.

When I heard the door close, I jogged upstairs to my room. I turned on the dual showerheads, stripped, and got in. Jerking off was high on my to-do list, and the way I figured things, keeping it just me and my hand for a while would do me some good. The less drama the better.

After I blew my load on the black-and-gray granite wall, I cleaned up, washed my hair, and got out. I fucked around the house for a couple of hours before heading out to my SUV to make the drive to the McRaes'.

One of my favorite things about them was how down-to-earth they were. Houston's parents had let him buy them a vehicle when he was signed to the Rush, but that was about it. They still lived in Denver, in the same house where he and Garrett had been raised—a two-story in an older neighborhood filled with middle-class families and manicured lawns. They fit there, and I liked that they did.

My father had blown his NFL career in just a few years —not from an injury he couldn't prevent, like Houston, but with bad decisions, a bad attitude, and a coke habit. He still tried to live a life he couldn't afford. I tried to minimize my contact with him. I was just starting to get to the point where people didn't mention my father in interviews, but he never stayed away for long. He didn't understand bound-aries. It was all about what he wanted and when he wanted it, and when it came to me, what he normally wanted was cash. He'd show up whenever he got a hair up his ass to try and get it too.

My hands tightened on the steering wheel, my muscles tense, the way they always got when I thought about him. He was the last person I wanted on my mind, so instead, I daydreamed about Ms. McRae's meatloaf, which was *to fucking die for*, and the look on Garrett's face if I alternated between calling him Little Man and Baby G. He was gonna be pissed, and I'd love the shit out of it.

I pulled into their driveway to see Houston's car was already there. I parked and headed for the porch, and just as I hit the top step, the door opened. I grinned when I saw Garrett standing there. "What's up, Little Man?"

He rolled his melted-chocolate eyes that matched his hair. He appeared to have put on a few pounds of muscle since I'd seen him last. He was tall and broad, with a runner's body that was big enough to knock the shit out of other players when needed. He looked like the boy next door, almost innocent, though I knew that wasn't the case. But his features were soft, and he had thick, dark lashes and a Captain America grin...

"That's *Mr.* Little Man, a.k.a. future Super Bowl ring winner to you. Wait...you don't have one of those, do you? I didn't think so."

I made sure his mom wasn't within eye shot and flipped him off. "Getting a little ahead of yourself, aren't you?"

"No."

"You don't even know where you'll land."

"I don't need to. I'm there, we win. We can head out back if you want some pointers."

"Aw, so cute. Baby G thinks he's better than me."

I reached out to pinch his cheek, and he swatted my hand away. He turned just as Houston walked up behind him. "Goddammit, bro. Why'd you tell him that dumbass name?"

Houston shrugged. "I'm your big brother. He's my best friend. It's in the job description to give you shit."

Shaking his head, Garrett walked away, and I'm not proud to admit, I watched him go. He had a great ass, tight and round—and definitely not what I should be thinking about. Even though my bisexuality was uncharted territory, if I weren't closeted and Garrett wasn't Houston's sibling, I'd definitely explore every inch of his body.

"What is it about Garrett that brings out that behavior in you? You always enjoy giving people shit, but it's even worse with him."

"I don't know." But he was right. I closed the door and followed Houston inside.

"Hi, Warner! You look sleepy. Are you getting enough rest?" Ms. McRae asked. She was one of the only people in the world who actually called me Warner—well, that I allowed to call me Warner, at least. The only others paid my salary so, ya know, I let them get away with it.

She was over a foot shorter than me, with dark hair, glasses, and reminded me of all the perfect moms on TV shows I'd watched as a kid.

"*Are you getting enough rest?*" Garrett mocked, but I ignored him. I was the perfect angel around their mom.

"Yes, ma'am." I walked over and gave her a kiss on the cheek. "Thanks for inviting me."

"You know you're always welcome here. And how many times have I told you to call me Connie?" She turned to Garrett. "Stop being a butthead."

I bit back my laugh as Houston said, "Yeah, stop being a butthead."

"What's everyone thinking?" their dad, Dale, interrupted as he came downstairs. He looked nervous in a way I didn't typically see him. He was tall like Garrett and Houston, but his hair was lighter and nowadays streaked with gray.

"Dad's freaking out," Houston said.

"You weren't this stressed about Houston getting drafted," Garrett said, the words playful, but he turned in a way that caught my attention. Like maybe he didn't want anyone to see he was upset.

"We're not worried about you getting drafted, dear," Connie said. "We know you're going to a team."

But they did worry about him. That much was clear.

"San Francisco needs a strong wide receiver," I told them. "They have a fairly high pick too. They might want to build their defense, but their offense has been pretty lacking the past two years, so if their main priority is the O, I can see them grabbing Garrett."

"I'd love to go to San Fran. It's a fun city, and I think me and Travers could rip shit up together," Garrett said, mentioning their quarterback.

"Who cares if it's a fun city?" Houston asked.

"Me. I mean, a boring city isn't going to make me turn someone down. I'll go wherever I can play football, but there's nothing wrong with hoping for certain places over others."

"Just make sure football is your first priority," Connie said.

"When has football not been my first priority?" Garrett's brows pinched together, the frustration evident on his face. The thick tension in the air wasn't typical of their family, so I was surprised by it today. The draft was stressful, though.

This was the beginning of Garrett's career. When you combined that with Houston's injury making him lose his, it made sense.

"Is everyone going to ignore the fact that *we* need a wide receiver?" Houston asked, and the room went quiet. I was pretty sure everyone did plan on ignoring that fact, because who wanted to think about the Rush replacing Houston with his little brother?

"Let's eat. I think we should eat," Connie said, breaking the silence.

"I've been craving your cooking ever since Houston invited me over," I told her.

That was that, and the Rush conversation was dropped when everyone headed toward the kitchen.

Except me and Garrett.

He shook his head, then ran a hand through his hair and sighed. The moment wasn't meant for anyone but himself. He hadn't been looking at me, so he didn't know I'd seen. A second later he had a smile so wide plastered on his face, I thought maybe I'd imagined him being upset.

Then he turned my way, stared at me, and winked. "What you looking at, handsome?"

I rolled my eyes. He was just the same ole Garrett as always. "Aw, you have a crush on me, don't you? I'm a little old for you anyway."

"Plus, you don't like guys." Aaaand, that's what he thought. "Eh, I'm out of your league anyway."

"You wish, Little Man."

"Not so little." He nodded toward his dick.

"That's not what I heard."

An expression I couldn't read flared in his eyes, but then Houston stuck his head around the corner. "You guys coming or what?"

"You're such a dork," Garrett told him, stepping away from me.

"I get it from you." Houston grabbed Garrett, wrapping an arm around his neck and pulling him into a headlock, the two of them wrestling around before heading into the kitchen. I grinned, watching them go, wishing Garrett had had time to offer me a comeback.

2

GARRETT

I was starting to wish I'd just stayed back in Silver Ridge for the draft announcement. I could've hung out at the frat house with my friends, or we could've gone to a bar or, hell, I could've accepted the football commissioner's offer to be flown to New York—which I'd not told anyone about. Any of those options would've been better than weathering the weird tension that kept popping up intermittently like a sudden rain shower on what should technically be one of the happiest days of my life.

The even stranger thing was, I wasn't the only source. The main one, sure; I had four years of all-out, ball-busting effort on the line. But Mom, Dad, and Houston seemed in on it too. In fact, the only one not contributing was Ramsey, though I could tell he was aware of it.

Wishing I'd stayed in Silver Ridge made me feel like an ungrateful little shit when my family had done nothing but be supportive, so I resolved to fight through it. The past year had been rough, due to Houston's injury. Maybe everyone would settle down once we all knew where I'd be going.

"Let go, jerk." I wrestled free of Houston's headlock as he

cackled, then claimed my usual chair at the dining table as Mom set serving dishes of meatloaf, vegetables, and mashed potatoes on the table—all my faves.

Sneaking a sidelong glance at Ramsey as he unfolded his napkin and laid it over his lap, I offered him a sweet smile. "Sure you want to roll the dice like that? Maybe you should just go ahead and tuck it in your collar like a bib." The last time I'd seen him had been over Christmas break, during a New Year's Eve party at Houston's loft. Ramsey had been wearing a white button-down, and even though he'd looked fine as hell in it, with the sleeves rolled up and a flash of skin where he'd left the topmost button undone, by now he should've known better than to wear white anywhere in the vicinity of football players, alcohol, and ribs.

"That wasn't my fault. It was Jace's clumsy ass. At least I wasn't walking around the whole night with my fly down."

Houston snorted softly. Mom ducked her head and smiled. Dad cracked a beer, while I wished I'd grabbed one for myself too.

"Pfft. I'm calling bullshit. What boxers was I wearing, then?"

Ramsey smirked. "Those stupid candy-cane ones."

Shit. I was pretty sure I *had* been wearing those boxers. I'd had them forever and always broke them out around the holidays, along with a couple of other festive pairs, because why the fuck not celebrate the season, even below the belt? I'd also been hammered at that party, meaning there was a high likelihood that might've happened.

"Aw, he's blushing." Houston chuckled. "Well done." He and Ramsey high-fived over the table, and I didn't even care that it was at my expense because it was better than thinking about the draft. Like Houston had ever so astutely

—and annoyingly—pointed out earlier, the Rush needed a new wide receiver, and if they decided to focus on their offense, there was no way I wasn't in the running. I was gunning for San Fran, though. Or even Philly. Anywhere, really, besides the Rush. Not that I planned to tell anyone that either.

"Anything happen with that offer from ASU?" Dad asked Houston, and the humor evaporated from Houston's face faster than water in the desert.

"What offer?" I asked, and Houston glanced at me with a dismissive shrug.

"ASU reached out about a possible assistant-coach position a while back. It wasn't a big deal, and I'm not taking it." He aimed the last part at Dad. "I'm all set here for now. PT is here, my friends are here, my life is here."

The fucker hadn't even told me, and it *was* a big deal. ASU had a great team, and Houston was more than capable of coaching. I narrowed my eyes, ready to ask him what the hell he was thinking, when I caught Ramsey give a single, sharp shake of his head in my direction.

I swallowed back my protests as Dad sighed.

"There will be lots of other opportunities," Mom said cheerily. "I'm sure some will be local, if that's what you want."

"What I want..." Houston exhaled an exasperated chuckle. "What I want is to hang out and celebrate with G. Let's keep the focus on someone who's actually still doing shit with their life."

Definitely should've stayed in Silver Ridge. Houston's comment solidified like cement in my chest, hard and heavy, and it wasn't anything that should've made me feel guilty—Houston didn't mean it that way, and I knew better—but it did.

AFTER DINNER, DAD, HOUSTON, AND RAMSEY DROPPED THEIR plates at the sink and headed into the living room. A second later, the blare of the TV filtered into the kitchen, and shortly after that, I heard the front door opening and closing as other folks arrived. My parents had invited a couple of their friends, my aunt Shereen, and some of my high school buds.

Mom tried to take my plate from my hands as I scraped it into the sink, stalling. "Let me do that so you can get out there. You're the man of the evening."

"I can do it. It takes two seconds," I insisted. As soon as I went in there, I'd be pelted with questions about what team I was gunning for.

"I know you can." She tugged harder. "But I'm doing it tonight. Shoo!"

The moment I let go of the plate, she set it down to one side of the sink and put her arms around me. "Don't think I didn't notice you hardly ate. I know you're nervous." In the living room, the noise increased as the TV volume and chatter of folks competed.

"As hell, yeah."

"You've worked hard. You deserve this. Wherever you end up, you'll make the best of it. And I know you're thinking about Houston, but..." She tilted my chin in her direction, her warm brown eyes insistent on mine. "Look at me. He's happy for you too. We're all happy for you."

"I know, Mom." I kissed the top of her head, wishing the twinge in my gut would go away, wishing Houston's career hadn't tanked right before mine was set to take off.

"Both my sons and—" Her breath hitched, and she

waved a hand. "Okay, get out of here so I can finish this before everything starts."

I took a deep breath, stepped out of the kitchen and into the living room, where I was immediately assaulted with back claps, well wishes, and hugs. And questions, of course, which I answered vaguely. Even my hermit-ass uncle Mick on my dad's side had driven in from his cave in Durango.

Houston's voice rose above the noise. "Everyone quiet! It's starting." He waved me closer, and I perched on the arm of the couch near him as Mom came in from the kitchen and did the same on the arm of Dad's recliner.

The room got quiet as the commissioner came on, made his opening announcements, and then the first pick was announced. Unsurprisingly, quarterback Colton Smith was going to Houston. That'd been the talk for months. He walked onstage to accept, and after that, a couple more picks were called out, the buzzing anticipation in my stomach growing with every passing minute.

Mom reached over and squeezed my knee as I jiggled it. I decided this process sucked. Why didn't they let players know beforehand, for fuck's sake? I couldn't even imagine how guys further down the list felt. The waiting blew, and I was crazy impatient in the first place.

After the seventh pick was announced, my phone rang. I gripped it tight as I put it to my ear.

"McRae, this is Coach Ray Baker." All the air in my lungs compressed into a tiny ball. "I've got our GM on the line too. What do you think about playing for the Denver Rush this year?"

Every eye in the room was on me as my heart sank to my knees. I forced a grin by sheer willpower, even as I felt, once again, like an ungrateful little shit. "I think that sounds amazing, and I'm happy to accept, sir." I was proud of how upbeat I'd been able to sound.

"Good man. We'll be in contact tomorrow to go over the contract. Right now, enjoy the moment. After this, the real work starts."

"Well?" Houston socked me in the arm as I ended the call, and I tilted my head toward the TV screen as the announcer came on again.

"Listen."

When the commissioner announced I'd been picked by the Denver Rush, the den erupted in cheers. Houston shot up and grabbed me around the waist, noogie-ing my head vigorously before he had to grab the arm of the couch to stay upright.

I caught him under the arms to keep him stable.

"Fucking knee," he muttered, then in the same breath shook his head, still smiling broadly at me. "I'm so goddamn proud of you right now, G. I hope you know that. The Rush is lucky as hell to have you."

I could see the pride in his smile, hear it in his voice, even if it was tinged with a bit of wistfulness. Houston never begrudged anyone anything, and I pushed aside my guilt to hug him fiercely before releasing him.

I was then bodily passed around the rest of the room for more congratulations, more back slaps, more hugs. Someone sloshed beer on my arm. Uncle Mick didn't seem to know what the fuck was going on, but matched the high spirits of everyone else. Probably he was just high in general.

I didn't think I'd ever been the recipient of so much affection in my life, and I couldn't deny it felt good.

When Ramsey closed in, he flashed me a mischievous

wink before hooking my neck and drawing me in, our chests smashing together.

"Did you know?" I asked.

"Nope. You know we're in the dark too. But they made a solid choice."

I was briefly overwhelmed by the sensation of his body against mine. The firmness, his scent. I realized I'd never been hugged by him before, and God, it was enormously distracting. And also, too short. The next moment, he let me go.

A FEW HOURS LATER, THE PARTY HAD DIED DOWN. DAD HAD fallen asleep in the recliner. Or maybe passed out was more appropriate. Four beers and he was toast. Mom rolled her eyes affectionately and covered him with a blanket, then made Houston and Ramsey come into the kitchen with her so she could fix them each containers of leftovers.

I walked with them out to their cars, Houston snagging me in another hug before heading around to the driver's side of his SUV. I noted the slight limp as he moved.

"See you in the a.m.?" Ramsey called out.

"Maybe," Houston called back. "Don't hesitate to start without me. I'm tapped tonight. I might need a day off. You heading home?"

"In a few. I want to talk to Garrett for a second."

The fact that he'd bothered with my actual name put me on edge, but I lifted a hand nonchalantly as Houston climbed into his seat. "His knee's bothering him."

"Yep. He'll probably skip tomorrow. It's getting better, overall, though. I know you worry about it. He worries about you too."

I didn't reply. I was well aware. He'd always worried about me.

As soon as his taillights disappeared, Ramsey turned to me, piercing me with his blue stare that hit me like the snap of static on a cold day.

"You don't want the Rush."

I'd never gotten used to the casual way Ramsey could cut to my core unexpectedly. I snorted in response. "Sure I do," I lied. "Like I said before, I don't care where I play, I just..." Ramsey's annoyingly placid, take-no-bullshit stare deflated the defense I wanted to mount. I sighed. "Fine. I didn't want the Rush. I wanted San Fran. Was it that obvious?"

"Nope. Don't think so." He backed up a couple of steps and dropped onto the brick retaining wall, then slapped the empty space beside him.

"Nah, I don't need some pep talk. I'm good with it, I swear." But when he smacked the wall insistently again, I let out another sigh and sat after a glance over my shoulder to make sure Mom and Dad were still inside. "You're annoying."

"I know." His smile was unapologetic as he shrugged, and as annoying as he was, and as annoying as my persistent crush on him was, it was that very first encounter with him four years ago, where he'd told me to keep my focus, and the earnest, intent way he'd said it, that had lingered in the back of my mind all through college. It was behind every time I thought about skipping a class or slacking at practice. It was behind the extra reps in the gym, the extra hours I spent watching tape and studying plays. Not that I'd been perfect. I'd definitely gone on the field hungover more than once, and done some stupid shit I'd been lucky not to get busted for. But I'd done everything I set out to do so far. And Ramsey was a part of it.

"Since I first met you, you've been wanting something of your own. Separate from Houston. And now you feel you're back in his shadow again. Having to live up to or live out his career in a way? Is that what's going on?"

"No," I bit off. Fuck his scary accuracy. "Okay, yeah. A little bit. Or a lot." There were other factors too. Life seemed like it might be easier without having to be around Ramsey all the time. Crushes were weird like that. It wasn't as if I'd spent day in and day out over the past four years thinking about him. I hadn't. I'd dated people, and fully explored my bisexuality—and I mean *fully*. I'd fallen in love and fallen out of love. But no matter how infrequently I saw him, that smolder I'd felt upon first meeting him came rushing back every single time, like something dormant inside me coming back to life.

"I get it." Ramsey shifted on the wall and, at my dubious expression, a half-smile twisted his lips. "No, I really do. I'm not bullshitting you. You know about my dad, right?" I nodded. Ramsey didn't talk about him much, and I'd always gotten a sense he was a sore subject, something Ramsey wanted to keep his distance from, and probably the reason he spent so much time with my family. From what I could tell, we were a whole other world away from what he grew up with. "It's kinda the same. Different shadow, though. I always feel like I'm on the line to not go the way my dad did. Not fuck shit up, not to squander my career, my money, my opportunities. Not to be like him."

All traces of the Ramsey who teased me and called me out relentlessly were gone, replaced by a somberness in his expression that filled me with a strange urge to smooth a thumb over his pinched brow. I didn't think I'd ever seen him so serious before. At least with me.

"I didn't want the Rush either, at first. I mean, my dad had played for them, after all, right? That seemed like bad luck. I was stoked when Tampa signed me. When I got traded, I was furious. Thought, fuck this, I'll play for a year and then ask to go somewhere else. Anywhere else. I thought I was doomed."

"You're still here."

"Yep. I got off to a rough start, but your brother and I became tight. Then, I don't know, I just settled in. Realized I really liked the other guys, really liked being back in Colorado. If I let the anger get the better of me, I was just as bad as my dad. I would've let someone else's shit fuck up my career, and that's just crazy."

"Easier said than done." I got what he was saying, even if his dad had been long gone by the time he got to the Rush. Everything with Houston still felt fresh. Hell, it *was* fresh. But I appreciated what Ramsey was trying to do, and that he wasn't patronizing about it by telling me to get over it. I already knew I should get over it.

"Just give it some time, see how it goes. Get settled in. Shit, you keep eating like you did tonight—or not eating, more like—and no one's gonna be able to see your skinny ass on the field anyway."

I laughed and stood, Ramsey following. "Kiss my ass. My appetite's already back."

He tucked the container of leftovers under his arm. "Good. See you at training camp sooner than you think."

"Hey," I said before he could turn for his SUV. It occurred to me that maybe I should thank him for the pep talk, but...nah. Not my style. "Was my fly really down the whole time at New Year's?"

Ramsey's grin skewed devious in answer.

"You fucker. How did you know what boxers I was wearing, though?" God help me if he said he'd been looking. But I knew better.

"Lucky guess. You only wear three pairs during the holidays."

"Paying attention to my underwear, huh?" I gave him my best scandalous smile, even if it was wasted on him. "What would Alice say?"

"Alyssa," he corrected me with a grin. "And it's kinda unavoidable since you more or less refuse to wear clothes at home."

"You're welcome." He wasn't wrong. I tended to roam the house in either PJ pants or boxers and a tee over the holidays, but fuck it, that was what being home was all about, right? Comfort. Letting it all hang out. Ogling my brother's best friend every time he was around. It'd been a time-honored tradition for years now.

Ramsey waved me off with a dismissive snort, and I lingered until his taillights had disappeared too, wondering what training was gonna be like with him and whether it was humanly possible to squash a rabid crush in the months before it started.

Two months later

This was exactly the life I've been dreaming of. It was a Friday night two weeks before training camp started, and half the team had taken over one side of Double Down, a popular downtown Denver bar. Ramsey had set up the outing as a kind of meet and greet. The drinks were flowing, and there was eye candy galore. On the way to the bathroom I got asked for my first autograph by an older blonde woman, which I was often down with, but tonight I was more interested in a table of hot guys I'd spotted earlier.

I signed the napkin she handed me, we took a quick selfie, and I continued on to the bathroom. I posted myself in front of one of the urinals, whistling—not something I usually did, but I was a little drunk. Okay, a lot drunk, and the acoustics were awesome.

"Christ, sounds like someone's murdering a cat."

I glanced over my shoulder and grinned at Ramsey as the door swung shut behind him. Somehow he managed to look hot even in shitty fluorescent lighting. "That's 'Rocketman' by the great EJ. Sorry your musical taste sucks."

He stopped at the urinal next to me. "First, you tight with Sir Elton? Second, no. That's the sound of someone plummeting toward their death."

I put all my lung power into the next bar, and Ramsey shook his head with a laugh. "How drunk are you?"

"I'm jussssst right," I informed him. Those damn Ss were getting trickier as the night wore on, though, no lie. "Hey, some lady asked for my autograph in the hallway."

"She was probably looking for me. Accepted you as a weaker alternative."

"Maybe." I considered. "But she seemed pretty into it when she asked for my number."

Ramsey's brows shot up. "Did she really?"

"Would it be that surprising?" I tucked my dick away and zipped up. "I'm a great catch and an excellent lay. I would definitely ask for my number."

"You're an egotistical little shit is what you are. So did you give it to her?"

"Nah." I shrugged. "I'm in the mood for Vitamin D tonight."

Ramsey snorted, waving me off and, realizing it was kind of awkward for me to still be standing there while he finished, I quickly washed my hands and bailed. I was proud of myself. I didn't even sneak a peek at Ramsey's junk, though the temptation was there. But I had my creeper limits, and urinal sneak-peeks were it.

Back at the table, someone bought a fresh round of drinks. Cross, the Rush's new tight end, led a raucous toast, and then someone broke into a legit sea shanty. Soon enough the whole bar joined in. After that, we hit the pool tables again, then the darts.

An hour later, my vision had gone a little swimmy, my limbs noodly, and I was pretty sure I was rocking a permasmile. Life was fucking good.

I was minding my own business, calling like a jerk as Cross busted his ass stumbling toward the bathroom, when Ramsey approached.

He'd looked good in crappy fluorescent bathroom lighting, but in the warm glow of the pub's overhead pendants, and with what was probably half a keg under my belt, he looked like the fucking answer to the meaning of life.

I forced myself to squint so I wouldn't accidentally give him googly eyes, but that made my forehead hurt, so I decided fuck it. I'd risk the googly eyes.

"I don't take requests," I told him as suavely as I could manage.

"'Pity,' said no one."

"But what would you request if you could?"

"For you to never whistle, sing, or hum a tune again. Ever."

"Damn." I put a hand over my heart. "Harsh."

He chuckled as he slid onto the seat next to me, and I had to physically bite back the instinct to tell him he smelled good.

I shot a look sideways as he smirked and muttered, "Thanks."

Wait, did I actually say it aloud?

"Yes, you said that aloud," he answered, confirming that somehow my inner monologue had turned inside out. Crap. *How do I make it go back inside?*

"You could start by shutting your mouth. Usually works for me."

This must be payback for laughing at Cross, I decided.

"Are you thinking of heading home soon?" Ramsey asked.

"Why do I feel like that's more of a suggestion than a question?"

"Because it is."

"Last I checked, I'm an adult, fully capable of making my own decisions, including when I depart this fine drinking establishment."

"Oh yeah, I'm well aware."

"That last beer might not have been one of the better decisions," I admitted.

"What about the one in your hand now?"

I looked down at the table to discover my hand was, in fact, curled around the handle of a frosty mug full of delicious beer. Excellent. "Hmm," I hedged.

"You didn't drive here, did you?"

"Fuck no."

He nodded. "Good."

He might have said some other words, but I'd gotten stuck on his angular jaw and sexy mouth. His whole face, really. "What happened to you?"

"Huh?" His brows bunched together in confusion.

"I just can't figure out how one human can contain so much genetic lottery winnings. It seems like even nature would say, 'That's not fair. Let's give him a weird eye or ears that stick out.' *Something. Some flaw.*"

Ramsey cocked his head, as if still not quite understanding.

Jesus, was the guy dense? I stared at him and spoke slowly. "You're hot. Ridiculously hot, is what I'm saying. And, ugh, it's sooooo too bad that only one portion of the human population gets a shot at you. You have no idea..."

Ramsey busted out in a laugh. "That's it. I'm cutting you off, Garrett."

"No, I'm just saying." I pulled my beer out of reach as he grabbed for it. "I figure since I already accidentally told you you smelled good, the rest might as well come out. It's true. I do think you're hot. There's also a seventy-one percent chance I won't remember saying any of this tomorrow, so it's all good."

"Seventy-one? That's oddly specific." He reached for my beer again. "How about I drive you back to Houston's."

"Ohhh, noooooo." I recoiled in horror. Fuck, I'd kinda forgotten I was staying with him until I found a place of my own. "I'm not going back to Houston's. That'll just give him ammo to mess with me or say I'm not taking this seriously, which I am." Ramsey arched a brow as if doubting the veracity of my assertion, which was fair, considering beer sloshed from my mug as I said it. Ramsey snatched the drink from me and set it down as I frowned petulantly. "I'm just gonna find someone to go home with."

"Oh yeah?" Ramsey plunked an elbow on the table, seeming interested. "You have any prospects?"

I ticked my chin toward the corner, where the table of hot guys had been earlier. "Those sexy dudes."

"All of them?" Ramsey squinted, then gave me the same narrow-eyed look. "I didn't realize you had a thing for huge age gaps. Or orgies."

"No, it's..." I looked again at their table. Sometime between beer five and eleventy-three, the hot guys had been replaced by a trio of white-hairs. "Shit," I muttered, then shrugged. "I'll find someone. It won't take long."

Ramsey shook his head. "I don't think so."

"I'm not going back to Houston's, dude. Not tonight."

I guess I said it so vehemently that I gave Ramsey pause because, after a couple of beats, he exhaled a long-suffering sigh and said, "You can crash at my place."

My lips twisted in a smirk, but before I could say a word, he frowned sternly at me.

"Whatever you're thinking? No. You're not doing anything but going to sleep."

"That doesn't mean no action can happen." I waggled my brows. "Pornhub says so, and I give you my explicit consent to have your way with me."

"Jesus Christ." He stood and gestured for me to do the same. "Don't make me regret this."

"Literally the same thing the last guy I took home said to me." I grinned as Ramsey groaned. "He didn't regret it, though."

"I'm already regretting it. Get your ass to the car."

———

"DAMN," I SAID, AS WE WALKED THROUGH THE DOOR OF Ramsey's Cedar Grove pad thirty-five minutes and multiple Journey and Gaga songs later—my request. "This is pretty sweet." It was a mansion, no doubt, but not ostentatious. I noted lots of windows and a contemporary vibe. The muted colors gave it a lived-in feel I dug immediately. "It is lacking a floor compass to tell me where the bathrooms are."

Ramsey shut the door behind me and locked it. "Down that hall and to the far left. That's also where the guest room is."

"Gotcha. Who's staying in the guest room?"

He rolled his eyes at me. "I'm gonna grab you a couple of bottles of water and some vitamins."

I waited for him to tack on, *Don't touch anything*, but he just gave me another amused up and down, then turned and walked off.

I went down the hallway, used the bathroom, located the guest room, and then wandered a little farther, peeking in doorways. There was a staircase to the second floor, so I figured I should explore that too. I found what must have been the master and checked it out while I was at it. Bed neatly made. Did he have a housekeeper? I was betting he did.

I ran a hand over some furry throw at the end of the bed that was softer than anything I'd felt in my life. I wondered if Ramsey liked a soft or firm mattress. I should find out for myself. I lifted my arms and free-fell face-first onto the mattress. Fuck, it was perfect. Firm, but not too firm. Soft, but not too soft.

I closed my eyes, deciding I'd just rest there a second.

"Hey."

I cracked one eye. Had a second passed, or had it been longer? "Sleeping. Go away," I mumbled into the plush comforter.

"Yeah, in my bed. Get your ass up. I put some water bottles on the bedside table in the guest room, which is where you should be heading now." Ramsey nudged the back of my leg, and I rolled over, offering him a bleary smile. Jesus, beer goggles just made him exponentially more attractive than his baseline smoking-hot status. Especially when he was standing over me at the end of the bed. Too bad he was still wearing all his clothes and staring at me sternly.

"Sure you don't want me to just stay?"

It was a testament to how drunk I was that, for a second, I could've sworn Ramsey was considering it. Then he shook his head with a chuckle.

"You're a hot fucking mess, G. Now get your ass out of my bed."

"Fine." I heaved myself upright and focused on moving toward the bedroom door with as much grace as I could manage, but slowly enough to give him time to change his mind.

He didn't.

3

RAMSEY

I groaned when my cell rang. I worried it was someone I wouldn't want to talk to. Scratch that. When it came to the phone, there was no one I *wanted* to *talk* to. In a world of texting, I didn't get why anyone called unless it had to do with business.

Ignoring it, I continued grabbing clothes from my dresser. I was leaving in the morning for training camp, where I'd spend two weeks participating in constant practice and fitness testing, where rookies always ended up running so hard, they puked. Not me, because fuck that noise. I was too old for that shit. I knew how to prepare to make sure it didn't happen. But for the rookies, it was a whole world away from college ball, and this would be their first introduction to that. Some might get cut from the team before it was over.

That immediately made me think of Garrett. *"You're hot. Ridiculously hot."* It wasn't the first time those words had played through my head since he'd spoken them two weeks before. I'd heard them before, so there was no reason for me to be obsessed with the tone of Garrett's voice when they'd slipped past his lips, or the way his eyes firmly held on to mine, like he couldn't look away even if he'd tried.

And that was maybe one of the dumbest things I'd ever thought.

Of course, he'd been drunk as fuck. He never would have told me in the first place if he hadn't emptied the bar of beer. But there was no doubt I'd liked hearing it, my dick perking up and taking notice because Garrett McRae was ridiculously fucking hot too.

I liked knowing he thought that about me. I'd liked hearing it even more.

My phone rang again. "Jesus." I tossed a few Rush T-shirts onto the bed, peeked at my cell, and answered. "Text. It's called texting," I told Houston while trying to pretend I hadn't been thinking about his brother and how adorable he'd been laid out flat on my bed before I'd forced him to the guest room. The fucker hadn't even been embarrassed about it the next day.

"I usually do. But I just had lunch with Garrett and wanted to talk to you about something."

"Shoot." I sat on the edge of the bed. I'd only seen Garrett a couple of times since the draft and our night out. Before things were confirmed, I'd been a little nervous because his contract negotiations had taken longer than usual. I thought maybe he'd changed his mind, and I cared a whole lot more than I should. While partly it was because I didn't want a guy on the team who didn't want to be there, I understood where he was coming from. Hell, I still couldn't believe I'd mentioned my dad that day. My first year in the league, every interview brought him up—they'd wanted to lay all his fuckups on the table, comparing me to him every step of the way, even though I didn't make any of the dumb mistakes he did. No drugs, no ego too big for the locker room, no missed practices, no drama. Things had chilled out since, and I didn't go around bringing him up, but hell, the last thing a guy should feel was disappointed on the night he got drafted to the NFL.

"You know how I'm worried something will go wrong?" Houston said. "That he'll get himself in trouble?"

"Wait. You are?" I teased.

"Somehow you're under the impression you're funny."

A soft chuckle rolled off my tongue. "I'm giving you shit. Yes, I'm aware." And while how drunk he'd gotten the night we went out wasn't a huge deal, it was another tally mark on the column that said Houston was right and Garrett needed to be careful.

"I was feeling some kind of somethin' about him going to the Rush, but you know, it's perfect because you're there, and I was thinking you could keep an eye on him."

Well, shit. I hadn't expected that and wasn't sure what I thought about it. "Garrett doesn't strike me as someone who would be okay with that."

"He wouldn't know. I'm not telling you to go on some top-secret mission here. Just watch out for him, keep him in line, make sure that big-ass ego of his doesn't get him in trouble."

"This sounds like the beginning of every rom-com I've never been forced to watch."

"You love that shit."

"Shh. You said you wouldn't tell anyone." Who could you share your secrets with if not your best friend?

"So I should cancel the skywriter I booked?"

I sighed. "Let's get back to my deep dark secrets later. What are you getting me into here, Houston? I'm the quarterback. It's my job to watch out for everyone on the team."

"I know. I'm not asking you to bend the rules for him. I

have too much respect for both of you to do that. Just don't let him be his own worst enemy." When I didn't reply, he added, "And you don't have to worry about the rom-com thing. He's my brother; that would just be weird. Plus, his name doesn't start with the letter *A*."

"You're a dick, you know that?" Also, was this a good time to tell Houston his brother was fucking hot? That them being related didn't make it so I didn't think he was spank-bank material?

"But you love me."

I did. He was the brother I never had, which sort of meant Garrett was too, only I liked to check out Garrett's ass and I didn't do that with Houston's. "Fine. Babysit the little man. Got it."

———

THE RUSH TRAINING FACILITY WAS ABOUT FORTY MINUTES outside Denver, but our team had a rule about staying in a hotel for camp. It wasn't mandatory because they couldn't really do that, but it was *strongly encouraged*, and we all knew that meant *keep your ass in the fucking hotel to be a team player*. Because that was what it was all about—building camaraderie, growing bonds so we were like a family before the season started. It wasn't my favorite thing in the world, but I got it, especially for the rookies. We needed to get used to each other, get to know and trust each other.

I headed toward the entrance while shooting off a text to Garrett. **How far out are you?**

Who dis?

I rolled my eyes. He was such a fucking idiot. **Your favorite person.**

It was ridiculous how I watched my phone for his

reply. I never knew what would come out of Garrett's mouth next, and I liked that. Most people were predictable, and I guessed in some ways he was too, but not in others.

Santa? Is that you? I knew you were real! Can I sit on your lap?

A flash of a naked Garrett riding my dick flittered through my head, sending blood rushing for my cock. Not a good sign. I shoved those thoughts away and answered him. **Get your ass here, slowpoke.**

Dad?

A laugh jumped out of my mouth, surprising me.

I'm waiting. I was pissed at myself for not playing up the daddy thing, but after I'd just imagined fucking him, I needed to get my head on straight.

Oh, it's someone boring...hm...Ramsey? I was really far off. You wouldn't make the top twenty on my faves list.

Somehow, I didn't believe that. **Liar. Hurry up.**

Then stop texting me!

I chuckled, leaning against the building.

Hammond, one of our defensive linemen, showed up next. "What's up, Rams?"

"Hey, man. How's it going?" We bumped fists.

"You ready to do this? Kick ass, whip the rooks into shape."

One rookie, specifically, was on my list, but I didn't tell Hammond that. "You know it."

"This whole Baby McRae thing... Is it me, or is that kind of fucked up? I mean, after losing Houston."

I shrugged. "We needed a wide receiver, and he is one, a damn good one too. That's all that matters. They stand on their own." That was something I needed to stress to the team. We teased and talked shit to each other—that was part of being teammates—but comparing Garrett to Houston wasn't going to benefit any of us.

"I got'chu, Cap."

"That was last season." Some teams chose a new captain each week and some by the year. The Rush went by season.

"I'm sure it'll be this year too. See you in there."

Hammond walked in just as—

"Jesus fucking Christ, a goddamned Aston Martin?" I said as if Garrett could hear me. Because I knew it had to be him. A lot of guys did it—got their paycheck and bought a badass car—so I couldn't talk too much shit, but of course he had to be as flashy as fucking possible.

Sure enough, once the car was parked, a long-legged Garrett climbed out. He grabbed his bag from the back and headed my way, a pair of Aviators hiding his eyes.

His brown hair was wet as if he'd gotten straight out of the shower and headed over. He wore a pair of nylon shorts, his college tee, and a big-ass smile. "Aw, you came out to carry my shit for me?" He held his bag toward me, and I bit back my laughter.

"Wouldn't want you to pull a muscle or something." I grabbed the handle of his bag, but Garrett didn't let go.

"Oh fuck you."

"I'm just sayin', you probably need to conserve your energy for training camp. You're finally out of the playpen and get to hang with the big boys. Might be too much for you. Don't worry, I got your back." Our fingers brushed, a snap of electricity shooting off between us. We both pulled back, and the bag dropped.

I adjusted the backward cap on my head, determined to ignore whatever the hell that had been. "Let's head inside."

Garrett's strong hand wrapped around my bicep before I

could head for the door. "Seriously, Ramsey, why'd you text? And wait for me?"

I shrugged. I should have been prepared for this question, but I didn't know how to answer it because I had a feeling that even without Houston asking me to watch him, I'd be standing right where I was. "Don't know really." Which was true. "Guess you kinda feel like my little brother too." Totally not true, though stepbrother porn was hot. I'd be down for some roleplay if he was.

His jaw tightened in a way I'd never seen in response to something I'd said to him. Clearly, he didn't like it. "I don't need another brother."

"I thought we bonded during the draft? And the night you spent at my house?"

"If we had, you'd know that the last thing I want is for you to treat me like Houston does."

Ah, hell. This was going to be a disaster. "Fine. Imightlikeyoualittle," I rushed out.

Now he grinned that cocky, mischievous smile I'd gotten so used to. "Oh shit. Warner Ramsey is obsessed with me. I can't take my brother's best friend."

"I said I like you *a little*. And would you look at that, I don't anymore."

"Liar." He winked.

"Come on, Little Man. Let's go inside."

He hefted his bag up on his shoulder and followed me. I led him to the conference room where we were meeting. Most of the team was already there. Coach Baker was standing in front, talking to a couple of guys on the team and our defensive coach, Todd.

"Look! It's one of the rookies!" Simmons, our starting cornerback, shouted.

"Been excited to meet me? I can give you an autograph if

you want." Garrett's delivery was smooth as honey, like the whole thing had been planned out. A few guys laughed.

"He's a cocky one," Jarrick jumped in. "I could tell at the bar the other night."

"Shouldn't we get going before it's time for McRae's nap? Did he already get his bottle?" Nichols, another teammate, teased. Joking around with rookies was normal, but clearly it was going to happen more with Garrett because of Houston.

"I feel like you guys sat around figuring out how to greet me. I know it's exciting having me on the roster, but I'm no better than the rest of you...okay, maybe a little better than the rest of you."

"Ooooh! Rookie McRae got jokes!" I wasn't sure who'd said that because everyone was laughing or talking shit. I clapped Garrett on the shoulder, not surprised he was already fitting in well.

"All right, all right. That's enough, guys. It's time to get to work," Coach Baker said, and everyone got serious fast.

We took our seats for our first team meeting of the season. Cross—Garrett's buddy—landed in the seat on the other side of him. We went over what we wanted for the year—a fucking Super Bowl ring—and then did a couple of exercises aimed at getting to know each other. Coach Baker had been with the Rush the past two seasons. He came with four rings under his belt, and while not all coaches stressed the teammates-are-family thing, Coach Baker was big on building strong bonds within the group and how that translated to the *W* on the field.

We went over some film from last season before starting an afternoon workout.

When we made it outside, we separated for offensive

exercises. While the defense did their d-line exercises, I kept my eye on Garrett between my five-step drop drills.

We ended practice with gassers. By the time we'd run the full length of the field four times in a row, two newbies had thrown up and everyone looked dead on their feet. I conditioned all year, but I worried my legs might give out on me anyway. Sweat dripped from my lashes. Still, I looked at Garrett and winked. He rolled his eyes but gave me a small smirk before bending over, hands on his knees and taking a few breaths.

"Bring it in!" Coach Baker yelled. Garrett pushed up and stood, jogging directly over. He was as sweaty as the rest of us, his face pink, and my brain went directly to where it shouldn't. Did his cheeks flush like that when he came?

Chill the fuck out. Get it together.

The motherfucker had me talking to myself. What the hell was it about Garrett?

As soon as the whole team was there, Coach said, "We're doubling up, two in a room, because you're all gonna become besties over the season." A few of us laughed as Coach started calling out names. I heard a few guys grumbling in the background, bitching about bunking with someone else and being too old for this.

I glanced over at Garrett, who had his arms crossed but wasn't complaining. "Good boy," I whispered playfully.

"Fuck off."

"Ramsey and McRae," Coach called out. Welp, that made my job easier, at least during training camp. He couldn't get into too much trouble if he was rooming with me. "Now, anyone who wants to whine or who has a problem with how I do things is welcome to sit out the season or find another team. *I* run this ship, and we do things my way. Come see me if you have an issue and want to ride the bench." With that, he walked away.

"He's no joke, is he?" Garrett asked.

"Nah, but he knows his shit. He's good. He's our best shot at going all the way." I nodded toward the building. "Let's go."

We headed back inside, got our stuff. Unfortunately, there were issues with the plumbing that were being worked on, so we had to head to the team hotel, stinking like a bunch of sweaty pigs. Luckily, it was only a couple of miles away. Security kept things on lockdown while we were there so fans didn't get in and guys didn't sneak women into their rooms. They always said women gave you weak legs, which was sexist as fuck. I wondered if guys did the same.

The team was all on the eleventh floor. Once we got our keys and room numbers, Garrett and I headed up together. The hotel had been remodeled since last year, redecorated in earth tones, and our room had a large window on one wall and a balcony on the other.

"You can shower first," I told him. Wasn't I just a gentleman? "Then we'll meet Coach and the team to eat, and the rest of the night is ours."

"You planned it this way, didn't you? Wanted me all to yourself." Garrett waggled his dark brows.

"Damn. You figured me out. Annoying-ass people are my kink, and you're top of the list."

"I live to serve." He tossed his bag on one of the beds and started pulling things out. "Want to save time and shower together?"

"No comment."

"No comment? Not even for the environment? Water conservation is something we all need to start taking seriously."

Not gonna lie, I was struck speechless for a minute, trying to think of some witty reply, but nothing would come to me. I landed on, "What in the hell is wrong with you?"

Garrett chuckled. "Straight people are so boring."

I kept my mouth shut. I didn't know why I kept my sexuality to myself with him. I trusted Garrett. Maybe it was just because sometimes I didn't feel like I had the right to claim the bi label since I'd never experimented with a man. Logically, I knew that was bullshit, but I still felt it.

I pulled Denver Rush track pants and a tee from my bag, then searched for my toiletries. Garrett's shower was quick, and less than ten minutes later, he came out wearing a towel.

"You're up." He walked to the bed, where I noticed he'd left his clothes, and dropped his towel.

"Jesus." I averted my eyes, but not before I'd accidentally gotten a peek at his soft cock. What would he taste like? How would the soap smell on his skin there?

"See? Not a little man, am I?"

"Not sure. I looked, but I must have missed it."

He laughed, the sound still drifting through the closed bathroom door when I fell against it. I needed to up my game. Garrett McRae was going to be the death of me.

4

GARRETT

Everything hurt, and my life was a lie. Play for the NFL, they said. It'll be fun, they said. And we hadn't even started the physical practice yet, where we dressed out and had full contact on the field. But that was today, and I knew a couple of the seasoned players were gonna get a lot of enjoyment out of trying to take me down. Jason Nance in particular. He'd been a wide receiver for the Rush for three seasons now and had been side-eyeing me since the start of camp.

Ramsey, like a damn sadist, laughed at my groan when he pulled the hotel-room curtains wide and bright morning light poured in. "I told you camp was going to tear your cocky ass up."

"Yeah, yeah." I rolled onto my back, trying to get my dick to ignore the tear-your-ass-up portion of that sentence because over the past couple of days I'd caught glimpses of what Ramsey was working with below the belt, and it definitely fell into the could-tear-an-ass-up camp.

I'd done, I thought, an impressive job of ridding myself of my crush on him in the intervening months between the draft and the start of camp. I was pretty fucking proud of myself, actually. I'd attacked it methodically, similarly to how I'd approached learning plays or studying for a test. I'd cataloged all the things about Ramsey that had annoyed me over the years, and if some of those things were also things I'd liked, well, whatever. The random nicknames, for one. Or how organized he was. That was definitely annoying. The way he rubbed his thumb along his jaw sometimes when he was about to disagree with something someone said. How his calf muscles were more defined than mine even though I ran my ass off every day. Unforgivable.

And since there was a huge mental component to football, I figured I was doing myself a solid by practicing that kind of sustained willpower and fortitude.

Because I was also rooming with him, it meant I had to run through that catalog several times a day, especially when he walked around shirtless. But again, I was looking at it as another opportunity to test my mettle.

Still, I was human, prone to relapses, and I was currently experiencing one as I watched Ramsey dig through a drawer and pull out a shirt. It was a damn shame he had to put it on. He was packed with long, lean muscle, like most QBs, but he had a back and shoulders even Atlas would've looked twice at. And that high, round ass...*was completely like any other guy's ass and not enticingly squeezable at all.*

Mine was better.

I gave my dick a punishing shove with the heel of my hand and winced. My hamstrings were fucked.

Ramsey said, "I know you know better than to do that newbie thing where you avoid seeing the trainer because you don't want to look weak as a rookie, yeah?"

I quickly averted my gaze from Ramsey's unremarkable ass as he tossed a pointed look over his shoulder.

"I would never do anything like that," I lied, and then resolved that I would take advantage of the trainer after practice today. The lactic-acid buildup was no fucking joke, and I knew it would help ultimately.

"You gonna consider trimming that bush on your face too, since they'll be doing interviews today?"

Coach Baker had told us that the league's marketing team would be filming parts of the camp later in the week to create short documentary-style pieces and highlight reels to get fans pumped in the preseason.

"I happen to appreciate a little bush." I rubbed my jaw, the scruff prickling my palm. It wasn't bad. Not even approaching beard status yet. I smirked. "Adds a nice little bite."

"I think that's called chafing."

"Not if you're doing it right." I didn't even have to see his eyes to know they were rolling, and that was enough to power me upright. I arched my back in a stretch that had my muscles twinging like crazy. "Let me know if you ever need any lessons. There's good prickle and bad prickle, and the difference can be a delicate balance," I said, like I was some connoisseur. I did like the feel of a man's stubble against me, though, and Ramsey's jaw was shadowed with the kind of stubble that would probably feel like perfect fine-grain sandpaper under my hand. No, someone else's hand. It wasn't ever gonna be mine.

"I do fine on my own, thanks. Better get steppin,' Scruffy."

I sighed as I caught a glimpse of myself in the mirror. Okay, maybe the scruff was starting to look a little untamed. Picking up my Dopp kit, I headed into the bathroom.

AFTER THE MORNING WARM-UP, WHICH THE TV CREW FILMED, Coach sent me and the other rookies off to the sidelines, where a guy in a T-shirt blazoned with the NFL logo stood with a microphone, chatting with what I'd determined was the director. While waiting my turn, I kept an eye on the various drills—the cornerbacks working on agility, the wide receivers clustered over on the opposite side of the field, catching and running, Ramsey and our backup QB, Ellis, talking to Coach.

"Garrett?" I jerked my attention back to the guy with the microphone. "Ready?"

"Yeah, sure." I should've been paying more attention to the interviews. I stood still as they mic'd me and led me over to a little backdrop blazoned with the Rush logo hanging from plastic piping.

"We'll do a brief intro and a couple of questions. Five minutes tops, very informal, and then you can rejoin the team. Why don't you start by saying your name and talking a little about what it felt like to be drafted to the Rush."

Softball questions like these were easy, and my posture relaxed as I introduced myself. "I grew up watching the Rush, so it's obviously a huge honor to be asked to play on the team."

"Being from Denver, and considering your brother played for the Rush, were you hoping they'd draft you too? Keep it in the family, so to speak?"

Ugh. There it was. I instantly hated the guy's casual chuckle that followed.

"That would've been cool, yeah," I hedged, "but you can't always know how the draft is gonna go, so I didn't have any preconceived notions about where I'd end up. I'm just happy to be able to play at a pro level."

"Houston's injury last season was a career ender, and I

know a lot of fans were heartbroken to see him go. I'm sure it was rough on you and your family too. Since you're both wide receivers, is there a sense that you've got some big shoes to fill?"

I bit the inside of my cheek until I tasted blood, reminding myself that this guy was just doing his job, looking for a potentially interesting soundbite among all the boring shit about training. Then I smiled. "I actually wear a size larger shoe than him."

He grinned. "So you're going in confident, huh?"

"I'm going in confident that I can help this team go to the Super Bowl, yeah."

The guy and the director exchanged a look, and then the reporter nodded at me with a smile. "We're good. Thanks for your time, Garrett."

I snapped the mic from my collar, handed it over to them, and jogged off. One irritating interview down, probably five hundred more to go.

THE FUCKING GASSERS DURING THE SECOND PRACTICE WERE what finally broke me. I'd managed to hold my own through play executions and full-speed drills, but every muscle in my body was on fire and my stomach was queasy going into the torturous fuckers. I swallowed bile the first three rounds and barely made a respectable time on the fourth. As soon as my toe touched the sideline, I curled over, spewing bright-blue Gatorade on the manicured grass. Relief was instantaneous.

So were the hoots and shouts.

"Got another!"

"Rooookkkkkiiiiieeeeee."

"How's lunch for the second time?"

I was pretty sure that last one was Nance, judging from the delight in his voice.

Cross trotted to a stop next to me. "Okay?" he asked, concern darting through his eyes.

"Yeah. I didn't hydrate enough." This fucking day. I couldn't wait for it to be over. At the end of the field, Ramsey turned in my direction and shaded his eyes. *Please don't come over here*, I thought, and for once, he didn't.

"McRae," Coach barked as I mopped my face with an icy cool towel one of the trainers had handed me. "Follow me."

Fuck my life. I had a brief flicker of terror that I was about to get cut—it was gonna happen to a few guys for sure —but they wouldn't have put up the money they did only to cut me. Not when I'd been keeping up just fine until today.

I followed Coach into the office and nearly moaned in relief at the air conditioning that blasted us as soon as we stepped inside.

Coach gestured to a chair. "Sit down before you fall over and break your nose."

"Not gonna happen," I said stubbornly, but I parked my ass against the arm of the chair anyway as he sat in the one behind his desk.

He rubbed a hand over his chest and looked out the window. After a long moment, his attention snapped back to me. "Bringing you onto this team right after Houston's injury was a calculated risk. There were a lot of good options this year."

"Yessir." Shit, was he already having regrets? What else had I fucked up and been unaware of? I racked my brain but kept coming up empty.

"The average person in your position would come into this kind of situation feeling a lot of pressure to fill in a gap.

Live up to something. That look on your face right now says you're well aware of it."

"Yessir."

"That's just part of the reason we chose you. My guess is, that pressure is gonna fuel you on this team in a different way than if, say, you'd gone to Dallas or San Fran. I know that sounds a little manipulative on our part, and it is. No doubt. But we also picked you based on your college career and what we think you can add to the team."

"Yessir." I was still waiting for the part where he said something about my performance or told me to step it up or I'd be cut.

"What I'm saying is, don't let your head get the best of you this season. Now go get cleaned up, then sleep off whatever happened this afternoon. Start fresh tomorrow."

"Yessir."

He shook his head with a chuckle. "Christ. You're definitely Houston's brother. Both of you say 'yessir' the same way."

I waited until I was well clear of the office before I slumped against the wall in relief.

I WASN'T FEELING DINNER, SO I GRABBED A PROTEIN SHAKE AND headed back to the room. While I was tempted to climb into bed after showering and soothe my bruised ego with some SportsCenter or *The Good Place*—my guilty pleasure—until I passed out, I forced myself to pull out my binder and study plays.

My eyes were starting to glaze over when the *click* of the door jolted me to attention. I awaited the inevitable teasing as Ramsey let the door fall shut behind him, but he only kept a thoughtful eye on me as he pulled off the long-sleeved tee he was wearing and reached into his bag.

He pulled out two mini bottles of Jack Daniel's and held them up to me.

"Isn't alcohol forbidden?"

Lips quirking, he tossed one my way. "The irony of you asking that... Yeah, it is. I keep them for emergencies."

"This qualifies as an emergency?"

He shrugged. "You had a shitty day, and you're wearing it all over your face."

I rubbed a hand over my face like I was trying to wipe something away. "Damn, must've missed a spot. Yeah, I had a shitty day," I confirmed. "I can't believe I puked."

"Everyone pukes at least once."

"Houston didn't."

"Like hell he didn't." Ramsey twisted the cap off his bottle of Jack, then grabbed a Rush Tervis tumbler and dumped it in along with some ice he'd stored in the tiny freezer of our mini fridge. "Maybe not at camp, but definitely during a practice. More than once, I think."

"Shit, see, even I compare myself to him." I pushed my binder aside, slid to the end of the bed, and grabbed another tumbler off the counter.

"It's hard when it's deeply ingrained. It'll get better with time, just wait."

"Hold up, what are you doing with that?" I asked when Ramsey pulled a Diet Coke out of the fridge.

Index finger poised on the tab, he looked at me like I was an idiot. "Pouring soda into a cup?"

"Fuck that. If you're gonna do Jack and Coke, do Jack and Coke. Diet Coke doesn't count." I slid from the end of the bed and reached around him, grabbing a Coke from the fridge and dumping it in my cup along with the whiskey. "God," I moaned, closing my eyes as the refreshing fizz and sugar rush of the soda mingled with the bite of the whiskey. "That's so damn good."

With a shake of his head, Ramsey put the Diet Coke back and retrieved a Coke. He let out a similarly satisfied groan seconds later as he took the first swallow, the sound doing some messed up shit to my willpower. The long day had weakened my defenses. It wasn't fair.

"God, my body aches." Ramsey set his drink on the bedside table between us, kicked off his shoes, and peeled off his undershirt. He flopped onto the bed and picked up his drink again. "You want to talk about it?"

"Not really, nope. I've had enough of that kind of talk today." When his eyes raked over me, I strongly considered sticking my tongue out at him like a child.

Then he grinned. "Never have I ever puked at training camp."

Really? I turned a scathing look on him that I hoped transmitted my extreme lack of interest in this game or rehashing my puking. Ramsey's stupid blue eyes twinkled with humor as he arched a challenging brow.

I took a small, acquiescing sip of my drink. Fine. I could return fire. "Never have I ever dated someone whose name starts with an *A* or"—I lifted a finger as his grin got wider—"who didn't pull some weird-ass behavior."

"All right, fair. No never have I ever." He picked up the remote and turned on the TV.

"You realize there are amazing, gorgeous women out there who would legit be interested in you, not your money or your career, and who wouldn't squirrel away weird photos of you—yeah, Houston told me about that—and wouldn't ask you to marry them after a month? Yeah, he told me about that too. Seriously, do you have some internal radar for crazy women the way I have bi-fi?"

"Bi-fi?" Ramsey snorted.

"Yeah, you know. Like gaydar." I ticked a finger back and forth like a probe. "*Beep, beep, beep.* Uh-oh, I think I'm in a dead zone."

Instead of laughing like I expected him to, Ramsey tilted his head, raking his teeth over his lower lip. "Maybe you need to get it checked."

I cackled and then stopped suddenly, blinking. "What?"

"What?"

We'd missed a connection. Or a sentence. Maybe a whole paragraph. "You said I need to get my bi-fi checked, as in it's not functioning properly. As in there is another bi in the room, and since I don't see anyone else in here besides you..."

He scratched his jaw. "I've never acted on it, so..."

Now I was thoroughly confused, and also something else, something I couldn't put my finger on yet. "What, is this like the sexuality version of if-a-tree-falls-in-the-forest argument? If a guy gives you wood and no one is around to see it, you've still got wood. So fuck yeah you can be bi without having ever touched another guy. Have you *wanted* to touch another guy?"

"Hold on, don't get me wrong. I'm bi. I'm just saying I've never hooked up with another guy."

For the first time in all the years I'd been around Ramsey, he'd struck me silent.

Briefly.

Then curiosity overwhelmed me.

"Have you been interested in someone before?"

"Not seriously." He shrugged. "It's more like...the idea of it. I thought about downloading an app, hooking up with some random guy. But I haven't done that either. Fuck, it's weird to be talking to you about this."

"Why? It's just me."

"Exactly."

I flipped him off. "Does Houston know?"

"Yes."

I stared at him. "And neither of you told me?"

Ramsey cracked up. "It wasn't any of your business. Why would it even come up?"

"Well, now it is." I guessed it made sense Houston hadn't said anything since he was Ramsey's closest friend, and yeah, it hadn't been my business. But it still felt like a brotherly oversight in my book. "Did you go down a Pornhub rabbit hole?"

"Fuck you." He laughed. "Maybe. I've watched stuff. I was into it, if that's what you're getting at. Very into it."

Do not get hard. Do not get hard imagining Ramsey watching two guys going at it and getting turned on enough to jerk himself off. Do not make the mistake of thinking this means there's any hope for you, because Ramsey is your teammate in addition to a shit ton of other things that would make him a very poor choice as a partner. And for fuck's sake, stop wondering whether he uses an overhand or underhand grip to stroke himself.

"Then there's the whole..." Ramsey gestured around. "Football thing."

"You're afraid someone would take advantage of that? I've hooked up with plenty of guys, and it's never been an issue."

"Yeah, but you're already out." He made a face. "I can just see some guy I hook up with talking to some tabloid or something."

"Well, sure, but that's a risk with a woman too." I kinda saw his point, though. Being established in your sexual identity was a different game than just starting to explore it, and Ramsey wasn't wrong to think someone might choose to exploit him. It was a vulnerable position to be in on a good day, and even more so when you were a star quarterback. *God, Warner Ramsey is fucking bi.*

I needed to get my bi-fi checked for sure. But first, I needed to push aside my own selfish desires. Ramsey might drive me fucking crazy in ways both annoying and sexy, but he'd looked out for me, helped me out, given me advice, and here was my chance to return the favor.

"What if..."

He put up a hand. "Every bad idea that has ever come out of your mouth started with 'what if.' No. Don't even finish the sentence. Just no."

"Harsh." I chuckled. "But hear me out. This is me being genuine. If you want to test the waters with someone, I can help you..." He got a funny look on his face and, worried that meant another denial was forthcoming, I rushed ahead. "No, listen. For just a hookup, you can set your location somewhere else, dress down, give yourself a whole different profession. A whole different persona, even. I can even help you vet the dudes if you want. I have great taste in men, I promise." What the fuck were these words coming out of my mouth? Since when had I had the desire to be helpful? And not just helpful, but helpful to the first guy I'd ever had a crush on.

"Is it anything like your taste in cars?"

"Tread carefully. That car could mow you down in .2 seconds."

Ramsey rubbed that spot along his jaw, then said, "I'll think about it," in a way that suggested he wouldn't at all.

5

RAMSEY

There was a large part of me that wanted to kill Garrett McRae. Okay, that might be taking it a bit too far. I didn't wish him bodily harm, but maybe I could gain the ability to render him speechless anytime I wanted. He'd say something like, *what if*—and I'd snap my fingers and those plump, kissable lips would be stuck closed.

I smiled at the thought.

Hell, maybe I *did* have a kink for annoying-ass people, and a slight sadistic streak too, and it all started with one offer to help me out. My mind had gone directly to an offer of a handy or maybe Garrett getting on his knees for me. That second one was what he said when I took myself in hand during my fantasies... *What if I sucked your cock, Ramsey? What if you shut me up with your cock, Ramsey?*

What if I was losing my fucking mind?

The odds for that were quite high.

I'd gone from wanting to bust his balls, to wondering what they'd feel like against my tongue. It was inconvenient as fuck...and I still wanted to bust them too because that was my favorite thing about Garrett. I had fun with him. He kept me on my toes.

I was also damn proud of him. I could tell he'd been nervous when Coach had called him into his office the day he'd puked, but Garrett hadn't let it get to him. If anything, it had fueled him. He'd had even more drive every time he shot off the line during practice, showing us his incredible speed. Every sit-up and catch drill too, and when I'd seen him after practice, working on his catches and hand-eye coordination with wall balls over and over again, it showed me how seriously he took this. His hunger was impressive, and it sometimes made me think we'd been quick to worry about him, but then he'd say some dumbass shit or I'd over-hear him talking with Cross about trying to sneak women into the hotel during training camp.

Sure, a lot of the guys did shit like that, but rookies needed to be more careful than the rest of us.

Garrett needed to be more careful. He had a lot to prove.

I let my eyes drift ahead a few seats on the plane, seeing him sitting with Cross. They were talking softly, and my nosy ass suddenly wished I'd sat behind him so I could hear.

We were on our way to Vegas for our first preseason game. When I wasn't thinking about *what if*, I was wondering how nervous G was about his first game in the NFL.

"Yo. What are your thoughts on Baby McRae?" Tucker nudged me from his window seat. Malik Tucker was our starting center. Since we lost Houston, Tucker was my closest friend on the team. We played as a unit, him snap-ping the ball to me on every play, so we had to have trust between us. Even if that wasn't the case, I'd like Tucker. He was good people, a big guy—two hundred ninety pounds, six feet four inches of heart.

"If he hears you call him that, he's gonna kick your ass."

"He can try," Tucker replied. "He's good. Cocky but good."

"Yeah, he is." My gaze drifted back to Garrett as he laughed at something Cross said.

"He's different from Houston. Not as serious."

"He wants it just as much, though." My defense of Garrett rolled right off my tongue, without any direction from my brain. Little shit had gotten all up in my head.

Tucker frowned, probably due to the accidental sharpness that had no business being in my tone. "Did I say he didn't?"

Fuck. What in the hell was wrong with me? "Sorry. I just have shit on my mind." That was true enough. I currently had two texts from my dad asking me to call him. I hadn't and didn't plan on it, but Mike Ramsey trying to get ahold of me was never a good thing. He screwed with my concentration, and I hated it. I'd spent the past four years—more, if I was being honest—making sure I did everything in my power to be nothing like him, but it still messed with my confidence. Part of me still thought that if I didn't keep my head in the game, I'd throw it all away just like he had.

But ignoring him also came with a set of problems because fuck, he hated that shit. Feeling rejected often led to him making even more random appearances in my life.

"No big, Cap. We all know you're a grumpy fucker sometimes." I'd been voted into the position after training camp for the second year in a row.

I gave my friend the finger. He offered back a cocky grin before popping his earbuds in. I pulled out my playbook and studied it. We were getting the fucking *W*. I'd make sure of it.

———

WE'D FLOWN IN THE DAY BEFORE THE GAME SO WE COULD GET settled and spend the afternoon in one of the conference rooms at the hotel, going over game film.

I sat with Tucker, Garrett with Cross, while Coach hammered home vital plays and what we had to do to beat Vegas. My attention drifted to Garrett more than it should, but every time it did, he was in the zone. No jokes, no cockiness, just studying Rush football, his eyes glazed over with that hunger that burned so damn intensely in him.

We ate low-fat, high-protein meals to keep our bodies fueled. Tonight it was grilled chicken breast, brown rice and grilled zucchini, and broccoli. After we ate, everyone headed for their rooms. Assignments had stayed the same so far, which mean Garrett and I would be crashing together again.

He was more subdued than usual. And I'd noticed he hadn't flashed his cock at me again now that he knew I was bi. I wasn't sure how I felt about that. He came out of the shower in his boxer-briefs, his bulge prominent, and goddamn, did he have a nice ass.

"You're up."

Yes, yes I am, I almost teased. I adjusted myself, but he didn't seem to notice.

Luckily, there was still hot water left for me. I rubbed one out in the shower. Everyone had their own routine, and part of mine was an orgasm the night before a game.

Garrett had his nose in the playbook when I got out. He sat on the bed, back against the headboard, legs out in front of him. "You guys are a strong running team—which is obviously good for me—but I'm scared as shit I'm gonna get out there and forget the plays."

I lingered beside his bed for a moment, then realized I looked like a fucking creeper and sat beside him. "*We* are."

"Huh?"

"You said *you guys*, but you're part of the team, so *we* are a strong running team."

"Guess I'm still getting used to it," Garrett admitted, quiet vulnerability in his voice, which surprised me. He didn't often show this side.

"I hear ya. You'll adjust. And tomorrow is our night to shine, Superstar. Vegas's defense is better at the short game than our long one. They can't match your speed. You'll have your way with them and—"

"What the fuck are you doing?" Garrett shouted, startling me.

"Um...making you feel better?"

"You're jinxing my ass is what that is. I know I'm the shit, but you're not supposed to *tell* me how I'll have my way with them the night before the fucking game. Goddammit, Ramsey."

I laughed. Hard. He shoved at me, but I could see he was also trying to bite back his smile. "Just how superstitious are you?"

"Enough that you'll be lucky if I don't smother you in your sleep."

Another laugh fell out of my mouth, and he playfully pushed me again.

"You're dead to me, *Captain*. I'm gonna...I don't know, freeze your underwear or some shit." His eyes darted down to the ones I was wearing, and I hoped like hell that didn't get me hard. That was the last thing we needed.

"You'd like to get your hands on my drawers, wouldn't you?"

"Eh. I mean, if I was really hard up, I guess. But I don't think I'm as desperate as you. Out of the two of us, you're the one who needs help getting laid."

And now the offer was on the table again. Fuck my life. "Oh yeah. Okay. Remind me again which one of us said the other is ridiculously hot? It was me who won the genetic lottery, I believe. Your words not mine."

He literally growled at me, giving me an adorable as fuck pouty face. Lucky for me, I didn't let those words out the way he did.

"I will regret that night for as long as I live. It was the alcohol speaking."

"Sure it was, Baby G." Getting back to the point, I added, "I have no problem getting my dick wet. I might not have fucked a guy—"

"Because you need my help."

"Why are you obsessed with my sex life?"

"Who's in whose bed right now? Awfully close too." Our arms brushed. He cocked a brow, and fuck if he didn't have me there.

"Just trying to help a rookie out." I scooted a little farther away but didn't get up. I could smell the soap on his skin. It was different from the hotel stuff I'd used. His had an outdoorsy scent to it, like we were lying under a canopy of trees instead of in a room off the Vegas strip that thankfully didn't stink like cigarette smoke. I hated that in the casinos.

"You download a gay hookup app yet?"

"We back on my sex life again?" Though I'd thought about it. My attraction to Garrett made me want to explore my sexuality more and more, but, as I'd told him, it was harder when you weren't out. If someone talked about sleeping with him, it wouldn't matter as much as it did if someone had a big mouth about me. I just wasn't ready for it to be public knowledge. I didn't figure I needed a reason not to be.

"We never got off the subject, and sorry for looking out. Just hoping your lack of an orgasm doesn't fuck up our game."

"Dude, I came less than an hour ago."

Garrett's brown eyes darkened, heat whooshing off him and wrapping around me, making us feel even closer, before settling in my balls.

"You...in there...just now?" I shrugged at his question. "Fuuuuuck..."

I laughed. "What?"

"Nothing. Fucking Warner goddamned Ramsey," he mumbled, then a few more things even lower that I couldn't make out. "I still think we should consider water conservation when we're rooming together, that's all I'm sayin'."

"You wish, Rookie."

What he didn't know was I wished too.

Before he could respond, my phone buzzed on the table between our beds. Garrett reached over and grabbed it, then handed it over.

"Fuck," I gritted, seeing the name on the screen.

Garrett peeked because that's the way he was. He had no shame. "I didn't know you and your dad still spoke."

"We don't. It's usually just him telling me how ungrateful I am because I wouldn't be where I am without him, how I ruined his life, and oh, that he's a better player than I ever could be, followed by, *You got some cash I can borrow, you ungrateful little shit?*"

Garrett stared at me, his eyes slightly squinty like he was searching for something. Then he plucked my phone out of my hand and powered it down. "You gonna go over these plays with me or not, Cap?"

I grinned. "Yeah, yeah I am." And that's what we did for the rest of the night, before I climbed out of his bed and went to my own.

"'Night, Ramsey."

"'Night, G."

"WHITE 80! WHITE 80. SET HUT!" I CALLED OUT JUST BEFORE Tucker snapped the ball. Our tight end ran forward, the rest of our offensive line blocking the Vegas defensive players coming for me or trying to defend all my offensive options. They'd been all over Garrett's ass most of the game. He hadn't gotten the yardage I knew he would have wanted his first time on the field, but they knew he would be our guy, and they weren't having it.

I tried to tell myself it wasn't my fault and that I hadn't jinxed us last night. It wasn't working.

My eyes scanned the field—left, right, the play I'd called not happening, just before I saw Ward, our running back, and handed it off to him. He dived into the center line and managed to get us two yards.

We had five minutes left in the fourth quarter, and we were down one touchdown. I called the guys in for a quick huddle, checking the plays attached to the cuff on my wrist.

"Your call," Coach said in my earbud, letting me judge what was best instead of calling something himself.

We didn't quite need a hurry-up offense yet, but if we didn't get our shit together, we would. Third and five, but we weren't even within field goal range yet. We just needed five more yards to get the first down.

I looked at Garrett. "You're faster than these guys, better than them." He was faster than he was running tonight. He didn't have his legs beneath him, which I understood. It was his first game, but I wanted this to go well for him for more reasons than just winning. It would inflate his already big ego, but damned if I cared. Nance huffed, but I ignored him. "Get open," I said, before calling out a play for him. I was hoping this would work. I'd backed off trying to get the ball to Garrett since they'd had their defense on point, but Nance, who clearly had something up his ass, wasn't on point tonight either.

Garrett didn't hesitate to nod his agreement.

We broke, everyone heading for their spots on the field. I'd taken a hard hit the last quarter and my side hurt, but I ignored it. The aches and pains never went away; we just learned to live with them on and off the field. "White 80! White 80. Set hut!"

Tucker snapped the ball, and I caught it, keeping my feet moving as I looked toward Nance, and then my eyes sought out Garrett, who wasn't open. It would be smart to hand off to Ward again, let him push his way through the *D*, but I really fucking wanted Garrett to have this.

My gaze darted to Nance again, who was covered, before darting back to Garrett. I watched as he faked right, then went left, not completely breaking away from his coverage but giving me what I hoped was enough space. I launched the football in front of him, just where I thought it could meet Garrett's outstretched arms when he ran. He caught it, pulled it close, and took off, dodging defenders before getting all the way down to the three-yard line.

"Fuck yes!" I shouted, jumping up like he'd fucking scored and won the game for us. I could see the glee in Garrett's eyes, even from a distance.

He hit his chest a few times with his fist, but didn't celebrate yet. We were still losing.

"First fucking down, baby!" Simmons yelled.

A few of the guys pushed him, congratulating Garrett briefly in the huddle. All we needed was another dive play or a short pass to the end zone, and we'd tie the game.

After the cadence and snap, Ward was where he needed to be to barrel his way through the defense, but by chance, I saw Garrett zigzag in the end zone—open, totally fucking open. I pulled my arm back, the ball flying toward him. He jumped up and caught it, just as a defender clipped him.

Garrett flipped and landed on his back. "Oh fuck," I whispered, my heart dropping to my feet, but then he leaped up, dancing. Both relief and pride flooded my chest. He threw the ball to the ground, dropped his head back, and screamed. I swear I *felt* his fucking happiness, the whole stadium vibrating with energy, all coming from him.

There was a defensive penalty on the play, which we denied, before our kicker came out and nailed the extra point. We were in the lead.

We ran off the field for our *D* to take over. I was proud of Garrett, but it was too early to celebrate. We had to stop them or get the ball back because time was running out.

Garrett stood next to me, his arm touching mine, my heart thudding as we watched Vegas try to work their way down the field. As soon as they were in field goal range, I worried we were fucked. I held my breath as their kicker ran out. Garrett reached out, hand on my bicep, squeezing, his nerves making his nails bite into my arm, and... "Hell yes!" Wide. The field goal he had no business missing was fucking wide!

Garrett jumped at me, the crazy motherfucker wrapping his legs around my waist, arms around my shoulders. I stumbled backward, almost falling on my ass, but managed to stay on my feet and hold him. He smelled like sweat, his body solid and so fucking hot against me.

As quickly as it happened, Garrett let go, everyone running over to celebrate with us.

We'd done it. We'd won our first preseason game, and I was pretty sure Garrett was flying. Damn, did I like to see him soar.

6

GARRETT

I'd thought the high of kicking ass at the Gator Bowl senior year of college was intense, but taking Vegas in our first preseason game blew it away. And it wasn't even a "real" game. Vegas was a strong team, though, so scoring that touchdown as a rookie had been validating, especially on the tail end of a brutal training camp.

My mood had soared in the clouds alongside our plane as we flew back to Denver, so of course, when a bunch of the team decided to go out and party, I wasn't gonna miss a chance to keep riding that high.

And also get laid. I deserved it, after all.

"Damn, the pickings are pretty slim tonight." Cross wrinkled his nose and polished off the rest of his vodka and soda.

"Since when are you so picky? Last time we were out, you hooked up with a woman who sounded like she'd swallowed a murder of crows." Seriously, I'd never heard someone with such a screechy voice, and I had a high tolerance for annoying people, obviously, since I myself was often one of them.

"The curves offset the voice." Cross waggled his brows.

I was unconvinced. "I hope you fucked in a soundproof room. I'd feel bad for any neighbors who had to hear all that squawking."

"Ca-*cawwww*." He grinned and flipped me off, then lifted his glass to signal for another as a waitress passed by, before rising. "I've gotta take a piss."

As he walked away, I scanned the crowd from where I sat on one of the club's low leather couches, the table in front of us littered with half-filled glasses next to a bottle of Grey Goose in a silver bucket. The Imperial Room had hooked the team up in their VIP area, which overlooked a packed, neon-lit dance floor, and came complete with its own private bar, bottle service, and dedicated staff—all the shit I'd always looked forward to and now planned to enjoy to the fullest.

Unlike Cross, I had no problem finding late-night potential, since men were on the agenda too. I'd been keeping track of a dark-haired guy who rocked the hell out of the business-exec look in a suit that fit like it'd been custom-tailored. He sat in a little enclave of chairs and tables with a bunch of other men dressed similarly. We'd caught eyes a couple of times, and did so again just then. He gave me an inviting twist of a smile, and I gave him the same back before continuing my visual recon. There was still a lot of night left, and it'd take a really promising lay to make me dip early, but if Business Executive was still around later, well...

I landed on Ramsey next, sporting one of his indulgent smiles as Tucker gestured animatedly. Tucker had been hyped about the win, and I'd put money on it that he was rehashing the game for the twentieth time. He wasn't a fan of the Vegas team, especially their QB, who he said was one of the most arrogant fucks who'd ever stepped foot on the field. I'd heard that too, but I didn't have a strong opinion either way. Still, overhearing him railing against their offense, their uniforms, and their missed field goal on the plane ride back had been entertaining.

As I watched, Ramsey lifted the shot glass one of our other teammates, Ross, handed him, and swallowed it back smoothly. I fought hard not to imagine him on his knees, swallowing me instead, but I needed to keep my eye on something I could actually have in this lifetime.

When after another couple of minutes, neither Cross nor the waitress returned, I stood, headed for the bar, and slid onto an empty stool. The bartender, a stacked dude with hair messily spiked in some kind of homage to punk, stopped in front of me, biceps popping as he leaned on the bar. "What can I get you?"

Late-night potential number 2. I matched his forward lean, getting close enough to see he had a darker ring of blue around his irises. "IPA. Whatever your favorite is that's on draft."

"You got it." He flashed me a wink.

Movement to my left caught my eye, and I turned my head in time to see Business Exec take the stool next to me and set his rocks glass on top of the bar. He gave a cursory glance to one of the flat screens above the bar before angling a playful look at me. "I recognize you."

"Me?" I feigned innocence. "I'm flattered."

He chuckled. "Having half the team here helped put you in context."

"Ouch." I put a hand over my heart. "You mean otherwise you would've just thought I was the hottest guy in the bar?"

He narrowed his eyes, looking me up and down. "Touché. I'm Alex, by the way. Buy you a drink?"

"Ordered one already. Maybe I should buy yours."

"You've certainly got the salary for it."

"My guess is you do too. We can make a game of it if you want. See whose is...bigger?" I joked, arching a brow.

He barked out a laugh. "You'd have me by a mile, I suspect." He cast a look over his shoulder. "I'm technically at a networking event. It's boring as hell, but they tell me I'm necessary. Will you be here for a while?"

"I might."

"Rain check on the drink, then." He tapped the bar in front of me and gave me a pointed look. "And on our discussion of whose is bigger."

I checked out his ass as he walked away—definitely promising—and then turned back as the bartender plunked my fresh beer down in front of me. His gaze swerved to the side as movement, again, caught in my peripheral. "You're a popular one."

I swiveled, ready to tease Alex for his impatience, and found myself staring at Ramsey's broad chest instead.

I forgot all about the bartender and Alex as Ramsey dropped onto the stool beside me. "I think I've had all the Vegas recaps from Tucker I can take in a night, especially knowing Coach is gonna go over all of it again tomorrow. We should just tell him that Tucker has covered it solidly and we're all good. Take the rest of the day off."

"Why's Tucker got such a beef with Hardin, anyway? Has he always been like that?"

Ramsey rubbed his jaw, considering. "I don't think it's really a beef. Tucker is just extremely competitive." One shoulder hitched. "You know how it is. Sometimes those random rivalries pop up for no real reason. Fortunately, it's always directed at other teams."

We both shot a look at Nance and laughed.

I could tell by Ramsey's looser posture that the alcohol had mellowed him. He wasn't stuffy in a general sense, but he usually seemed keenly aware and tuned in to everything going on around him, which was part of what made him a great QB. But the relaxed vibe looked damn good on him too.

"Do you have one?" I asked him.

"A rivalry?" Ramsey's mouth twisted to one side, but then he shook his head. "Nah, not really, aside from LA. Their cornerback Whitt is a dickhead—was in college too. When I was playing for Michigan and we'd play Franklin U, he always acted like his shit didn't stink. And I'm not a big fan of Daryl Rogers, but that wasn't all his fault." Rogers was one of the first players to make contact with Houston after he'd been injured, before the rest of the defense had piled on, which probably made it worse. Ramsey inclined his chin in the direction of the executives. "Who's that guy you were talking to? Your next hookup?"

"Maybe. His name is Alex. Seems cool. I don't know, I might just go back to Houston's and crash. I'm beat." I frowned at the words coming out of my mouth. What the hell? I wasn't lying, I *was* beat, but I'd been full-steam ahead about getting laid until Ramsey had sat down beside me.

"Hmm." Ramsey seemed distracted as he continued eyeing the execs, before his attention veered back to me. "You're still looking at places, right? Or did you decide you'd keep living with Houston?"

"Still looking. I'm picky," I joked, even though it had kinda come as a surprise to me. I'd expected to roll into town and immediately plunk down a large sum on some opulent downtown loft or maybe even a house over in Cherry Hills Village, but despite looking, nothing seemed right yet, so I continued living in one of Houston's spare rooms for the time being. "It's harder to find places with compasses embedded in the floors and shrines to my greatness than you'd think."

"Imagine that." Ramsey chuckled.

"If only it was as easy as getting laid." I mock-sighed, but Ramsey's expression remained thoughtful as he rubbed his thumb idly around the rim of his glass.

"I'm starting to come around to the whole bi-fi thing. Is there a way to tune it or home in on the mother signal or something? You've got guys simping for you left and right." He glanced pointedly at the bartender.

"Requires a lot of practice and study. Dedication. Perseverance." He rolled his eyes at my confessional tone, and I laughed. "It's called eye contact, Ramsey. Jesus. Take the same shit you'd do with a woman and make it...a little less subtle."

"I'm not about to walk around eye-fucking every hot guy I see."

I stared at him, wondering what he considered hot. Hell, for all I knew, Ramsey preferred twinky blonds with a penchant for glittery eyeshadow, or slender intellectual types who drank single-malt scotch. Sweet, nerdy bookstore owners or baristas. None of which I was ever gonna be. "You just have to pay attention," I told him. "If you spot someone you like, see if you can make eye contact. Then gauge the interest from there. A straight guy will usually give a quick acknowledgment—up-nod, grin, whatever—then look away. Someone interested is gonna linger." I picked up my drink and slid off my stool.

"Wait." His brows drew together. "You heading out already?"

"No. I'm about to give you a demonstration. Don't move."

"Jesus, this ought to be good."

"I'm very good," I promised.

I stepped a few paces away from the bar, put my game face on, and then paced back to the empty stool and slid atop it. I set my drink on the bar top as I gave Ramsey a sidelong, lingering look before focusing on the TV screens.

Ramsey threw his head back and laughed. "That's it? That's the shit that requires practice, study, dedication, and perseverance? You looked like you were casing me to see if you could take me in an alley later." I arched a brow, and he rolled his eyes. "I meant 'take me' as in murder me, you pervert."

"I've considered it before." Both murdering him and taking him. The latter was far more enticing. Damn, now I had back-alley shenanigans with Ramsey on the brain. Talking to him was counterproductive sometimes.

"Likewise."

I shook my head, moving my focus back to the TV screen. "That's part 1: tossing the anchor." Time to invoke part 2. Before he could come up with some smart-ass reply, I turned my head and looked him over again, really looked him over, the way I rarely allowed myself to. Letting my gaze roam slowly from the crown of his head, I paused on that stern mouth of his I'd fantasized about, open and gasping in pleasure, or wrapped around my cock, or whispering dirty shit as he fucked me. I dropped lower, just for a beat, to his lap, where his jeans stretched tight over his quads, to the mouthwatering bulge that had tempted me way too many times while wrapped in a towel, then moved back to the piercing icy blue of his eyes. I held eye contact, unleashing all the desire and damn want I'd kept at bay for years, feeling it speed up my pulse as I leaned closer and dropped my voice so he had to lean in too. "Wanna get the hell out of here so I can fuck you inside out?"

His lips parted, pupils flaring wide and dark, and for just a second I could swear I saw something close to interest, *genuine* interest, that scorched through me like a lightning bolt.

Then he set his jaw and huffed out a laugh as he leaned back. "That actually works?"

"Yep. Also..." I pulled my phone from my pocket and opened Grindr. "There's a cheat code."

Ramsey stared as the screen populated with available guys nearby. "Damn, they're all over the place." He ticked his head toward the executives. "So were you already talking to that guy over there?"

"On the app?" I laughed. "No. I've got my profile hidden, but I found his, yeah." I clicked and pulled it up. "You know, you're awfully interested for someone who said they weren't interested."

"I'm just curious how it usually goes down."

"Houston is your best friend. You haven't picked up on it yet?"

"You know how low-key he is about everything. I never knew when he was hooking up or with whom. He'd just disappear."

That sounded about right. I extended my palm. "Give me your phone."

His hand flew to his pocket protectively. "Fuck no."

"You downloaded apps." My smile grew as he scowled. "Holy shit, do you already have a profile up and you're just playing dumb?" I scanned my screen again and clicked on a random profile before blinking my eyes wide at Ramsey in faux shock. "Dirty4Daddy69, is that you?" I scrolled down the listing and read aloud. "'Foot fetishist who will let you spank me all day and top me all night.' Mmm, you kinky fucker. Who knew?" And even though there was no way that was Ramsey, just wondering whether or not he was a little kinky got me hot.

He burst into a laugh. "No. Goddammit, I don't have any apps, and I don't want you to put any on my phone. I'm just asking questions."

"Offer still stands. Just saying."

"Nope." He grabbed his drink and stood, touching his brow in a mock salute. "I'm heading home. Good luck with your hookup."

Luck wasn't necessary, but a half hour later, my interest in Alex had waned. I really was tired. Plus, we'd have to go to his place, and then I'd have to jet back to Houston's in the morning before football. Or we'd have to fuck in a bathroom, which I wasn't usually against but wasn't in the mood for tonight. It had absolutely nothing to do with that split-second look in Ramsey's eyes earlier. Nothing at all.

THE NEXT MORNING I WOKE UP TO MY PHONE VIBRATING incessantly.

Ramsey: Hey
Ramsey: You awake?
Ramsey: We're going out next Monday night.
Garrett: I usually like to be asked, but I can appreciate alpha male initiative. Pick me up at 8. I hate roses and daisies. Tulips are fine.
Ramsey: FFS. I can see you're still typing. Don't even bother with some dumb two-lips joke.
Garrett: Fine. Okay, so where are we going?
Ramsey: To find me a hookup.

Ramsey: If you've got that stupid cocky grin on your face right now, wipe it off.
Ramsey: You're now my default wingman option due to proximity.

I did have a cocky grin on my face, and when it ebbed, it wasn't because of his second comment but because I was beginning to suspect my generosity was about to bite me in the ass.

Damn.

7

RAMSEY

I'd finally found the way to shut up Garrett McRae.

I tilted my head down, took in the sight of him on his knees, looking up at me with big, brown eyes full of heat and a mouth stuffed with my cock.

Fuck yeah.

He bobbed on me, taking me to the back of his throat, working his tongue just right, swallowing around the head every time I thrust my hips forward to fuck his pretty, smart-ass mouth.

"I like this Garrett. Hard to talk shit with my dick stretching out your lips."

Mischief and fiery want sparked in his eyes, making Garrett's pupils blow wide. He pulled off, leaned close, inhaling deeply before lapping at my balls. "Of course you like this Garrett. I'm gonna make you come so hard, all your future orgasms will fail to compare."

My dick jerked, and my knees buckled. Why did he get to me so fucking much? That shouldn't have been hot, but it was. "You wish, Little G. Now shut up and suck my cock. I'm getting bored."

He laughed. "Only because I want you to remember that the

best orgasm of your life was from me...and I might want to drain a load out of your balls too."

I held his head, pushed past his lips, and snapped my hips forward. Garrett took it like a champ, like if there were a cock-sucking Olympics, he'd win gold every fucking time.

One kiss. All it had taken was one goddamned kiss to get us here.

He whimpered, and I grinned. "Yeah, there we go, take that dick like a good boy."

He lifted his arm and gave me the finger. Only Garrett would flip someone off during head.

But then that hand lowered to my balls next, cupping and tugging on them just a little before his finger sneaked back to rub my taint. Tingles started at the base of my spine, my vision went blurry, and—

Ding! Ding! Ding!

"Oh fuck." My eyes popped open at the sound of my alarm going off. "Goddamn, son of a bitch, Garrett fucking McRae." Even Dream Garrett, sucking my cock, was annoying, because somehow, it was his fault he didn't coax an orgasm out of me before I woke up.

It had been like this all week. I didn't know how he managed to get inside my head so thoroughly, but he had. It was unnerving as hell. I'd never experienced something like this before. I sure as shit hadn't had sex dreams about someone days in a row just because they'd mock-hit on me. He threw out the anchor and somehow caught my ass, but I would never tell him that.

My alarm went off again, so I reached over, grabbed my phone, and turned it off before plucking the lube out of my nightstand drawer. I slicked up, dropped my hand below the blanket, and took my dick in hand. I was aching, balls full, precum pooling in one of the valleys between my stomach muscles.

I kicked free of the comforter. My hand didn't feel as good as Fantasy Garrett's mouth, but it would get me off. I needed to get laid. It had been too long. Hell, was Alyssa the last one? I was pretty sure she had been. I didn't ever go this many months without getting my dick wet.

I had a feeling I knew the culprit behind why I'd waited.

I tightened my hold, stroked myself with long, lazy pulls before speeding up, jacking myself quickly, then taking it down a notch again. I focused on the crown, twisting my slick palm around my glans, little bursts of pleasure going off inside me, multiplying as I rubbed myself just right.

Before I knew it, my whole body was tingling, all those pinpoints of satisfaction coming together to explode in one giant *fuck yes* when my balls drew up and I shot all over my stomach, chest, and hand.

Damned if brown eyes and a cocky grin didn't flash behind my closed eyelids when I did.

With a frustrated growl, I climbed out of bed and went straight for the shower. Tuesdays were our only days off, which was why I'd chosen Monday to go out with Garrett. Hopefully, I'd have enough fun that I'd need to sleep in the next morning.

Depending on our schedule each week, Fridays were often reserved for games or traveling. Football season was a grueling six months, but there was nothing I loved more. Where my dad had floundered under the curfews, schedule, and discipline, I flourished. It was possible to have a good time *and* be in the NFL.

I cleaned up, threw on a pair of shorts, a Rush tee, and my Adidas. They'd sponsored me for the past two years, so it was lucky they were actually my preferred brand.

After whipping up and sucking down a smoothie, I headed toward my vehicle so I could get to the practice facility early. The sun was riding behind me, and over one of my favorite trails at Cedar Grove. When we didn't have practice, it was where I ran. I didn't feel right without some kind of physical activity every day.

Like fucking.

That was physical.

Fucking Garrett would be physical as hell because I could see both of us battling for control... *Get a fucking grip*, I chastised myself. Jesus, what was it with this guy? He screwed with my head, and I didn't like it. At all.

That would all change tonight. He'd play my wingman, even though I had to admit, I still had my doubts. How did I know I could trust whoever we found? But Christ, I couldn't keep going this way either. I'd find a guy, and once I had my dick in a man who wasn't Garrett McRae, my desire to explore my bisexuality would be quelled, and with it, my obsession with him.

It wasn't him I wanted, just a dude.

Or so I told myself.

WE'D DECIDED TO STEER CLEAR OF THE IMPERIAL ROOM because a lot of the team partied there. I had no desire to run into any of the guys when I was trying to meet someone to figure out if I liked sucking cock. I mean, I knew I would. I was attracted to men. I wanted men. I always had. I just hadn't had the behind-the-wheel practice yet.

G said he'd heard Fusion was a popular bar with a pretty diverse clientele. Like the Imperial Room, it was frequented by businesspeople—local and those traveling. It was also known as a popular spot for both queer and straight people to drink. If anyone saw us there, it wouldn't out me before I was ready like it might if we hit up a gay bar, but I also didn't have to worry about most of the guys around me only looking for women.

I took a car service there in case I had a few drinks and couldn't drive home. When I pulled up, Garrett was already waiting for me, leaning against the redbrick building and looking hot as hell in a pair of perfectly fitted jeans and a black tee. My style was slightly all over the place—half jock, half sophisticated. I wore jeans, a button-up white shirt, sleeves rolled to my elbows, and a backward hat.

"Thanks, man," I told the driver before climbing out. If he'd recognized me, he hadn't said so. Then I turned to Garrett. "You're early. You miss me, Little Man?"

Garrett pushed off the wall, and fuck if I didn't watch his body move as he did. Despite his size, he was graceful in everything he did, agile and smooth, so that even something as easy as standing up straight drew a person's attention just as much as when he dodged the defense while rushing down the field.

Okay, not just as much, because Garrett playing ball was a beautiful thing to watch, but he looked good just *being* too.

"I've got a lot of work ahead of me tonight. I figure with me here, I'm not sure how much anyone else will want you."

I barked out a harsh, deep laugh. "In your dreams." His gaze started at the top of my head and traveled down my body, hot and appreciative, burning with both confidence and blatant desire. I rolled my eyes. "Stop trying to hit on me."

"I'm giving you a lesson again. You're a newbie, so I thought you might have forgotten my previous instruction."

Aaaaaand, maybe it was time to knock Garrett down a

peg or two. I let myself appreciate him, let myself take in each muscle as it moved and his chest while he breathed, the way his Adam's apple suddenly bobbed like he was struggling to swallow. I stepped closer, then closer still, not stopping until his back was against the building, my chest against his, Garrett's warm breath on my skin when he let it out shakily.

Fuck, he felt good, hard muscle and the scent of some outdoorsy cologne. I willed my dick to be good and not try for a meet and greet with his. I pressed my hands flat against the wall, one on each side of him. "I can assure you," I whispered close to his ear, rubbing my cheek against his temple before lowering my lips close to his other ear. "If I want someone in my bed, I have no problem getting them there."

He trembled, fucking *trembled*, and damned if blood didn't rush toward my groin. *Mayday! Mayday!* This was a dangerous game I was playing, but it was fun too. I couldn't lie, I liked a little bit of forbidden, and Garrett felt very much like a favorite toy I couldn't play with.

"Wow...someone is speechless?" I asked, still close, our body heat wisping around us like invisible ropes tying us together.

His hands went to my waist, fingers pressing in with enough pressure that I couldn't deny he was there. "If I'm the one you want, all you have to do is ask." This time, the tremor rocked through me, vibrated along my fault line before setting off an earthquake inside me. He was playing with me, testing me, I knew that, but it took everything in me not to teach the cocky little shit a lesson and take his mouth with mine. Garrett cocked his head, lips close to my ear like I'd done to him. "Cat got your tongue?"

"You're playing with fire." My voice came out on a growl.

What the fuck was going on here? This was not the plan, but I couldn't seem to stop myself.

"Or maybe you're all talk and no bite?"

Fuck if my dick wasn't completely hard then, throbbing and pulsing with desire for him. This was getting out of hand quickly, but I'd never met a challenge I couldn't accept, so I leaned down and bit his bottom lip, my teeth sinking in, tongue swiping at the puffy skin here. It was quick, too quick, but definitely enough to elicit another sharp inhale from him.

With one more swipe of my tongue, I let his lip go.

His hold on me tightened, enough to leave bruises now, and damned if I didn't want the evidence of this moment on my skin for later.

Our gazes locked. Fuck, fuck, fuck. This was bad, so goddamned bad. I had no business wanting Houston's little brother...my fucking *teammate*.

Hoooooonk!

The long blow of the horn snapped us out of whatever lust-trance we'd been in. We jerked away from each other like a bolt of lightning struck between us. Jesus, I'd almost kissed Garrett...I'd *bitten his fucking lip* on the street, where anyone could have seen us. What had gotten into me? I'd lost my head. I couldn't imagine the mess that could have gotten us in. Two NFL teammates caught kissing? It would be a media circus, something I wanted nothing to do with. I wanted to be known for how well I played football, not for weekly stories about how I fucked up, even if it was different from the mistakes my dad had made.

Garrett spoke first. "We should, um...go inside."

Or we could go back to my place and finish what we started...
"Yeah, we should."

The entrance to Fusion was on the other side of the

building. We headed that way silently, not looking at each other, hell, nearly five feet of space between us.

"I got it," I managed to say to Garrett while I handed money to the bouncer to get in.

He must have still been in shock about whatever we'd done outside because he didn't argue.

Bass made my chest vibrate when we went inside. The music was loud, some fucking pop song, but I didn't know the artist. Garrett went straight for the bar, and I was right along with him. I needed a fucking drink. Stat.

We were lucky enough to grab two open seats there. "What can I get you?" the bartender asked.

"Whiskey, please," Garrett said.

"Make that a double for me," I added.

Garrett signaled for the same, then absently reached up and touched his lip where I'd bitten him. I must have done it harder than I'd thought because it was slightly swollen.

Would you like me to kiss it better?

The second the bartender finished pouring, we downed them in long gulps until the glasses were empty, and Garrett said, "Another."

I held out mine as well.

Garrett paid for the drinks, and I let him. The bartender went to help someone else, leaving us nursing the brown liquid that burned when I swallowed.

"Let's see what we have." Garrett pulled out his phone, wasting no time.

"G."

"Shit. We scored. There are lots of options here, especially for a Monday night."

"G," I said again.

"What?" he snapped.

"I'm sorry...for biting your lip." We stared at each other

again, his eyes matching the whiskey, gazes holding before laughter fell from both of us. It was the most ridiculous thing. Had I really just apologized for biting him?

My stomach muscles hurt, I laughed so hard. Luckily, he found it just as funny. When we finally settled down, he said, "It's all good. I'm hard to resist."

"I still have a bad taste in my mouth."

"Fuck you." He took a drink. "Now shut up and let's find you some dick."

We looked at his phone together, and damn, there *were* a lot of men here looking to get laid.

He clicked on the first profile.

"Nah, not him," I replied.

Garrett chose another. "Fuck, he's hot."

"He says he's a top only. I'm not looking to get dicked down my first time out."

He cocked a brow. "But that's a possibility for you?"

I winked. "Wouldn't you like to know?"

He went to the next, then the next, but every one he chose, I found something wrong with them. "Jesus, Rams, you're trying to suck some cock, not marry someone."

"I'm picky, what can I say?"

"Stalkers only need apply?" he teased, referring to my ex.

Actually, my dick was currently on the Garrett-McRae-only train, and I needed to find a way to get off it. "Pick another one," I said, just as someone slipped onto the open stool beside me.

He had blond hair, wide blue eyes, and dark lashes. His mouth was fucking hot, all plump lips, which then made me think of Garrett's bruised lip *from my teeth*.

"Can I buy you a drink?" he asked, giving me an appraising look, so I knew just what he was looking for, which apparently was me. This wasn't a bro thing; this was an I-want-to-fuck thing. Garrett had been right about the anchor-stare method because Blondy used it on me.

A hand came down on my shoulder, squeezing, before Garrett slid out of the seat. Where the fuck was he going?

"Umm...yeah. That'd be cool." That'd be cool? I sounded like an eighteen-year-old virgin.

Blondie signaled for the bartender and ordered two more whiskeys.

"I'm Bailey."

"Warner," I replied. Even the media called me Ramsey, so it felt safer to use my first name.

"Nice to meet you, Warner. I haven't seen you around before. I definitely would have noticed."

I shrugged. The guy was fucking hot, but I was pretty sure this wasn't happening. It felt like too much of a risk. When I came out, I wanted it to be on my terms, and how the hell did I know if this guy realized who I was? Or what if he did later, and all of a sudden the league would be talking about me getting blown in a bathroom stall by some dude? Even though there were a few out guys in the league, it was still always something that was discussed in a way it wasn't with het couples or hookups.

Still, I didn't want to be a dick. "You from around here?" I asked.

"Yep. Hence why I know I haven't seen you here before."

Shit. That was a dumb question. "What do you do?"

Bailey started rambling about tech stuff I had zero interest in, and I couldn't help spinning my stool around and scanning the crowd for Garrett. Where the fuck had he gone?

Bailey did the same, the two of us drinking slowly, him rambling and not seeming to notice I wasn't interested. It was a good thing he excelled at talking about himself so I didn't need to add much input— "What the fuck?" I said softly.

"What's wrong?"

Garrett was dancing...*with a guy*, who had his ass against Garrett's groin, feeling the dick that had been against me just a little while ago. And Garrett was running his hands up and down the guy's chest like his lip wasn't swollen from my bite.

Discomfort pooled in my gut before turning into thick lava that rose until it filled my chest. The guy turned and kissed Garrett's neck, and G's hands were on his hips like they had been on mine, and...oh God. Was I *jealous*? I was going to kick his fucking ass. I couldn't believe I wanted him that much, but I did.

"I gotta go," I told Brandon...Bailey...whatever the fuck his name was. I set my drink down, then handed him some cash so I wasn't a complete asshole.

Garrett's gaze landed on me as I worked my way through the crowd. He was still touching the guy, rubbing him and tilting his head so the guy could make out with his neck. But the whole time, that feeling in my chest was mirrored in his eyes.

"Let's go," I said the second I reached him.

"Say please."

"You're such a brat. Let's go. Please." I was too annoyed to even argue with him.

Garrett kissed the guy on the cheek, and then the two of us made our way to the door. We were silent like we had been when we came in, me leading, Garrett following. I didn't know what the fuck I was doing, or where I was going, or why I suddenly wanted him so much, it was hard to breathe. Yeah, I'd always been attracted to him. He amused the shit out of me. I loved how he never stopped giving me hell, but this *craving* for him was different.

The second we were around the backside of the building, alone in an alley that, unfortunately, stank like trash, I pushed him against the wall and took his mouth with mine.

There I was, straggling after Ramsey out of the club and trying to suss out his sudden desire to bail—had the guy he was talking to pissed him off? Been a prick? Been pushy?—when he whirled around on me, a feverish intensity in his eyes.

For one brief second, I thought he was about to yell at me.

Next thing I knew, my back slammed into a wall for the second time that night.

This time with more force.

And this time with the addition of Ramsey's mouth sealing over mine. Not in a bite, but a kiss that short-circuited every thought zipping through my head.

Full of heat and need, his kiss simultaneously crashed over me like a wave and shot through me like lightning. The warring sensations left me light-headed, and I gasped for breath as my lips parted beneath his. His tongue slid over mine, smooth as silk, and I tasted him for the first time.

Long-term crushes were weird. I'd gotten so used to the unrequited part, at first I didn't know what the fuck to do with the fact that it was now being requited, at least physically.

In my fantasies, I'd touched Ramsey a hundred times, grasped him firmly, confidently, plundered his mouth, tugged him closer, pushed him away, yanked his pants down, his shirt off, his socks, shoes. A hundred imaginary articles of his clothing had been destroyed, ripped, or torn off in my daydreams, and now that this moment was actually happening, the tremor that'd run through me earlier returned. My stomach went all jittery, alive with bone-deep desire that spread outward, seeking an outlet that finally came in the form of a moan that rumbled through my chest.

Then instinct kicked in, reminding me what I was supposed to be doing: enjoying the hell out of this, saturating myself in it. Later I could question motivation. Right now? I just needed to give in to the primal urge that always came alive around Ramsey.

I needed to *take*.

The jittery feeling subsided, hunger surging in its wake as my fists unclenched and I sank into the kiss. When Ramsey's grip on me slackened, as if he might pull away, I snaked a hand into the waistband of his jeans and hauled him around the side of the building where the darkness was thicker, and then shoved him against the wall the same way he had me.

He let out a short, sharp grunt as he smacked into the bricks, and before he could get a word out, I closed my mouth over his again, determined to savor this singular event down to its marrow.

He tasted like whiskey and the bite of pepper, and the kiss morphed from fervent savagery to a more exploratory tempo, like he was enjoying the taste of me too. A minute shift of his hips sent a torturous, tempting pleasure corkscrewing through me.

Just to see what would happen, I rolled my hips once, my aching dick gliding firmly against his in one long, slow slide. Ramsey let out a groan that made me want to reach deeper behind his waistband, wrap a hand around his shaft, and get him off right there in the alley, but I resisted, just barely. This being Ramsey's first guy-on-guy kiss, it might've been overkill, and fuck knew, I didn't want to overwhelm him. Too much.

It occurred to me I was thinking with my upstairs brain, and I didn't like it. I reengaged the downstairs brain and focused on the kissing part again because it turned out that Real Ramsey was just as stellar a kisser as Fantasy Ramsey.

Letting go of his waistband, I slid both palms up to his jawline, his stubble biting into the skin of my palms, and held him close, our cheeks brushing when we finally broke for air or risked passing out.

"Fuck," he muttered on a gusty exhale that warmed the side of my neck.

"Okay," I said in a teasing murmur. "Your place or your place? Because I'm kind of squatting currently." I had no idea how it would go over, were I to trot into Houston's loft with his best friend in tow and every intention to get loud in the bedroom next to his.

Turned out, that was the wrong thing to say.

Ramsey's laughter was too soft, too brief. He leaned back, lifting his gaze to mine. It was enough for me to read the caution in his eyes.

I changed tack. "That was a joke, obviously." I didn't want things to get weird, and I was well aware that we were about one second away from that happening. "I didn't realize your annoyance kink was so strong."

His mouth quirked into a smile that was more familiar. "I guess it took over."

"You might need to work on that self-control." I definitely didn't want him to work on self-control. In fact, I wished he would set fire to all the self-control he possessed right then so I could get him someplace private and work him over the way I'd wanted to forever.

He did that laugh again, the soft chuckle that told me the gears were cranking in his mind. I took a step back, giving him space, and he ran a hand over the top of his baseball cap.

When he looked down, my gaze followed. His dick and mine sported matching denim tents.

He sighed. "You know that was a bad idea, right?"

"Nope." I offered an innocent shrug. "I have idea dyslexia, remember? Good, bad, they get all mixed up." It was probably true, if I really thought about it.

Ramsey muttered another curse. Since the party was clearly over, I swiveled around and rested my shoulders against the wall next to him. "So what happened back inside? Does someone need their ass kicked? Did you embarrass yourself and totally choke?"

"Nah." Ramsey hesitated, then shrugged. "I don't think I'm going to be able to force this, like, just dive in with some rando. I wasn't feeling that guy. Wasn't feeling any of them. Not enough to take anyone home."

"And it pissed you off enough to storm out and rage-kiss me?"

He snorted. "Rage-kiss? That's a new one."

"I just made it up, but you defined it. It's canon now."

"I guess I did." He quirked another small smile, then rubbed a hand over his face. "Fuck, that was bad form. I'm sorry. I just came at you out of nowhere."

"It was a kiss, Rams." And it'd been fucking awesome, but whatever. "It's not third grade. It doesn't mean you're my boyfriend. We don't have to make a thing about it. It's possible for people to hook up and for it not to be a big deal, you know."

"Well aware, but that usually works out better when it's not someone on the same team as you and not your friend's little brother whom you have to see every day."

"I think you're gonna have to drop the 'little' thing, considering that noise you made when my dick rubbed against yours."

"Fine. Brother. My friend's *brother*. And teammate." He glanced at me. "And I reserve the right to reinvoke 'little' at any time."

"I reserve the right to make you regret it."

"Our status quo, basically?"

"Yep." The banter eased some of the tension in my shoulders. I'd said what I did about the kiss not being a big deal because I didn't want any awkwardness between us. But it was also true. Or could be. It would take two of us to make that happen, though. "So..." I slanted a sidelong look at him. "Your first kiss with another guy... How's it stack up? Your dick seemed to give it a rave review."

"It was all right." Ramsey knocked his shoulder against mine and smirked. "Could've used more tongue. Or maybe less. I don't know. I wasn't paying much attention. Got distracted thinking about paint drying."

"Please. I'll go up against any Ashley, Alyssa, or Arnold any day." I narrowed my eyes, catching an equivalent heated flash in his that almost had me lunging for him all over again.

"It was good, okay?" He averted his gaze, staring off into the distance. Okay, message received. No second servings of

Ramsey for me. "I definitely enjoyed it, and it definitely shouldn't happen again."

He wasn't wrong. Once more, the part of my brain I usually despised engaging in situations like these reminded me that it would be a long season—hell, career—if we were hooking up and shit went south.

"Fine. Just try to not to jerk off too many times tonight thinking about me. Wouldn't want that golden arm to be sore for practice." I shoved off the wall and ticked my head toward the front of the club.

"Somehow I think I'll manage." He trailed after me with a laugh.

Bad idea to think about Ramsey jerking off. "Share an Uber?"

HOUSTON WAS SPRAWLED ON THE COUCH, WATCHING ESPN, when I got back to his place. I grabbed a water from the fridge and flopped onto the couch next to him.

He glanced down at an imaginary watch, then eyed me suspiciously. "You're home early."

I shrugged one shoulder lazily. "Club sucked." I *wished* there had been sucking. Odds were a hundred percent I was gonna go to bed, relive the sensation of Ramsey's mouth on mine, jack off, and still manage to have a wet dream about him. God, I was becoming pathetic.

"What's that look on your face?"

I blinked. "What look?"

"Dunno." He shrugged and looked back at the TV. "You getting along with everyone on the team?"

"Yeah. Nance doesn't seem to like me very much, but whatever. He'll get over it eventually." Or he wouldn't, but I was trying not to sweat it. I'd gotten along with everyone on the team at Silver Ridge U.

"I think that's just how he is. He gets jealous easily. Don't take his shit, though, just because you're new."

"It's all good." I eyed him sidelong. "You know you can come out with us anytime. The guys would love it. They're still your friends."

Houston blew out a long breath. "I know. But it's not the same, and every time I've done it before, it just reminded me that's no longer my life."

"You can't hide in here all the time." I got it, but I still hated the idea of him hanging out solo week in and week out.

He snapped a sharp look at me. "I do other things. I have other friends."

"Yeah? Like who?"

"Don't do that pity shit. I texted Rams a while earlier to see what he was up to, but he was busy. See, social interaction attempt made. You can stop worrying now."

The memory of Ramsey's body against me, his mouth on mine, roiled through me with fresh heat. I studied my brother's profile. He'd dated and hooked up, but it'd been a long time since he'd been involved seriously with anyone. Like, since before he'd gone pro. "Did you ever have a thing for Ramsey?"

"What?" He chuckled and rolled his eyes at me.

"I'm serious. Rookie year y'all were always together, so I just wondered if you had a thing for him." I had to tread carefully since Houston didn't know Ramsey had told me he's bi.

"I might have had a small crush on him." He spread his thumb and forefinger an inch apart. "For five minutes, but it would have never been reciprocated. Plus, half the US does.

And that was never gonna happen anyway for a shit ton of reasons. He's so focused on not fucking up his career, he's never gonna do anything that could potentially be slanted in a negative light or draw unwanted attention to himself." He gave me a longer look. "Word of advice, G—"

"Oh Jesus." I sighed and waited for the inevitable.

"Don't even think about fishing from the team pool. That's a shit idea. Find other ponds."

I raised my brows. "I don't remember saying anything about fishing from the team. I was just asking about you, asshole. Fuck off."

He kept giving me that stern look until I finally flicked condensation from my water bottle at him and told him I was going to bed. He was right that there were plenty of other ponds to fish in. I could totally be content that I'd made Warner Ramsey's head spin at least once. And now we could go back to our usual routine.

Except, it didn't exactly work out that way.

9

RAMSEY

K*issing your best friend's brother and NFL teammate is a great idea*...said no one ever. I didn't usually lose my head like that. I was good at determining how much damage something could do before making the decision whether to go ahead or bail on the plan. Life would be boring without a little bit of fun, so it wasn't like I always toed the line. I was just smart about when I chose to cross it, and I hadn't made that decision with Garrett. It had just happened because I wanted him so fucking much.

Twice. It had just happened *twice*. First when I bit him, then when I kissed him.

I was so fucked.

The rest of preseason we steered clear of each other. Yeah, we were together at practice and games. We talked shit and gave each other hell because we wouldn't be Garrett and Ramsey if we didn't, but there was no more touching, no more dumbass ideas about going out together, or playing wingman, or *how about I shove you against the wall and stick my tongue down your throat?*

We were good boys, but I was pretty sure neither of us

wanted to be. The heat in his gaze damn near scorched me every day. The evidence of the desire in my stare showed in the flush of his cheeks and the inferno in his eyes. We tried to ignore it, like we were right now, him on his hotel bed, me on mine, while we went over our playbook after just finishing hours of game film. I'd just put my heating pad away after trying to soothe sore muscles.

We could work out the Houston part a whole lot easier than we could the teammate part. The NFL had worked hard since Anson Hawkins, a former tight end for the Atlanta Lightning, had come out. He'd been the first in the league, followed by his teammate Darren Edwards, but... they hadn't been fucking each other. Therein lay the problem. Players screwing other men behind closed doors in their own homes was one thing. Players fucking each other was a hard limit I was fairly certain the NFL would safeword out of before the fun even started.

And even if they were okay with it, I didn't want to be their poster boy. All I wanted was to play ball.

Well, and fuck Garrett McRae. There was still that.

Our first game of the regular season was in Pittsburgh. We'd lost once during preseason, which was one too many for my liking. It was all part of the game and blah, blah, blah, but I fucking hated to lose. Most of the guys who really gave a shit did.

Pittsburgh was known for their short game. They were big-ass sons of bitches who were better at barreling through the defense than throwing long bombs down the field. None of their defenders matched Garrett's or Nance's speed, though. Hell, they couldn't match Ward's either, but despite Ward's experience in the league and the fact that he was an incredible running back who played smart football, no one was as fast off the line as G. Once he got his legs under him a bit and got used to football at this level, no one would be able to fuck with him.

"You nervous about tomorrow?" I asked.

"Nah, I'm good." Garrett adjusted himself, and I didn't hide that I was watching.

"Stop looking at me like that."

"Like what?"

"Like you're two seconds away from tearing my clothes off."

"In your dreams. You do that, you know? Dream about me... Say my name in your sleep over and over again."

"The lie detector has determined that is a lie. I don't even want you anymore. Kissed you, wasn't that good, got it out of my system."

I laughed my ass off, and then for shits and giggles, laughed some more. We both knew that wasn't true, but then, Garrett could say the same thing about me.

"Shut up and go to bed, Rams. We have a game tomorrow."

I hit the lights, then climbed into bed before getting serious for a minute. "It's okay to be nervous."

"Is it okay to want to strangle you in your sleep? Asking for me."

When I passed out, it was with a smile on my face. Why the fuck was Baby G so much fun?

WE WERE KILLING IT. WE WERE UP BY TWENTY-ONE POINTS, and it was the last drive of the game—Pittsburgh with the ball. We were running off the field as the defense took their places on it. The second I hit the sideline, I opened my mouth for one of the water guys to hydrate me. It was weird as fuck, other people squirting water into your mouth, but it was a thing that happened, so I went with it.

I glanced over to see Garrett doing the same, and the motherfucker winked at me, because of course he did.

We'd been on fire tonight. If Garrett had been nervous, it hadn't affected his game. We'd come in expecting to beat Pittsburgh, but not a blowout.

We didn't allow ourselves to celebrate early on the sideline. I turned and watched as Hammond pummeled their running back just shy of the first down.

"Jesus, I feel like I can't fucking stay still." Garrett slid up beside me. "Like I'm going to burst out of my skin."

"Yeah, great, isn't it? I love the adrenaline of a game, and the high that comes with winning."

"Me too."

Pittsburgh fought their asses off, trying to make some dent in our lead despite having no chance of winning, but the time ran out just as Bette tackled their tight end.

The *W* was ours.

"Fuck yes!" Garrett screamed as our *D* came running off the field.

We were back-slapping, ass-grabbing, congratulating each other, when Alice Andrews, from NBC Sports, came jogging over. "Ramsey, Garrett, can I grab the two of you together?"

"Sure thing. Just make sure you get me from my good side." Garrett tugged off his helmet.

"You have one of those?" I teased, making Alice laugh.

She shoved a mic in our faces, and the camera was rolling. "The two of you have great chemistry on the field, but it seems you have it off it too."

"Eh, he's all right," I joked.

"Do you think that has anything to do with Garrett being

Houston McRae's little brother? You and Houston were a beautiful thing to watch, and now it's his younger brother trying to fill his shoes."

I felt Garrett stiffen beside me.

"He's not trying to fill anyone's shoes. Garrett's a great player, who's playing his game and helping the team get to where we want to be, just like Houston played his. Think we can stop with the comparisons and appreciate the fact that the Rush have been lucky enough to have two McRae brothers who are their own people and are both class acts on and off the field?" I hated this shit. Unlike G, if I could play ball and not have the rest of the hoopla, I would. I hated this side of it—the attention and being a star.

Alice paused for a moment, the surprise clear in her wide, blue eyes. "Oh, I didn't mean... That pass in the third, though, when Garrett had a man on him, but you still managed to get the ball in his hands."

"He was good enough to leave me just the amount of space I needed to get the ball where it belongs—in his hands. We're teammates. It's what we do."

She turned to G next. "Garrett, there's a lot of talk about you around the league already. Your first game of the season, and you ran for 175 yards, got one touchdown, and helped get your team to 1:0."

"I'm here to play football and win games, one at a time. That's what we did tonight, and that's what we plan to keep doing."

I smacked him on the shoulder, hoping he knew I was telling him he did a good job, before he was pulled away by another reporter. I watched for a second while more questions were thrown at him—thankfully just about Garrett's game and none about Houston. He fielded them like a pro, a wide smile on his face, totally enjoying the attention. This was exactly what Garrett had wanted—to win and to be in the limelight.

My body ached as we went into the locker room. Most of the time, we flew out after the game, but we were staying tonight and leaving early. We showered at the stadium, then loaded up on the bus to head back to the hotel.

Garrett sat with Cross, the two of them loud, clearly buzzing from the night. I remembered what that had been like—my first real game. Houston and I had been the same, though, maybe taken down a couple of notches.

As we unloaded at the hotel, Coach said, "We're out of here at four a.m. No going out, no women, get your sleep, and then get your asses up to get back to Denver. We won tonight, but the work's not done."

They led us in the back door. Garrett squeezed in beside me in the elevator, he and Cross giving a play-by-play to each other on the game. His hand brushed against mine, making sparks zing up my arm. The hairs on my arm stood on end, my nerve endings sparking and somehow connecting with his, before he immediately pulled away.

I didn't want him to.

I wanted to tease him, and to have him tease me, in plain sight of everyone who would be none the wiser.

Goddamn, he made me feel *reckless*.

I really needed to get ahold of myself, but as I stood there listening to him talk shit to Cross, as I smelled the familiar woodsy scent that always clung to his skin, my fucking dick twitched. Yeah, I was always boned up some after a game because all the endorphins gave me a bit of a high, but this was ridiculous.

My stomach tumbled, muscles tight with pent-up energy. Maybe we shouldn't have pulled the brakes the other night. Maybe we needed to get this shit out of our systems and move on.

Maybe G was right and he was actually the best person for me to explore my sexuality with. It wasn't like either of us would want more. We could keep a secret. A little sex on the side wouldn't screw up the team because it wouldn't be anything more than getting off.

Aaaaand, sixty seconds in the elevator with him and my wires were already getting crossed. That should tell me I needed to stay away.

We hit our floor, and the doors slid open with a *ding*. The group of us made our way out.

"Wanna chill in our room for a bit?" Cross asked him, and damned if I didn't hold my breath waiting for the answer. This whole situation was getting out of hand quickly.

I glanced over at him, trying not to make it obvious, but of course G's gaze darted to mine at the same time. They locked for one crackling moment, before he turned back to Cross.

Say yes and *say no* played tug-of-war inside me.

"Nah, man. I'm gonna hit the sack. I'm beat."

Be a good boy, Ramsey. Stop wanting your teammate to suck your cock.

Well, if that wasn't something I never thought I'd hear myself think, I didn't know what was.

When we were safely...*unsafely* tucked away in the room, I went straight for the mini fridge. "I need a drink. Do you need a drink?"

"That's not very responsible of you, Cap."

No, no it wasn't. "We can have a drink before bed."

"Thank fuck," Garrett replied. I tossed him a small bottle of whiskey and kept one for myself.

He went to his bed and me to mine, both of us toward the center, too fucking close while we took off our shoes.

"Jesus," Garrett said, "I'm almost coming out of my skin after that game."

"Get you that hot watching me play?"

"You played?"

I laughed. The motherfucker always gave just as well as he took. Great. That couldn't have sounded more sexual if I'd planned it. Now I was thinking about Garrett taking my cock. "I get it. It's that endorphins rush. Makes you feel invincible. Like you wanna fly or fuck or..." I shrugged. "You know, whatever." It was probably better if I didn't talk about sex.

I opened my bottle and took a drink. Garrett did the same, the long column of his throat moving deliciously while he did.

He set the drink down, stood up, and pulled his shirt off. "You, um...done anything else?"

It said a lot that I knew exactly what he was talking about without having to ask. "Nah, doesn't feel safe. Like I said, I don't want my business out there like that."

I shoved to my feet too, slowly working the buttons on my shirt. When he didn't respond, I added, "We did the right thing." *Did we, though?* drifted through my head.

"Yeah, I know. I don't want you going and falling in love with me or anything," G responded.

"Not likely." I tossed my top to the bed just as Garrett tugged his slacks off, the bulge behind his tight boxer-briefs looking like it matched my aching prick. I cocked a brow at him.

"I can't help it. The fucking game and then... I mean, it was a hot kiss so..."

Lust consumed me, damn near swallowed me up, and I

knew there was no escaping this. We'd drive ourselves out of our minds if we tried.

I watched him, not speaking, hell, maybe not even breathing as I unbuttoned my slacks and pulled them down, my dick aching for release.

Garrett groaned and adjusted his erection.

"I've been thinking about it," I admitted. We were in nothing but our underwear, close enough that I could feel his hot breath mixed with that goddamned scent that made me crazy.

"Me too."

"Would you want to do it again?"

Garrett's hands twitched like he was fighting back the need to reach for me. "What about the teammate stuff?"

"If no one knows, is it really a problem? If you think about it, not only are you the safest person for me to explore bisexuality with, but is there really anyone safer for you to fuck than me?" I took a step closer, got all up in his space, watched him tremble. "Neither of us wants more. Neither of us will talk about it. No risk of drama, stalkers, or any of that other shit that can get in the way." I brushed my thumb over his pebbled nipple and watched goose bumps play chase down his arms.

My good sense was gone. I wanted him too much. So much that I wasn't acting like myself.

"Look at you...coming up with a good plan. Is that your first time? So we what...do the friends-with-benefits thing?"

"Yes."

"I'm down for an easy lay." Garrett acted nonchalantly, but it was clear we were both keyed up.

"G...when did I say I'd be easy?" But fuck if I wasn't. At least tonight.

We lunged together, arms wrapping around one

another, fighting for purchase, bodies pressed tightly as I ravaged his mouth. My brain clicked off, desire taking over and muting the part of me that made responsible decisions. Basically, dick on, brain off.

The two of us battled, each trying to gain control. Garrett reached down, his palm around my cock, grinding on it. I melted into the touch for less than a second, which was all he needed to gain the upper hand leading the kiss, his tongue plunging into my mouth while he pushed me toward my bed.

"You got lucky," I said as he kissed down my throat.

"No. I'm that good." His teeth dug into my shoulder.

"Oh fuck."

"I had to explain my bruised lip, asshole. Maybe I should give you a hickey so you have to do the same."

"Only everyone knows it wasn't there today, and tomorrow morning, after spending a night with you…"

"Good point." Our mouths crashed together again, teeth clacking. I pushed at him, and Garrett stumbled backward. "Friends with benefits? What are we doing?"

"Aren't I supposed to be the one asking that?" I should be the levelheaded one here.

"You're slacking on the job," Garrett taunted.

"Don't remind me. I blame my cock."

Garrett laughed. "The whole my-brain-is-in-my-dick defense?"

"You talk too much." I pushed him down on the bed and tugged my underwear off while he did the same. My balls were aching and full.

He looked up at me, half on, half off the mattress, on his back, hand around his shaft. "Now that you have me here, what are you going to do with me?"

Oh shit. This was real. I'd been so blinded by my lust, I overlooked one tiny fact: I'd never been with a man before.

Reading my hesitation, Garrett's gaze softened. "Come here."

He scooted over, head on the pillows. I went down beside him, and Garrett leaned in to take my mouth again. Our tongues wrestled, teased, tasted. It was slower than it had been, like he was making sure I was okay. While I appreciated it, I also didn't want to be treated with kid gloves.

"Hey...so my dick was wondering if he could say hello to your mouth. It looks nice and comfy in there."

Garrett barked out a laugh. "But if I blow you, I'll never get rid of you. No other BJ will ever compare."

"Not likely...I just want to shut you up."

He winked. "Guess it's a good thing I like sucking cock."

Garrett went down on me, head in my lap, and— "Holy fuck!" He immediately took me to the back of his throat, lips stretched around my girth the way it had been in my dreams —yeah, unfortunately not singular.

I thrust up. Garrett took it, seemed to fucking crave it, his mouth and hand giving me the best kind of pleasure. Every time his nose was in my pubes, he swallowed around me, worked his throat just fucking right.

Jesus, my balls were already tight. I fisted my hand in his hair and pumped my hips, reveling in the sound of the wet suction of his mouth and the heat and talent of his tongue while he drove me wild.

"You look good with your mouth full of my dick."

He lifted off, nuzzled my balls, then said, "I always look good."

"I like it better when you can't talk."

"Shut up and let me work a load out of your balls, Rams."

Before I could respond, he got to it again, and I couldn't think of anything other than the feel of him pleasuring me, the sounds he made when I fucked his mouth, and how he groaned and thrust against the bed when he choked on my dick, like nothing got him hotter.

"Oh fuck...I'm gonna come. You better pull off if you're not taking my load."

But he didn't, and I whispered a silent prayer. My balls drew up, and pleasure shot up my spine and to the goddamned moon. I cried out, bursting in his mouth, Garrett taking it all down, and...fuck, did he lick his lips afterward?

I was so fucked.

He pushed up to kneel beside me, wrapped his hand around his shaft, but I batted it away. "Fuck no. That's mine."

"I won't last in your mouth. Just jerk me. When I shut you up with my cock, I want more time to enjoy it."

There was a quiet voice in the back of my head that said he was easing me into being with a man, which made me stumble.

I pushed those thoughts aside, wrapped my hand around his erection, and almost fucking whimpered at the feel of his hot, hard length, which was embarrassing as shit.

It wasn't every day a guy had his hand on another man's dick for the first time, and I wanted it to last, wondered how many ways I could make Garrett come, before concentrating on this moment. I jerked him hard and fast. He leaked more than me, precum dripping down his shaft to help with lubrication. I let go of him just to spit in my palm, before jacking him again, watching his fat cock slide in and out of my fist.

"Fuck, Rams. You're lucky I'm horny. I'm already gonna blow."

And he did, his balls pulling up, thick, white ribbons spurting on my hand, my arm, my chest, until Garrett fell onto his back, and I did the same.

We were both breathing heavily, the room suddenly thick with tension.

Garrett was the first to speak. "So...that just happened."

Yeah, yeah it did. I couldn't find it in myself to regret it.

10

GARRETT

The way I saw it, hooking up with Ramsey, no strings, benefited us both on the field and off. Ramsey got to exercise his bi-curiousness with me, and I likewise didn't have to hunt someone to get off with when I got tired of looking at my own hand. I could devote myself completely to football. No external distractions, no need for apps or the make-sure-the-person-isn't-a-psycho text exchanges before hooking up.

It was easy.

It was efficient.

It was hot as fuck.

We'd been messing around for a couple of weeks with no signs of slowing down. I'd had FWBs before, but Ramsey took thirsty to a new level, and I couldn't get enough. I'd had more handjobs in a span of days than I'd had in years, and his cock had been in my mouth so often, I'd know the shape of it even with my eyes closed. Introducing him to frotting had been especially fun. We'd both come within seconds, Ramsey had immediately demanded a do-over, and then we'd stuffed ourselves stupid with pizza at his place while watching *The Good Place*.

I looked forward to practices even more, not just for love of the game, but now also because watching Ramsey in action got me all worked up, and I knew that nine times out of ten, we'd be working off the stress of an upcoming game or a grueling practice with each other.

Wednesday's practice was particularly brutal because our next game was against Tennessee, and they, like us, hadn't lost yet. We'd watched hours of film until my eyes glazed over, and then spent the rest of the afternoon on the field in shells, running drills and plays.

"Good practice. Go wash it off," Coach barked, and the team broke for the locker room.

My legs were heavy, and my arms felt just as leaden after all the conditioning we'd been doing, but it was the good kind of heavy that made me feel like I was pushing my body to its limits and improving. I planned to buckle down that night, go over more film and revisit the plays we were working on.

"Better work on that grip strength before Sunday's game, McRae." Nance had turned around to face me, walking backward as he grabbed his crotch. And yeah, I'd fumbled the ball during goal post drills earlier. So had a couple of our other receivers. The dude never missed a chance to fuck with me or call me out, though.

"Shower next to me, and I'll show you all about grip strength." I flipped him off, and a chorus of hoots followed from Simmons and Jarrick. It was an easy quip, mostly light-hearted, but Nance sneered.

"Don't bring that kind of shit in here."

"The fuck are you talking about? You think I meant on you?" I rolled my eyes. "Fuck off with that homophobic shit.

I listen to your dumb asses talking about pussy this, pussy that all day. We're suddenly PC now?" It got to me sometimes. The guys would banter sexually all day, but the second someone who wasn't straight did it, it was suddenly a problem. It was tiresome. Weirdly, it'd been less an issue in college than it was in pro, I'd noticed.

Nance took a step forward, his chest puffing up, so I took a step forward too.

"Cut it out." Ramsey came out of nowhere, cutting between Nance and me like we were about to throw fists.

Nance lifted his hands with a chuckle. "I'm not doing shit. Baby G's acting up. Maybe he needs a nap."

God, I'd never hated a nickname more in my life. I took another step forward and cocked my head. "Come closer and tell me that."

"You'd probably like that, wouldn't you? Having me all up in your face?"

"That's enough." Ramsey glanced pointedly at my clenched fists. "Nance, shut the fuck up and stop with the bullshit. Both of you go cool off."

I glared as Nance looked between us, then huffed out a chuckle and walked off. I followed a second later, brushing past Ramsey and his stern expression. I wasn't heated. I just wasn't going to back down. Okay, maybe I was a little heated.

In the locker room, I waited until Nance vanished into the showers, then stalked toward Ramsey as he undressed.

"Don't do that swoop-in-and-play-savior crap." I peeled off my shirt and tossed it on the bench. "I can handle myself."

Annoyingly, Ramsey merely lifted a brow. "How about you check that ego?"

I tugged my pants off, catching myself on a locker when they got hung up on one ankle. "I managed college by myself. I can handle Nance. I don't need anyone watching out for me or whatever the fuck Houston told you to do."

Ramsey barked out a laugh, and goddamn, I wished his amusement didn't get me as hot as it frustrated me. "Right now you seem like you're more in need of a babysitter. You think I was doing that just for you?"

I frowned. Well, wasn't he?

Ramsey snorted. "Tension on the team is bad news, dumbass, you know that. And I'm the captain. Of course I'm gonna chime in. It'd be fucking weird if I didn't." He balled up his shorts and sent them sailing toward my stomach. "Like I said, get the fuck over yourself, McRae." Spinning on a heel, he headed toward the showers.

McRae. He never called me by my last name. I wasn't sure I liked it.

Tossing his shorts on the bench, I trailed after him.

In the shower, I stood under the spray with my eyes closed, letting it pelt my body as I sucked in a few long, deep breaths. And even though I made sure to grab a spot far enough away that I wouldn't be tempted to check out Ramsey's arrogant ass, I still did a couple of times.

———

THE LOCKER ROOM WAS EMPTYING OUT AS I MOSEYED TOWARD Ramsey's locker, whipping the towel from my waist and scrubbing briskly at my hair as I went.

He gave my approach a sidelong, wary glance. "You cool your jets?"

"Yep." I checked a smirk when his gaze doubled back and dipped lower. I'd had plenty of locker-room experience, so there was no chance I was gonna get inconveniently hard, even if Ramsey's gaze moved over me with an edge of hunger that darkened the shade of his eyes.

"Good." He tightened the knot of the towel around his waist. "We need to go into this game strong. Tennessee wants the win just as much as we do."

"Yeah, I got it. Relax. I'm lying low tonight, going over the plays, watching film." I remained where I was, unmoving, and he looked over at me again, arching a brow.

"Something else I can help you with, then?"

I shrugged nonchalantly and threw the towel around my neck. "Can't find my comb. Thought I could borrow yours." Our shoulders brushed as I leaned in and grabbed the black plastic one off his shelf, then ran it through the messy tousle of my hair a couple of times.

He shook his head, a half-smile tugging at his lips. "You think you're so smooth."

"Aw, nah, this is me being obvious." I cut him a wink and leaned back in, the same brush of our shoulders he didn't back off from, the same spark of electricity rolling over my bare skin. I tossed his comb back on the shelf and pitched my voice lower as I eyed his crotch. "Looks like your dick is struggling with subtle, though."

"Yeah, well, there's a whole new playground for it to explore lately." He glanced away, and I followed his sightline to where Cross, Simmons, and Boswell were huddled together, cracking up at something on Simmons's screen. The rest of the guys were finishing dressing or zipping up their bags. "It's like a kid in a fucking candy store. It'd be annoying, except it feels so fucking good. I'm horny all the goddamn time."

So basically what life around him for the past four years had been like for me. Still, the frank admission stunned me as much as the grin that followed, which, if I didn't know him better, almost seemed a little self-conscious.

"Welcome to wonderland." I grinned shamelessly.

"Get your ass dressed, and c'mon," Ramsey said as he snagged a clean pair of track shorts and started pulling them on.

"Where we going?"

"You said you were gonna be studying all night, yeah?"

"All night."

"Uh-huh." He inclined his chin and gave me an appraising stare that threatened to undo all the confidence I'd had in myself earlier not to pop a boner in the locker room. "So we're going to eat first. I'll drive."

The way my pulse sped up under that stare told me not to question him. I motored back to my locker and yanked my clothes on.

"Yo," Cross yelled back at me from the front entrance. "We're going to Boswick's. Want in?"

"Can't. I'll catch you later." I flashed him a wave, then grabbed my bag, throwing it over my shoulder before turning around. Ramsey was already heading down the hallway toward one of the side entrances. I picked up speed to catch up with him and knocked into his shoulder. "Why didn't you park in the front?"

"I did."

"Then what—" Ramsey stopped short and turned a handle on one of the doors lining the hallway. "Oh shit," I exhaled as he shoved me inside and realization set in.

The small supply room smelled like lemon cleaner and bleach. Buckets and mops hung from pegs. Shelves were lined with solvents. There wasn't a lot of wiggle room. I opened my mouth to make a joke but snapped it closed as voices sounded from outside.

"Keep that loud mouth shut," Ramsey whispered, pressing me against the door. His heart beat rabbit-quick against mine, his breathing soft and shallow as we held still.

The voices passed a second later.

"Is this a good idea?"

Ramsey exhaled a quiet chuckle. "Fuck no. It's a terrible idea, but probably not worse than one of yours." His knuckles skimmed down my sides and then over the fly of my jeans. My dick, weary from its valiant effort in the locker room and the showers, lost all its willpower. I tilted my hips into his touch with a soft groan of satisfaction when he turned his hand over and cupped me. "I saw you looking at me in the showers."

"Wasn't the first time, won't be the last," I admitted easily, then stifled another moan as he squeezed my balls, then grazed his fingers over the fabric. "No one else saw. *Fuck*. Quit teasing me and touch me for real."

His laughter was warm in my ear, but thankfully his fingers moved to the button of my jeans, then the zipper, lowering it as his mouth closed over mine in an unhurried kiss that smoldered through me. My dick throbbed with anticipation, eager for his grip and the slide of his cock.

But that wasn't what I got.

Ramsey pulled back. "So you're done being pissed at me for earlier?"

"Yeah." I clamped down on my lower lip as he brushed his fingertips over the head of my cock. I was dripping already. "Shit."

"Good."

"You were right. Team dynamics, focus on the game...*goddamn*." Ramsey was a fucking sexual prodigy if there ever was one. Or maybe it was just that I was so attracted to him and, like the good QB he was, he paid attention to everything. It'd taken maybe one handy for him to figure out I was a sucker for a little twist over the head of my dick, and my balls were already tight just from the sweep and slide of his fingers.

I arched into his touch harder, then sucked in a loud breath when he dropped to his knees. Eyes still locked on mine, he pulled me out and gripped the base of my cock. My mouth opened for words, but nothing came out. I'd sucked Ramsey's dick as often as I got the chance, but hadn't gotten the same in return. I didn't press it, wanted him to go at his own pace, and if it wasn't his thing, that was cool too.

But now he'd caught me completely off guard.

"Wow." The corner of his mouth lifted. "Good to know I can shut you up by putting your cock in *my* mouth too."

I nodded mutely on another deep inhale and sank my fingers into his hair as he edged forward slowly. His tongue flicked out, dipping into my slit a second before he wrapped his lips around my head.

Heat engulfed my body, concentrated heaviest on the seal of his lips. My grip on his hair tightened, and I had to fight the urge to thrust and choke him as every nerve ending in my body was bathed in pleasure. "Oh shit. Oh fuck." I clamped down on my lower lip until it hurt, trying to keep myself under control.

Ramsey licked around my head and stroked my shaft. "Good?" The hint of tentativeness in his eyes made my stomach clench. That he wanted this to be good for me, to please me, made it all the more erotic.

I exhaled a shaky breath. "Very."

"I've been paying attention when you go down on me, and thinking about what you like when I jerk you off, and—"

"Holy shit, I finally get how annoying it is when I talk

too much. Shut the fuck up and get my cock back in your mouth."

Ramsey's eyes gleamed as he licked a hot stripe up the length of my cock and rubbed his lips over me. He was spot fucking on, though, because everything he was doing was driving me straight crazy.

"I swear to—" I lost the rest on a breathless grunt as he sucked me into the back of his throat. His eyes watered, and the cough as he choked and got ahold of himself almost undid me. I squirmed and clutched his head, probably too hard. "I'm about to lose it."

Ramsey went to town then, working his own cock with one hand while he lapped and slurped at mine, making an ungodly sexy mess of it until my balls tightened. I barely hissed a warning out before he doubled down on the suction, his arm moving faster. My orgasm seared through me, spiking the backs of my eyelids with dancing pinpoints of lights as I blew my load down his throat. "Swallow it," I whispered, another shudder of pleasure racking me when he complied with a hard bob of his throat. He exploded a second later, spattering the floor.

His fingers were still digging into my hips, slow to release, as I slid down the door and slumped beside him.

"Fuck," I breathed out. Ramsey rested against me, his pulse still hammering where we touched. I ran my fingers lightly through his hair.

"It's sweaty," he said.

"I know. I was making sure I didn't accidentally rip out a whole hank of it. Goddamn, that felt good."

"I think I'm sitting in my own cum."

"Lucky us, there's plenty of cleaning supplies."

Ramsey's lazy chuckle ebbed, and he thunked his head against the door. "Shit. I can't believe I just did that."

I glanced over, a teasing retort dying on my lips when I saw his expression. "Hey." I frowned. "Listen."

He darted a look at me. "What? Did you hear something?"

"No." I nudged his leg with mine. "That's the point. Stop freaking out. No one's around."

"I wasn't—"

"You were."

He blew out a breath and laughed softly as he ran a hand through his hair. "Okay, maybe a little."

"It's fine. I promise. Trust me?"

His eyes met mine, and he was silent for a beat before speaking. "I do. Sometimes I don't even know why, but I do."

"Good." I tugged the collar of my T-shirt straight and stood, extending a hand to him. "Are we still going to get something to eat, or was all that some kind of innuendo? Because I'm fucking starving now."

He grasped my hand and let me tug him upright. "I could eat, yeah."

"Despite the mouthful I just gave you?"

"Goddammit, Garrett."

11

RAMSEY

I was really good at sucking cock.

I'd only blown him twice so far. Once at the practice facility, which had been dumb as hell, and I was still trying to wrap my head around the fact that I'd done it. Then again that same night when Garrett had come over. A couple of weeks later, I still couldn't get the noises he made out of my head. I still felt the sting in my scalp, his pleasure and want for me, showing in the way he'd gripped my hair and spilled down my throat.

I really *liked* sucking cock too, and I couldn't wait to do it again.

But I also needed to tell Houston. I hadn't planned on letting it go this long without talking to him. I'd considered it when we'd hung out the day after the Tennessee game, which we'd won but just by a field goal.

How did a guy even do this? *Hey, I'm exploring my sexuality by hooking up with your little bro. There's nothing like the sight of him on his knees, draining my balls. Is this what you had in mind when you asked me to keep an eye on him?*

Somehow, I didn't think that would go over well. *Fucking Garrett*—that was my new catchphrase. He was too tempting. I still couldn't figure out why he was so different. What was it that made me want him so much that I lost my head. Like blowing him in the supply closet. Coach was cool, but he would kick my ass if he found out, fine the shit out of me, and likely take my captain position away, if not worse. And that whole not-ready-to-come-out thing would be out the window.

But knowing wasn't enough to make me stop.

I pushed myself harder, my feet smacking against the trail as I took a morning run, while I tried to exercise away my thoughts of Garrett. Coach had worked us hard at practice yesterday, but from here on out, we'd only have light training before our game on Sunday.

We always wanted to win, but I think it was even more important to G this week. Not only because it was against another undefeated team, but because it was his first home game of the regular season, which meant his family would be there.

Maybe playing in Denver this weekend was why I'd decided it was time to tell Houston. We didn't need that shit weighing us down. When I'd talked to Garrett about it before he left last night, he'd agreed.

The trail wrapped around, so I followed it back to my house, leaves crunching beneath my shoes, one of my favorite true-crime podcasts talking about blood-splatter patterns in my ears.

I got inside just as my phone rang. I glanced down to see it was my agent. Allen had pushed hard for me my senior year in college. I liked his grit and business sense. He was one of the best.

"Hey, Allen. How's it going?"

"Just checking on my favorite golden boy."

I rolled my eyes. I couldn't blame him for the nickname. When I first got signed, it was what I'd told him I was going to be—the complete opposite of Mike Ramsey. An angel. A badass angel who was going to win a motherfucking Super Bowl ring. "Come on. You're never just calling to say hi."

"You're right. I got an offer for this new vitamin water on the market. They're coming in with a lot of cash. They really want you to endorse their product. *Our motto is go big, or don't go at all. We want the very best representation for our brand, and there's no one better than Warner Ramsey.* That was a direct quote, by the way. They want you bad, and luckily for us, they have the funds to back it."

"Well, clearly they have good taste," I replied, making Allen chuckle.

"You never change."

"Why mess with perfection?" I teased, before getting back to business. "I need to try it first. I'm not agreeing to pretend to love drinking something that might taste like ass." Though...I sort of wanted to taste Garrett's ass, so maybe I should rephrase that.

What would Allen think if he knew about me and G? Not that he ever would, since we were just fucking around. But at some point, I should tell him I was bisexual. I didn't think Allen was a homophobe, but it wasn't a conversation we'd ever had. It was shitty that I even had to question it.

"Of course. I'll get every flavor out to you and send you the details of their offer. We'll take it from there."

"Sounds good."

"And the team has that hospital visit coming up too."

It was one of the hardest and most rewarding things we

did. It was a fucking honor that we could light up a kid's life, give them something to look forward to, but damn, there was nothing worse than seeing sick kids. I wanted the power to fix them all.

"Anything else I need to know?" Allen asked. It wasn't a pointed question. Allen always asked that when we got off the phone. He was a pretty hands-on agent.

The vitamin water motto popped into my head, and I figured now was as good a time as any to test the waters. Not that I was ready to tell Allen, but I could at least get a feel for what he thought of my situation. "I have a hypothetical question for you."

"Shoot," he replied simply.

"What would you say if you found out one of your clients was hooking up with one of his teammates?"

The line went quiet. I could hear Allen breathing, so I knew he was still there, but other than that, the silence stretched between us. Shit. Fuck. This had been a mistake. Now I was going to find out my agent was a homophobe, and he would basically know I was bi because why else would I be asking?

"I'd tell them to be careful. That I'd have their back, of course, but I can't promise the league would feel the same. It's one thing to be queer, but fucking a teammate adds a new set of problems."

Shit. I knew he would say that. He was right, but I'd hoped his answer would be different.

"It also depends on who it is. If it's someone like you, for example, I'd tell him it would likely bring the kind of attention I know he doesn't want. It would be a big deal, even if the league supported it. They would get asked about it, commentators would talk about it, comment sections on social media posts would be...not so pleasant."

I dropped my head back. Allen wasn't telling me anything I didn't know. "Thanks, Allen. I was just curious. Asking for a friend, ya know?"

"Of course."

We chatted for a few minutes, and before we hung up, Allen said, "Be careful, Ramsey? But whatever happens, I'll support you."

"Thanks. I appreciate that." I hung up feeling a little shitty but also not surprised. *Go big, or don't go at all.* I kept the honesty train going by shooting off a text to Houston, telling him I was cleaning up and then heading over to his place. I had a few free hours before the team was meeting to go over more film.

I jacked off in the shower to the memory of Garrett's dick on my tongue and his hands fisted in my hair. I mean, it was sex. It had nothing to do with the fact that it was *him*. Orgasms were one of my favorite things, so it would make sense I would relive moments with the only person I was currently blowing my load with.

When I climbed out, there were two texts, one from Houston telling me he'd be there and the second from Garrett.

Garrett: I'm meeting Cross before we head to the practice facility. Good luck with Houston.
Ramsey: Think I'll need it?
Garrett: Nah. I'm irresistible. It can't be helped. He'll get it.

I rolled my eyes, but damned if I didn't also have a stupid smile on my face, one I had embarrassingly too much when it came to Garrett McRae.

"The team's playing good football—oh fuck, I should have caught that."

"Even my avatar is better than you," I teased. Though I was only up by one touchdown, and it was almost the end of the fourth. There was nothing like a good game of *Madden* among friends.

"Real life, you can suck my cock. I always kick your ass, and today won't be any different."

I can't suck you because I'm blowing your brother. Houston hadn't been serious, but my brain kept trying to kick my ass into telling him.

"Interception, baby!" Houston shoved to his feet.

"Fuck." I stood too, pushing buttons like crazy, trying to catch up with Houston's player, but he made it to the end zone and did a stupid fucking dance.

"You're getting a little rusty, Rams."

"*You're getting a little rusty, Rams,*" I mocked because I couldn't think of anything else to say.

He made the extra point next. I tossed the remote to the couch because both of us knew time would run out before I could make it downfield.

"Just don't play like that on Sunday. It's going to be your first real test of the season—even more than Tennessee. LA is on fire. They have the most sacks in the league right now. Plus, Whitt is fucking fast. Garrett and Nance will both struggle to get away from him."

Blah, blah, blah. I hated LA. They'd been our rival for years now, and more often than not, got the upper hand. I was really fucking tired of all the hoopla between LA and Denver every year. And Houston wasn't telling me anything

I didn't already know. It was just making me second-guess whether it was a good time to tell him about me and Garrett. But man, I felt like shit keeping it from him. Houston was my boy, and he trusted me. I didn't want to feel like I was lying to him. "I think G'll be good. He needs to be tested. He's stronger than we thought, up here." I tapped my temple. The corners of Houston's lips curled down slightly. I was pretty sure I'd fucked up somehow, cluing him in that we were a little closer than he thought, so I added, "Also, Nance is pissing me off."

Houston turned off the game and sat back down. "I worried about that—him having trouble with Garrett. Nance doesn't like it when someone is better than him, especially a rookie. Plus, I'm pretty sure he's homophobic."

"Yeah, he's been giving Garrett a hard time. Nothing too bad. He's handling it."

Houston nodded. "How's he doing? Keeping his head in the game? He's getting close with Cross. Are the two of them going out when you guys travel? All we need is another pregnancy scare like he had in high school."

Well, shit. I hadn't heard about that, but then why would I have? I hadn't known the McRaes back then. "Make sure Garrett sticks to dudes. Check."

"Make sure Garrett sticks to football," Houston countered.

"He is. Cut him some slack, McRae. He's got a better head on his shoulders than we gave him credit for. He's doing his thing. I'm proud of him. Don't ever tell him I said that, though."

Houston chuckled, then leaned against the back of the couch on a sigh. He sank into the plush gray material and closed his eyes. "I'm proud of him too. I trust him. He's just my little brother. It's my job to bust his balls while also looking out for him. He can be impulsive sometimes. You think everything is fine, and then *bam!* He calls you from Wyoming because he and his friends were bored and went for a drive and, *Oh shit, the car broke down and I have a game tonight. Can you hurry to come and get me?*"

I couldn't help noticing that most of the stories Houston had about Garrett were from high school or his first two years of college. Still, how many rookies had fame and fortune go to their heads? How many players fucked up and ruined their careers because they had their first taste of the lifestyle, money, and attention being in the NFL gave you? For someone who had a tendency to make rash decisions, it was a valid concern.

Except...that didn't feel right when it came to Garrett. Just a few months ago I would have agreed with Houston, but now that I knew him better, now that I saw how hard he practiced and how much he loved the game, the puzzle no longer fit together. "Like you said, he's your brother. It's your job to worry, so I get it, but Garrett's got his shit figured out. He's still a cocky, flashy, hotheaded little bastard, but he's got his head in the game. He got all pissy at me yesterday because he thought I stepped in with Nance just because it was him and—"

"Why are you smiling like that?"

Huh? I was smiling? "Because I like to think about your brother making a fool of himself?" I mean, that was partly true. His cheeks had been all pink in anger, a cute little scowl on his kissable lips.

"Good point. Just, be careful. You guys have gotten close, and Garrett's always had a bit of a hero-worship crush on you."

Hero worship? I couldn't wait to tease G about that. "Can you blame the guy?"

"I'm serious. All we need is Garrett crushing on you his rookie season."

Aaaaand, now I felt like the biggest prick on the planet. Houston had been my best friend for over four years, and I was hooking up with his brother behind his back?

I opened my mouth to tell him, to confess I was attracted to G and the two of us were friends with benefits. No big deal, right? But what came out was, "I want to fuck Garrett." Followed by, "Shit. That's not what I was supposed to say."

Houston's eyeballs damn near popped out of his head. "You wanna back up and start over? Because I'm pretty sure I missed a step."

I leaned forward, rubbed a hand over my face, and groaned. This definitely wasn't going as planned. "Let's pretend I didn't just say that—"

"You wanting to stick your dick in my brother? Bet. I'm down with scrubbing that from my brain."

"Sorry." I shrugged. "Every once in a while I have an open-mouth-insert-foot moment. What I was supposed to say is...good news! I'm finally exploring my sexuality. The questionable part is it's with Garrett. Does that sound better?"

"Not the time for sarcasm, Rams."

He had a point. "Listen...you know I've been attracted to men for a while. I was just stressed about getting outed or the whole thing turning into a sensationalized news story, so I kept that shit in check. But...I don't know...he's hot. He gets under my skin somehow. I bit his lip in a club, and then we were at a hotel and—"

"Oh my God. Shut up!" He shoved me. "What the fuck, Ramsey! He's my brother. Gross."

"He's also sexy as hell." I held up my hands in defense when he tried to push me again. "I'm sorry. He is. And his smart-alecky mouth makes it worse. The way we talk shit to each other really gets me all boned up."

"I'm going to kill you. All these years you've managed to keep your attraction to men in check, and now you can't shut the fuck up about getting a hard-on for Garrett?"

He was right, but I also knew Houston, knew the relationship we had. Treating Houston like I always did, showing him that nothing had changed between us, was the best way to deal with this. "If I can't tell my best friend, who can I tell?"

He shook his head, but there was a small smile tugging at his lips. "I can't believe you like Garrett."

My heart rate spiked, the thing jumping into my throat. "Slow your roll there, big guy. No one said anything about *liking* him. Not what way, at least. It's just a FWB thing. It works with him. Neither of us wants a relationship, and we don't need the extra work involved in finding people to hook up with. I have to have someone I can trust, who won't out me until I'm ready. Sex is always the perfect way to burn off a little steam after a game. And you asked me to keep an eye on him. I mean, you gotta admit, it's almost like it was destined to happen."

"I hate you."

"You love me." I wrapped an arm around Houston, tugged him close, and kissed his temple.

"Gross. You've had your lips on my brother. Don't touch me with those things."

We both laughed before the weight of the situation made the air thicken until it threatened to suffocate me.

"Are you sure this is a good idea? You don't want the media going crazy, but I think that would happen on a hell of a smaller scale if they just found out you like guys than it will if they discover two NFL players, *on the same team*, are sleeping together."

It being me, that would likely make it an even bigger deal. Sometimes I felt like the media was waiting for me to screw up, waiting for me to show I was like my father.

But walking out on his own team, fighting with coaches, the DUIs, and getting caught snorting coke off a hooker at a party, that was all different from having mutual sex with your teammate...or it should be. I forced those thoughts away. "How would they find out? Only me, you, and G know. None of us will tell anyone." But that probably meant sucking his cock in the supply closet shouldn't happen again.

He paused, looked at me in a way I'd never seen Houston look at me before—all seriousness and sharp with a warning. "I don't want him to get hurt."

"It's not like that. We're on the same page. It's just some orgasms between friends."

He gave me the finger. "You're gonna keep being TMI about this, aren't you?"

"Would I be me if I didn't?"

Houston sighed. "I guess not. I just...you know what you're doing, right? I'm trusting you, Ramsey, with Garrett and with his career."

"I know. It won't get fucked up. We're not going to let this get out of hand."

Houston nodded, picked up his drink from the coffee table, and swigged some down. "I still can't believe you're having sex with Garrett."

"Apparently, I give great head."

He jumped on me, and we wrestled around until Houston jerked back. "Ouch. Fuck."

"Your knee? You good?"

"Yeah." He pushed off me, his brows pulled together in what looked like frustration.

I hated this for him, hated that Houston had lost something he loved so much.

12

GARRETT

The game was way too fucking close for my liking. Too close for anyone's, judging by the solemn expressions on my teammates' faces. But then we'd known it would be. The films had been right, Coach had been right, Ramsey had been right. LA had moves and players that made lightning look slow. Especially fucking Whitt.

But I'd prepared for this. I was ready for this.

Every muscle in my body was fired up and soaked in adrenaline as Ramsey called the play.

As soon as Tucker snapped the ball, I was gone.

The stands around me vanished. My family, Houston, the bright lights beating down on the field were all reduced to a vague glow in my periphery. My world became the pump of my legs, the position of the defense as I took off down field, running a play I now knew like the back of my hand.

I broke left and twisted around, the ball arcing toward me like a dark bullet, exactly how it was supposed to, exactly how we'd practiced. Fucking beautiful. The second it barreled into my grasp, one layer of tension peeled off, leaving another behind.

But I had this. I fucking *had* it.

I raced toward the end zone, seeing the touchdown in my mind's eye, the interviews afterward. I could almost feel the clap of Ramsey's hand on my shoulder, Houston's, my parents'.

Yard lines sped by in a blur. My heart threatened to explode, filling my ears with the rush of blood, mingling with the roar of the crowd as the end zone loomed.

And then it was all gone.

A hard thump to my side threw me off-balance. I careened around, stumbling backward, my hands suddenly way too empty, just in time to see Whitt dive on the ball and smother it with his body.

A roar went up from the crowd as Whitt was helped up. He punched a victorious fist in the air that might as well have landed in my gut.

I'd fucking fumbled the ball mere yards from the end zone. No touchdown. No glory. Not a damn thing except humiliation and defeat that settled over me like a lead blanket.

"Shake it off." Cross knocked me in the shoulder as I gasped for air. "C'mon."

I trotted after him, still trying to get my bearings over what had gone down and how badly I'd just fucked up.

"We've still got time," Ramsey said as we walked off the field.

But we never fully recovered.

We lost by six points they wouldn't have gotten if I hadn't fumbled.

The walk back to the locker room felt like one of the longest in my life. Conversation buzzed around me, but I barely made out the words until my name cut through the air, and I glanced up in the midst of yanking off my cleats.

"Hey, maybe next time you want to make a fumble like that, you could just hand it over to the other team. Save everyone some energy."

I wanted to punch Nance in the face, but he was right. I'd seen the playback, and no doubt everyone else watching had. It would be all over highlight reels for the next week.

So I punched a fist into the bench instead.

The ball hadn't been tucked close enough to my chest. That was Football 101. I'd practically given Whitt an engraved invitation to knock it out of my hand. And he'd done so easily.

It was a rookie move. A total fucking rookie move, and I'd made it. I still couldn't believe it.

Coach let me have it in the post-game recap. I wasn't expecting any less. And I wasn't the only one—we'd fucked up other key moments and were staring down some brutal practice sessions in the next few weeks, no doubt—but I might as well have been the sole reason for our loss the way heat crawled up the back of my neck, spread over my cheeks, and decided to camp there the entire time he spoke.

I managed to hold my composure for the reporters who stuck their mics in my face once they were allowed into the locker room, even when the inevitable references to my brother came up. I rubbed at the tightness along my jaw in relief as they moved on to Dominguez, questioning him about sacking LA's QB. It was one of the few good highlights from our game. And there was Ramsey, of course. They loved talking to Ramsey. I watched him as he spoke, the perfect white flash of his grin, how his expression sobered, became more serious, an occasional nod. The ultimate pro. No doubt he was being grilled about the rookie's fumble.

When his gaze moved in my direction, I looked quickly away, finished getting undressed, and headed for the showers.

He caught up with me as I dressed. "You okay?"

"Peachy keen."

He gave me one of those appraising looks that felt like it left score marks on my bones. In the right setting I loved them. In this one I didn't. After a beat, he shrugged. "All right. I'm not gonna blow sunshine up your ass right now. You hanging with the fam tonight, or you want to come over for a while?"

God, I dreaded going out to the players' parking lot where my family was sure to be waiting. "Nah, I think I'm gonna crash after I talk to them. I'm beat." And humiliated and hating the taste of the ground I'd crash-landed into after flying high for weeks.

Ramsey studied me a moment longer. "All right. If you change your mind, you know where to find me."

I almost changed it in that second just because he fucking read me so well, pushed at the right times, left me alone when he sensed I needed it, and I appreciated it more than he'd ever know. But when he turned away, I let him go, finished stuffing my gear in my bag, and headed to the parking lot.

Houston was the first to wrap me in a big bear hug. "I know you're being hard on yourself right now. Don't."

I grunted, fully embracing my sour attitude. "Did any reporters find you?"

"Sure did."

"Ugh." I groaned again. "Did they ask what it was like to watch your brother crash and burn?"

Houston chuckled lightly and ruffled my hair before I could duck away. "Not in those exact words. I asked if any of them had seen you absolutely killing it in the Pittsburgh game. Then told them to piss off. Politely, of course."

I grumbled some more, even if Houston's nonchalance about the loss and his defending me did make me feel a tiny bit better. Like, an ounce better. Or if there was something smaller than an ounce, that.

Mom and Dad were next. Mom, full of optimism and opinions as usual, chattered about how fast I'd looked on the field, and how "distastefully unsportsmanlike" some of the behavior from the other team had been on the final touchdown, until I started cracking up.

"Mom, the guy just fist-bumped a teammate. He wasn't out there doing the chicken dance."

"He was practically taunting you all."

That was totally not the case, but her vehemence made me smile. And then Dad chimed in.

"They'll get theirs. They think they're hot shit with that Whitt asshole. Pfft. Just wait."

Mom patted my arm. "You want to come home for the night?"

"Jesus. And what, you'll put a Band-Aid on my booboo, then tuck me in bed?" I teased, but wrapped an arm around her shoulder and squeezed it. "Nah, I'm good. I'm gonna crash early."

Houston lingered when they left. "I honestly expected a win. I'm supposed to meet up with friends—see? Social life." He gave me a pointed look. "How about you come with us for a while? Grab a beer? Or more than one?"

I shook my head. "Not in the mood. It's cool. You go. Have fun."

"You sure? I can cancel. Actually..." He pulled his phone from his pocket. "I'm gonna cancel. We can hang and watch reruns of that dumbass show you and Ramsey love." A funny expression crossed his face, but it vanished quickly. We mostly avoided the subject of me and Ramsey, and I sure as shit wasn't inclined to change that now.

I reached out and shoved him. "Don't cancel. Go. I mean it. I'll be pissed otherwise." He tucked the phone away, and I cocked my head, narrowing my eyes at him. "So are these real friends or imaginary ones?"

He snorted lightly. "There's the asshole I know and love. Here I was worried you were gonna go home and curl in a ball on the couch."

"Nope. I'm solid. Promise." I was, mostly, and hey, if I curled into a ball on the couch, it wasn't like anyone was gonna be there to see it.

After a quick hug, we separated to head to our respective cars.

Idling at a red light where I'd make a left to go home to Houston's, I imagined getting home, sprawling on Houston's couch, staring numbly at the TV, then crawling in bed alone. It'd seemed like the perfect plan ten minutes ago.

But when the light turned green, I turned left, made a U-turn, and headed in the other direction.

THE CORNER OF RAMSEY'S LIPS TWITCHED AS HE OPENED THE door and found me on his steps, but he didn't say anything, just opened it wider and gestured me inside.

I closed it behind me, and he eyed me, shoving his hands in the pockets of the sweats stretched tight over his thighs. "Want something to eat? Drink?"

"Got a keg?" I joked weakly.

Ramsey huffed out a quiet laugh. "Nope, fuck that.

You're not gonna come in here and mope around the rest of the night."

"Okay, what're we doing, then?" I'd kinda planned on that. Oops. And maybe receiving a sympathy blowjob at some point. Hell, I should be the one giving the sympathy blowjob, considering how I'd wasted Ramsey's perfect goddamn pass.

Mostly, I just hadn't wanted to be alone.

Ramsey's gaze narrowed slightly, and then he spun around. "C'mon," he called over his shoulder.

I followed him onto the deck, watching the muscles of his bare back ripple with his movements. A fucking gorgeous man if there ever was one. I decided he was probably the only guy that could make me sigh just by looking at him.

We stopped in front of his hot tub.

"Get naked and get in. I know that big-ass ego of yours isn't the only thing that's sore."

He wasn't wrong. I ached all over, so after a second, I did as told and stripped down.

I climbed in, groaning as the hot water enveloped me, sinking deep enough to cover my shoulders and the bruises all over my body. Not that they would faze Ramsey at all. I wriggled around until I found a jet that hit my back just right. Ramsey slipped in across from me. "So does this happen to be the deluxe version hot tub that also massages bruised egos?" I rested my head back on the edge of the tub and closed my eyes.

Ramsey's chuckle was soft. "Nah. That was another ten grand, and I didn't anticipate having too many guys in here with one the size of yours. Couldn't justify the added expense."

I peered at him through hooded eyes. "So you're admitting I'm huge."

"Your ego? Fuck yes."

I cracked a smile, the first one that had felt real all night.

After a couple of beats of silence, Ramsey spoke again. "We got outplayed tonight. Wasn't the first time and sure as shit won't be the last. You fumbled the ball—"

"I ruined a perfect pass."

"You ruined a perfect pass. Won't be the last time for that either. It's not the defining moment of your career, though, Garrett, unless you're planning on starting to suck ass from here on out."

"Depends on whose ass."

"Goddamn, you're an idiot sometimes."

I deserved the splash that followed, but Ramsey was right. I knew he was, and maybe coming over here had been the thing I needed after all, because some of the weight in my chest had already vanished. I'd fucked up, and all I could do was try to be better next time.

I swiped water from my eyes. "Thanks." I meant it sincerely, and Ramsey nodded, just once, to show he knew what I meant, then tipped his chin up. "C'mere."

Fuck, his confidence with men was definitely growing, and it was a total turn-on. I closed the short distance between us and straddled him, expecting him to wrap a hand around my cock immediately. Instead, his fingers cupped my chin and pulled me in for a gentle, lingering kiss. My lips parted for the press of his tongue, and I groaned as he plunged inside, his other hand smoothing down my back and pulling me tighter against him until our cocks rubbed his stomach. I rolled my hips against him, then pulled back. "Sure you didn't splurge for the upgraded tub after all? My ego's already feeling a little better."

"Don't you dare give the hot tub credit for my skills, jackass."

My chortle was cut short by another searing kiss. I snaked a hand behind me, guiding Ramsey's hand lower, over the curve of my ass and down the seam until his fingertips brushed over my hole. He went momentarily still. Even our kiss paused, but then he rubbed over the tight muscle once, a palpable tentativeness in the movement, his eyes flicking up to mine, the question within them clear.

"Fuck yes," I whispered, choking back a moan. "That's perfect. Keep going." This was what I needed, what I wanted, and after another beat of hesitation, Ramsey's fingers started moving, circling, rubbing, softening me up. His other hand tightened on me, guiding my hips back and forth, our cocks bumping and brushing against each other, the friction far from perfect and a little awkward in the water, but pleasure still raced through me with every second of contact.

I reached behind me again and laid my hand over his, pressing down on his middle finger as it circled my rim until it sank just barely inside, and I hissed at the immediate, familiar sting. It'd been a while. "Fuck me with your fingers." Ramsey muttered a curse as I slid my hand to his wrist, guiding him deeper. "Slow and steady," I told him, and sucked in a sharp breath as he pushed in all the way to his knuckle, then pulled back slowly.

"That how you like it?"

I nodded mutely, clamping down on my lower lip as he pushed inside again. The increased momentum as he grew surer in his strokes made our trapped cocks rub together.

Ramsey threw his head back on a moan, and I took advantage, attacking his throat, licking and sucking the stubbled skin. "You like the way I feel?" I whispered.

"Fuck yeah." His voice was a throaty rasp. "Goddamn tight as hell."

"Mmm..." I worked my way back to his mouth and licked over the seam of his lips until they parted for me and I could suck on his tongue like the hungry motherfucker I was while I rode the finger inside me. It wasn't enough, though. When I clamped down, he exhaled a stuttered breath. "I wanna feel your cock stretching me open, fucking me hard and deep until I come all over you."

"Jesus, McRae." Ramsey's eyes blinked half-open, a lust-filled glaze shading them a darker blue as they narrowed. "Get your ass in the bedroom, then."

13

RAMSEY

I was nervous as shit but hoping it didn't show. I was about to fuck a guy for the first time...who also happened to be my best friend's little brother and my NFL teammate. But this was Garrett, the cocky little fucker that, hell, made me smile more than I wanted to admit. Since training camp, he'd quickly gone from Houston's bro to my friend and the guy letting me explore this part of myself I'd kept buried for too long.

I watched his tight ass as he ran upstairs, me trailing him. We didn't even dry off, leaving tracks of water along the way, but I didn't care. I wanted inside that ass, wanted to feel his tight heat around me, his hard body against mine as I blew his fucking mind.

Because nerves or not, I planned to do exactly that.

I caught up with him just as he skidded to a stop in front of my bedroom. I wrapped my arms around him, reeled him in easily, like he was happy on my hook. His ass pressed against my hard cock, Garrett pushing back like his hole was begging for attention while I peppered kisses along the back of his neck. "I can't wait to fuck you."

"You planning on doing it sometime tonight?" I felt him move and looked down to see him stroking his thick erection. He hadn't been lying; he was big. I loved the feel of his fat dick stretching out my lips, wondered if one day he would want to fuck me and if I'd let him. I thought maybe I would.

"Stop being an asshole."

"Get inside my asshole."

We laughed, our bodies vibrating in sync like the moves had been choreographed.

I walked toward the bed, still holding him and pressing my lips to his skin, sinking my teeth into his shoulder, but not enough to leave a permanent mark.

It was awkward to move, but finally, we got to my king-size bed with the massive dark-cherry headboard and footboard. I pushed him down so he was still standing but bent over, hands braced on the mattress, his perfect ass in the air.

I grabbed the lube and a condom out of my nightstand, and G didn't move, just waited for me. "See? You can be a good boy," I teased.

"Fuck you," he replied, but goose bumps took a journey up and down his arms, making me wonder how much he liked it.

Nerves waged a war in my gut, but I tried to ignore them, let the want I felt for Garrett override everything else. I tossed the supplies to the mattress and stood behind him, kissing each knob of his spine, my fingers seeking his hole again.

I rubbed his tight rim, hoped I didn't blow my load the second I got inside him. My mouth trailed down, and when I reached his ass, I started to work my way up again. Fuck, his hard body felt good.

"You know...you can kiss him hello first. It's proper

manners and all," Garrett said, and I paused because damn, I hadn't even thought of that. It wasn't as if I hadn't seen guys rim each other in porn. I'd eaten a lot of pussy over the years, but I'd never fucked a girl in the ass, and I'd never let my tongue travel there either. "You don't have to. It feels fucking great, though. I'll tongue-fuck you first. I'm amazing at it."

Of course, I wasn't going to let myself be one-upped, so I dropped to my knees. "Yeah, that's not gonna happen. Not that you're not, but you won't be first. I'll show you how it's done."

"You've never done it."

"Doesn't mean I won't be the best at it." I playfully smacked his ass. Garrett chuckled while kneeling on the side of the bed, at just the right height for me. Why was everything so *much* with him? I wasn't even sure that made sense, but that's how it felt.

I ran my hands over his ass cheeks, spread them wide, and took in his tight, pink hole. Jesus, I couldn't believe I'd have my cock inside him soon.

"Come on, Rams. Show me what you can do. I can't wait for you to eat me out before you dick me down."

White-hot lust shot through me. Somehow, Garrett knew just what to say. He was talking me up, distracting me so I didn't worry. I appreciated it. We did that, I noticed, gave and took, led and followed, whether it was football, sex, or life.

I leaned in, swiped my tongue over him, drew circles on his tight muscle.

"Fuck yeah. Just like that. Make me feel good, get me ready for your fingers and that big dick of yours."

Said cock jerked against my belly. It was so hot hearing him talk to me like that. I reached around him, stroked his dick while I licked and probed at him. Garrett pushed back, like he couldn't get enough, practically riding my face and moaning, telling me how much he wanted me, how hard I was going to make him come. I hadn't even gotten inside him, and my balls already begged to empty, to paint him with my load.

"If you're not careful," Garrett said, "you're gonna drain my balls too soon."

I smiled against his ass. "Told you I'd be good at this."

"Get the lube and open me up some more."

"Good boys say please," I teased.

He laughed, then moved over, head on the pillows and lying on his back. With a sexy smirk curling his lips, Garrett stroked his cock. "Who said I want to be good?"

An electrical storm went off inside me, my nerves cracking and popping with hungry sparks. I crawled onto the bed, settled between his spread thighs. "I'm gonna ruin you for anyone else, gonna make you come so hard, your head spins."

"Sounds like I'm possessed, not orgasming." His voice was playful, but also husky with want. "But I'm game. Go ahead, ruin me, Warner Ramsey."

A growl pushed past my lips. I lubed my fingers, then leaned in to kiss him. Remembering where my tongue had been, I paused, but he pulled me in, our mouths searing together. I slipped my fingers between his ass cheeks. The angle was awkward, but we made it work, Garrett spread out wide and lifting his legs for me. One finger sank into him, but it wasn't enough. I worked two in, fucking and stretching him the way I'd done in the Jacuzzi, swallowing down his moans.

When he loosened, I breached him with a third, twisting

in circles, sliding them in and out, kissing while I did, our cocks rubbing together with delicious friction.

"That's good...I'm ready. Get your cock in me." When I didn't move, didn't stop, he slipped out a soft, "Please."

"That's what I want to hear." I bit his earlobe.

"I hate you."

"I hate you too."

I suited up, then slicked up my condom-covered erection. My eyes scanned his torso, all the black and blue marks from the game. Our bodies took a lot of beating.

I kissed a purple mark on his chest, then said, "Turn over." Garrett got on his hands and knees. "Your body is so hot. I love how hard you are, how muscular." We both were, but it was different having that in bed with me, having a build that matched mine. It was maybe the sexiest thing I'd ever experienced.

"Fuck me," Garrett ordered.

"Gladly." I pushed at his hole, watched it open for me, stretch around my cock. Shivers ran the length of me at the feel of all that tight heat around me. I wasn't going to get tired of his ass soon, I knew that. Friends with benefits with Garrett was maybe the best idea we'd ever had. "That's it...take my cock."

"Give it to me. You don't have to go slow."

His words unleashed something inside me. My hips snapped forward, the two of us hissing out a deep breath when I was buried deep. I held on to his hips, pulled back, and thrust again. Over and over and over again, I railed into him, savored the slide of my cock inside Garrett. He moved with me like he couldn't get enough, fucking himself on my dick, hands fisted in my blanket.

I wanted his mouth, wanted to make him come so we could hurry and do it again. I pulled him up so Garrett knelt too, his back against my chest. I slicked my hand, wrapped it around his steely length, jacking him while I pulled back, then fucked into him. He turned his head so we could kiss, tongues delving and tangling.

My balls felt like they were going to burst, so full and ready to let loose. When I felt Garrett tense against me, his body going rigid, his lips leaving mine, I knew he was about to blow his load.

"Fuck, Rams. Right there. Right fucking there."

I sped my stroking and my thrusts. He cried out, his hot release coating my hand, and damned if it didn't push me over the edge too. I buried my face in his neck, riding out my own orgasm, fucking through it as my dick jerked and shot, filling the condom.

We fell into a sweaty heap on my bed, breathing hard.

When I was finally able to speak, I joked, "Blow your mind?"

"Eh, I've had better."

I laughed. "Lies." My words had just come out before Garrett sealed his mouth to mine. We lay there, kissing and touching, sweaty and cummy.

Eventually, he pulled back. My dick was soft, my load pooled in the rubber. I pulled it off and tossed it into the trash can.

"I'm beat," Garrett said.

"Might as well stay." I shrugged.

"Don't you go falling for me," he teased.

"I'm pretty sure that's my line," I played back.

He climbed under the blankets while I got up and turned the lights out before joining him. We didn't touch at first, like neither of us knew what to do, or if we should. But considering I'd had my tongue and my dick in his ass tonight, I figured a little cuddling was okay. "C'mere," I said, and he did. I was on my back, Garrett's head on my shoulder. Seconds later my world went black.

———

Buzz! Buzz! Buzz!

Garrett pulled out of my arms in the darkness. "What the fuck is that?"

"Shit," I groaned. I knew without looking exactly who and what it was.

My doorbell rang three more times before the banging started. "It's my dad." I flipped on the lamp and looked at my phone. It was after two in the morning. I tugged on a pair of track pants, just as Garrett got out of bed. "You don't have to go."

"I wasn't. I was just going to come down with you and make sure everything is okay. Shit, Rams. Does he do this often?"

"Often enough. When I don't pay enough attention to his phone calls or do what he wants, this is what happens." And I'd never shared it with anyone. Not even Houston. It was embarrassing as shit. I was lucky that I'd rarely had this happen when someone was staying the night, but when it did, I usually just asked them to stay in my room. I didn't tell them Mike Ramsey got off on making my life hell.

I grabbed a pair of shorts out of my drawer and tossed them to him.

"Should I come down with you?" Garrett asked, his eyes filled with concern.

"He's not stupid enough to try and lay a hand on me. He's probably just drunk and wants money."

Buzz. Buzz. Buzzzzz.

Still, Garrett tugged the clothes on and followed me out

of my room and to the stairs. It was cute, him trying to protect me, but this was embarrassing enough. "I'll be fine. Stay here. Maybe tucked around the corner some so he doesn't see you."

"Okay, but I'm watching. If he tries something, he'll have both of us to fuck with."

"Aww, my hero." I pressed a kiss to the tip of his nose, which was...what the fuck was that? It felt more intimate than having my dick in his ass.

I jogged downstairs before either of us could say anything. Once I had the door open, my dad staggered inside. "Why the fuck don't you answer my calls? You think you're too good for me? Big fucking NFL player in the goddamned league that fucked over your dad, and you can't even pick up my phone calls?"

"They didn't fuck you over. You ruined your career. You have no one to blame but yourself."

"Don't you talk to me like that." He pressed a finger into my chest. I heard movement upstairs and knew Garrett was there waiting.

I grabbed his wrist tightly. "Don't. Touch. Me." God, I fucking hated him so much. Hated that when I was young I wanted to be like him, and now all I cared about was being better than him, on and off the field.

He jerked his hand back. "I need some money."

It was never anything new. In the beginning, I used to give it to him, but that just made him ask for more. I'd decided a long time ago I was cutting him off and hadn't faltered since. "Get a job."

"Fuck you, Warner. I raised you. I gave you everything. I put food on the table and a roof over your head. You wouldn't be shit if it wasn't for me, and you sure as hell wouldn't be in the NFL. You have a career because I built you!"

I inwardly flinched, hating that a part of me was still that scared, insecure kid who thought he might be right. Usually, I would have just tried to pacify him so I didn't have to deal with the drama, but I was so fucking tired of this...of him. Of the fact that I had a gorgeous man waiting for me, and I had to be down here dealing with this shit.

That Garrett had to hear him say these things about me. I couldn't even imagine what he thought, and that made embarrassment light a fire under my anger. "I worked my ass off to get where I am. Me." I hit my chest. "Not you. All you did was tear me down, blow your career because you think everyone owes you and you can do what you want. Then you blamed me. I'm not that fucking kid, and I won't deal with it. You want help, I'll be there if it's to straighten up your life, but I sure as shit am not going to give you money to blow on what-the-fuck-ever you want, and I'm not going to be your verbal punching bag."

He spun around, pacing. "I built you," he said again.

"You need to leave, or I'll call the cops." But we both knew I wouldn't, not because I cared about him as much as I didn't want to bring the media's attention.

"Sometimes I can't believe you're my son. Your mother would have been disappointed."

This time, my flinch showed. He knew exactly where to strike to hurt me, exactly what to say. In my heart I knew she wouldn't. I knew she'd loved me, and she had to have seen him for who he was, but...what if she hadn't? What if I'd built up this image of her in my mind and that wasn't who she'd been? What if I really was a bad person? What if I was just like him? "Get out," I said between clenched lips.

"Such a fucking disappointment." He turned and walked away, leaving the door open behind him.

I closed my eyes, didn't move for a second, a minute, maybe ten minutes or a hundred years. I didn't know how much time had passed when I felt strong arms wrap around me.

"He's wrong, ya know? You're where you are because of no one but yourself. You worked hard to make it. He can't take that away from you."

I sighed. "Fucked-up family, huh? You're finding out all my secrets."

"Stop." He kissed my shoulder. "It's okay to be upset. And she wouldn't have...been disappointed in you, I mean."

"You never knew her."

He dropped his forehead between my shoulder blades and whispered, "But I know you," before his arms dropped away. He closed and locked the door. "Come on, Rams. Let's go back to bed. Maybe in the morning, I'll let you fuck me again."

"Who said I want to?" I teased, but we both knew I did.

Garrett took my hand, and I followed him up.

14

GARRETT

Waking up next to Ramsey was strange...in that it didn't feel all that strange. It felt nice. Weak predawn light streamed through the skylight as I burrowed into covers that smelled like him. The sleepy warmth of his body heat surrounded me as he turned toward me and cracked one eye open.

"You're still here."

For a split second, I panicked it was about to get awkward. Instinctively, I started to roll upright, defaulting to my usual script. When someone stayed over or vice versa, morning was usually met by sliding out of bed and dragging clothes on. Conversation was exchanged about hooking up again soon—which sometimes happened and sometimes didn't—followed by getting the hell out.

"That's a joke, dumbass." Ramsey planted a palm in my chest and pushed me back into the mattress as he rolled toward me, his body half smothering mine. His erection pressed against my outer thigh.

"Damn, I think I've created a monster." But did I reach beneath the covers and stroke it lightly? Yes, I did.

"Something like that."

Before I could toss out another quip, his mouth covered my nipple, his teeth clamped down, and we were off to the races again.

Forty-five minutes later, we lay sprawled on our backs, catching our breath. I turned my head, glanced at the clock on the bedside table, and groaned. "Shit, we've got thirty minutes before weight-training, and I already need a nap." When Ramsey chuckled, I elbowed him. "Don't say a goddamn thing about Baby G needing a nap," I warned him.

He rolled his lips inward and shook his head. "Not what I was about to say. I was about to say I need coffee."

"Fucking liar."

He shrugged with a grin and rolled upright. "I'll make us some. You need to borrow clothes or anything?"

"Nah, I've got it." There was no way I could get home and back to practice on time. Fortunately, I had a change of clothes in the car.

I followed Ramsey to the kitchen and leaned against the counter, watching him fiddle with his fancy Nespresso, and once again, I was struck by how not awkward it felt.

Ramsey glanced over his shoulder. "When's the last time you did this?"

"Stand in someone else's kitchen while they made coffee? A long time. You?"

"Alyssa, I think." He ran a hand through his hair and shook his head.

"What?"

He mashed a button on the machine, then twisted around to face me, palms braced on the counter. Jesus, he looked good in the morning. Sweats hanging low on his hips, the dark stubble peppering his jaw. No wonder Ashley or Alyssa or whoever the fuck it was had sneaked pictures of him. "I dunno... Sometimes when I think back on relation-ships...hookups...whatever, there are a lot of them that in retrospect feel like distractions more than me actually being into the person."

"I don't know if I'm following."

"The game and everything around it...it takes a lot out of you, you know? And the average person has no clue what it's really like. A lot of them just see the big player, the glamour, the money. Not the bruises, the injuries, the stress. I guess that's plenty of other jobs. Feels different sometimes, though. Know what I mean?"

I nodded. Maybe I hadn't had the long-term pro experi-ence he had yet, but even in college I'd dated people who'd been disappointed or frustrated once they realized exactly how much of my life was devoted to moving a pigskin down a field.

"That's part of the reason this setup works." Ramsey gestured between us. "You get it."

Oh, I got it. Maybe it was too easy, but I was trying not to question it and keep the faith that I could fuck Warner Ramsey out of my system before he got tired of me and moved on to the bi big leagues.

"Pretty sure I don't even need to ask where you were last night," Houston said as I walked in after practice. He was in exercise clothes, one leg hiked up on the back of the couch. He switched to stretch the other one as I shut the door behind me.

"Probably not." I dropped my bag by the door, walked into the open kitchen, and grabbed a water from the fridge. I had enough time for a snack and a shower before the team's hospital visit. "Hey, you know about Ramsey's dad, right?"

"That he's an asshole? Yeah, everyone knows that."

"No, I mean that he bugs the fuck out of Rams, shows up randomly?"

"What? Really?"

"He showed up last night, wanting money."

Houston groaned.

"Yep." I was silent, then shook my head, thinking back on it. "It pisses me off that Ramsey has to deal with that all the time."

"Same, but you can't fix that shit. You know that." Houston gave me a long look. "Are you sure you know what you're doing with this whole hooking-up-with-Ramsey thing, because..." He blew out a breath. "Fuck, part of me knows it's none of my business, but the other part hates the idea that one of you might hurt the other. How the hell am I gonna know whose ass to kick?"

"You ain't kicking anyone's ass with that bum leg," I teased, grinning when he flipped me off, but then I sobered because obviously, I'd given some thought to our situation. "Seriously, don't worry about it. We'll figure it out as we go."

"Just...you know. Watch yourself. Both of you. I don't want either of you getting caught up in something that's gonna eventually crash and burn. God, I can't believe I'm even saying that to you."

"Not necessary. We know what we're doing." Kinda counter to my previous statement, and definitely counter to my thoughts, but I said it confidently as I headed toward the shower.

Because what I did know was that I'd liked waking up next to Ramsey maybe a little too much.

AT ROCKY MOUNTAIN CHILDREN'S HOSPITAL, WE WERE corralled into a conference room and briefed by HR. A couple of the Rush's PR guys were in attendance too, along with a small film crew.

I bumped Ramsey's elbow. "Nothing says charity like a film crew there to capture every second, huh?"

Ramsey bumped mine back. "Don't be a cynic. They take pics for the kids and give them the tapes. The kids love it. It's one of my favorite things the team does, even though it breaks my damn heart."

I could read it in his expression, an added brightness in his eyes, the set of his mouth. After the episode with his dad last night, it was good to see, softened something inside me that'd been tense.

After the briefing, we split into small groups, signing footballs and jerseys and taking pics with the kids. Their faces lit up, their laughter filled the rooms. Ramsey was right. It felt amazing to make them smile.

He glanced over at me in the hallway as we moved to the next room. "You all right?"

"Yeah." I rubbed a hand over my chest. "Sick kids are..." I shook my head. I lived a privileged life, that was for damn sure. My biggest complaint walking in here had been that my ass was sore. "Fuck, that's hard, thinking about them suffering."

"What, you mean there's a heart behind those giant pecs?" he teased, but his smile was sympathetic, and he reached out a hand, giving the back of my neck a quick squeeze before we ducked through a doorway. "That's why it's good to come here. Puts things in perspective, you know?"

A cute guy in scrubs was fiddling with the IV lines hooked to a kid who couldn't have been more than ten. He wore a Rush hat, the brim way too big. I made a mental note to check the gear we had on hand for a smaller one.

The guy in scrubs looked up with a smile as we entered and poked the kid. "Look who's here to see you. Guys, this is Jared."

"Holy..." Jared's eyes got huge, his grin even wider. "Freaking Warner Ramsey, Brandon Cross, and Garrett McRae."

Ramsey stepped forward and plopped on the edge of the bed. I was too nervous I would fuck up something, so I just stood next to it. Cross seemed to share the same fear, but Ramsey seemed perfectly at home as he brandished a football and held it out to Jared. "We all signed this for you. Come spring, you'll be out tossing it. I hear you've got a younger brother probably itching to do that with you, yeah?"

"Jude." Jared wrinkled his nose a little even as he accepted the ball. "He's only five. Not so great at the whole catching thing."

Ramsey thumbed toward me. "McRae here has an older brother who used to play, and he turned out pretty good, wouldn't you say?"

Jared looked me up and down assessingly. "Yeah, you're pretty good, except that last game. Man, what even happened?"

Cross choked back a laugh, and I could tell Ramsey was trying to do the same. The guy in scrubs didn't even try.

"Damn, harsh critic." I scrubbed my hands over my face with a grin. I couldn't even be mad about it now. "I'll try to do better next time. Promise."

"You will." Jared nodded with all the certainty of

someone twice his age. I felt like my mom was talking to me. "My dad says you're just getting your legs under you."

"Something like that." I elbowed Cross, who was still snickering.

"You don't remember me, do you?" The guy in scrubs approached while the camera crew snapped some pictures of Cross and Jared.

I looked him up and down. There was something familiar about the dark hair and eyes, but I couldn't come up with a name. I gave him an apologetic smile and glanced at his badge: *David*. I hadn't even paid attention to it before. "I'm sorry, I don't. Don't hold it against me."

He laughed lightly. "It's okay. It was a...umm..." He shot a glance toward Jared, then lowered his voice. "A short encounter, and I looked a little different. We..." He gestured vaguely, but enough for me to get the gist. Still no recollection of him, though. "While you were home on break one time. You were a junior, I think."

My eyes went wide as the memory caught up with me. "Holy shit!" I said, way too loudly, and apologized quickly when everyone looked over at me. We'd traded blowjobs at someone's holiday party. I couldn't remember whose, but I remembered the action had been good. "You look completely different. Your hair used to be—"

"Platinum and spiky. That was back in my burgeoning emo-twink days. I was going through a phase."

I looked him over again. "Damn, you've made some serious gains." He was stacked as hell and had definitely graduated from twink to twunk.

He preened teasingly. "Thank you."

"So I guess life's treating you pretty good these days, huh?"

"You could say that." He tapped his badge. "I ended up

getting my BSN and got hired here right after. Love working with these kids." As he glanced over at the camera crew, I caught Ramsey staring at us. I smiled. He didn't. David's gaze moved back to me. "Anyway, I know you've got to visit other rooms, but I'd love to catch up sometime."

"I—"

Ramsey's hand clapped down on my shoulder, and he gave me a pointed look. "We've gotta go to the next room."

"Yep." I turned back to David. "We'll see if we can make that happen."

"I'm easy to find on social. Hit me up." He winked.

"Who was that?" Ramsey asked once we were back in the hallway. Cross had veered off to use the restroom.

"Guy I hooked up with once at a party. He looks *totally* different. Like mind-blowingly different." I shook my head and gauged Ramsey's expression with a smirk. "He just wants to catch up."

"I'll bet he'd like that." Ramsey snorted. "I get it. You're hot."

"You feeling okay?" I reached out, and Ramsey smacked my hand away before I could press it to his forehead. "Was that an actual compliment?"

"I'm just repeating what I've overheard. Doesn't reflect my personal views."

"Uh-huh. Jealousy makes your jaw get all tight. It's kind of attractive."

"That wasn't jealousy. That was me keeping you on track. We're here to spend time with the kids, not at a fraternity mixer, you gigantic fucking flirt."

I cracked up. "That wasn't even flirting."

He gave me a level stare. "You did the anchor look."

"The anchor look... Oh, you mean this one?" I let my

gaze drift over him, up and down, lingering around his mouth. It was one of my favorite parts of him.

He smacked the back of my head, making me crack up all over again, then started off down the hallway.

I trotted after him, still grinning. "It's cool. I'll give you a compliment back to make you feel better: your ball-handling skills are incredible." I leaned in closer, mouth near his ear. "And that ass is something else."

He shoved me away and picked up speed, but the fucker was definitely smiling.

After we finished up at the hospital, we all headed to the parking lot. Tomorrow was an off day in the sense that practice was lighter, but I still planned on getting in a solid workout and spending some time watching film. I didn't want a repeat of the last game, and I'd promised Jared, after all.

Ramsey caught up to me as I walked toward my car. "You want to come over later?"

It would have been way more suave if I'd hesitated longer than the nanosecond it took me to respond. "Bet."

15

RAMSEY

"We should go out and get laid tonight." Tucker tugged his shirt on, then straddled a bench in the locker room. My gaze automatically traveled to Garrett, who cocked a dark brow. I wanted to wink at him but figured that might be a little too obvious. I could cover it up when I flirted with him in other ways, but likely not in a conversation where Tuck wanted me to go out with him and find someone to fuck.

"Yeah, Rams. You should get laid tonight. I plan to." Garrett grinned. Leave it to the little bastard to playfully start shit up. Sex was one hundred percent in my plans for the evening, though it would be him I had my dick inside of, not anyone else.

"Don't get started. We don't wanna hear about how you take it up the ass," Nance sneered, making my blood run hot and spots dance around in my vision.

"Keep talking about my sex life, and I'm gonna start thinkin' you're jealous. You want a turn on my dick?" Garrett replied, way more coolly than I felt. The muscles in my arms twitched, my hands automatically balling into fists. I'd never liked Nance, but I'd never had the all-consuming need to beat the shit out of him until Garrett got drafted.

"Don't even fucking joke like that. I'm not a fa—"

Before Nance could get the word out, I'd leaped over the bench and slammed him against the locker, my forearm across his throat. "You finish that sentence, and we're gonna have a real problem, you and me. You don't want to have a problem with me, Nance." Years after Anson Hawkins and Darren Edwards came out, and the league was still dealing with pieces of shit like Nance. I hated homophobia, hated that he brought this shit out in me. Fighting in the locker room felt like something my dad would do, but at least I had a good reason.

"Rams," Tuck said, warning in his voice. I could feel the hot stare of every guy on the team. Nance was breathing heavily, hand on my arm, but he couldn't pull me off. "Rams," Tuck said again. I knew without looking that Garrett would be fucking pissed. It was why he hadn't said anything, but I was tired of Nance's bullshit.

"Jesus, taking this babysitting gig for Houston's brother a little too seriously, aren't you?" He had no way of knowing that Houston had really asked me that at some point. He was talking shit and I knew it, but his words would be like a dagger to Garrett's heart.

"Nah, just don't like you. Never have. Keep your mouth shut."

"Warner! What the hell are you doing?" Coach interrupted.

My eyes fell closed, and I whispered a quiet, "Fuck," before letting go of Nance. "Nothing."

"Are you sure? Because it looked to me like you had your hands on one of your teammates. That shit doesn't fly here."

But Nance could be a homophobic asshole? "Then he needs to learn to watch his mouth."

"What did he say?" Coach asked, but I didn't repeat it. G wouldn't want his shit out there like that. He was way better at this than me.

Tucker sighed. "He was about to call McRae the *F* word."

My gaze snagged on Garrett, who scorched my skin with the anger in his gaze. Yep, I was fucked. I didn't think the but-I'm-the-captain line was going to help me this time.

"You're both fined twenty thousand dollars." Coach looked at Nance. "We're a team, and I expect you to act like it. Keep your opinions to yourself." Then to me. "You don't put your hands on my players. If anyone has a problem with that, come and see me. You're lucky we're going into our bye week, or I would have benched both your asses, record be damned." Coach's gaze shot toward Garrett, then back to me and Nance.

I shoved away from him, my gut tight, my pulse banging against my skin.

Nance was the first one to barrel his way out of the locker room.

"Christ, Ramsey. He's a fucking dickhead, but you can't let him get to you like that."

I gave Tucker an up-nod before looking over just as Garrett slammed his locker, jerked his bag onto his shoulder, and stormed out. "G, wait up." I grabbed my duffel and bumped fists with Tucker. "Catcha later, man."

Garrett was halfway down the hallway when I caught up with him. "Garrett," I said, but he ignored me and kept going. Neither of us spoke as we went past security, one of the guards opening the door. When we stepped out into the bright sunlight, I tried again. "Garrett."

"Fuck you, Ramsey. I already told you I don't need you

fighting my battles for me." He jerked out of my hold, Nikes beating against the pavement of the team parking lot.

"I'm the cap—"

"We both know that's not what that was. It's because we're...whatever the hell we are."

Shit. He was right, and we both knew it. I followed him to his car. "It was like...ten percent because I'm captain," I said, hoping to get a smile out of him.

He shook his head, tossed his bag in, said softly, "Just because we're fucking doesn't mean you get to do that. I don't need a knight in shining armor. Every time you come to my defense, all it does is make me look weak in his eyes. And I get it—homophobia is bigger than me. This is your battle too. But when it's in response to what he says to me, that just makes it seem like I need you to fix it for me."

Fuck. I could see where he was coming from, but it was hard. I would defend anyone I cared about from shit like that, but I got what Garrett meant. "I'm sorry. I hate bullies. My dad is one."

His gaze softened. He dropped his head back, looking up at the sky, and let out a deep breath. I stepped closer, wanting to bury my face in his neck...maybe bite it and then kiss it better, wondering what it would be like to bend him over his car and take him right here.

"It really sucks that you're such a good guy, Rams."

"Because you can't stay mad at me?" I fluttered my lashes, but then sobered. "I get you, G. I do. I won't do it again, but for the record, if the situation were reversed, I think you'd do the same for me. It has nothing to do with thinking the other person is weak and more to do with giving a shit about them."

Garrett's lips curled up, and he winked. "Get off my nuts."

I laughed, stepped closer again, leaned forward, before his eyes went wide and reality shocked through me, making me jerk backward. Holy fuck, I'd almost kissed him in the parking lot of our facility.

"So, um...yeah...you forgive me?"

"No."

"Still wanna come over tonight and have sex with me?"

Garrett laughed. "Yes. But only because I like your dick, not you."

It had been three weeks since the first night Garrett slept in my bed, and he'd made it there numerous times since.

"What did you say that night you were drunk all those months ago? I'm the hottest guy you've ever seen? Oh, no, it was *ridiculously hot*. That's what you said."

"I'm pretty sure that was you dreaming."

"Nope." I nodded toward my SUV. "Hurry up and get your ass to my place. We'll get cleaned up and go grab some dinner or something." We'd never been on a date, not that I was saying that's what this was, but after practice today, we had a whole fucking week to ourselves—no game, no practice, nothing. I hoped he'd spend a lot of it with me.

"You're getting awfully bossy."

"Hurry and get your ass to my place, please?"

"That's better."

I walked away with a smile on my face, though I always wore one when I was around Garrett McRae.

GARRETT HAD FOLLOWED ME HOME. HE'D KEPT SHIT IN HIS car for when he stayed at my place. We'd sucked and fucked all over my house like we got some kind of prize for how many places we could come together. Though I hadn't let him take my ass yet, I had a feeling I would soon. I'd let him stick a couple of fingers up there, and I had to say, Nance didn't know what he was missing. Garrett had rubbed my prostate and basically made me shoot my brains out of my cock. It was one of the most intense orgasms I'd ever had.

We showered together, then climbed into my SUV to head to Stella, a popular restaurant in Denver that was used to serving high-profile customers. It wouldn't be odd for the two of us to be seen together there. I didn't worry about it, didn't think people would assume we were on a date or anything. I'd been with both Houston and Tucker how many times? It was shitty that I had to think that way, which was partly my fault. I shouldn't care if people knew I was queer, but I just...didn't want to be known for anything other than football. I'd finally taken hold of my own career and wasn't asked about my dad in every interview. I didn't want my game to be overshadowed by something else.

But if I was being honest, I'd admit my little act in the locker room likely wasn't helping me any.

"You're being quiet. Change your mind?" G asked when we were seated. We'd chosen to eat outside. They had a patio with outdoor heaters at each table and fairy lights strung across the lattice ceiling.

"Nope. I'm good." I wanted to be out with Garrett tonight. I should worry about what that meant—this was only supposed to be a friends-with-benefits thing, after all— but I liked spending time with him. He made me feel...more *real*, if that made sense.

"You're being weird," Garrett said.

"I know you are, but what am I?"

"An idiot?"

We each ordered a beer, steak, potatoes, and veggies.

When we were alone again, after getting our drinks, Garrett leaned back in his chair, watching me.

"What?" I asked.

"Nothing."

"You're so gone for me."

"You wish." He lowered his voice. "Any trouble with your dad lately?"

The hairs on the back of my neck stood on end. I wasn't used to people talking to me about him this way. How the media did it, yes, but not with the concern Garrett had in his voice. "He hasn't shown up, but it's only a matter of time before he does. He's still calling, though."

"You don't deserve that."

I didn't. But then, did anyone? "It sucks, ya know? I used to wonder what it was like to have a real father, one who gave a shit. He only cared about himself—not me, not his career, just himself, money, fame, and having a good time. All I am to him now is what I can give him." I took a swallow from my beer, surprised I'd shared that with him. I didn't typically crack open my heart and show my insecurities that way. "Fuck, I have no idea why I said that."

I could see it in his eyes, that he was as shocked as me, but pleased I'd opened up to him. I also knew he wouldn't make a big deal out of it, and there weren't enough words for how much I appreciated that.

Garrett shrugged. "That's kinda how we've been from the start. I told you about how I feel getting compared to Houston."

"True. You're a strong player on your own, G. Even if the comparisons are out there, it doesn't take away from how badass you are."

"You're just saying that because you want in my ass," he countered.

"You'll let me in there regardless. You're always begging for this cock." He laughed, and I plucked a piece of ice out of my water and threw it at him. "I'm sorry again about today."

"I've been dealing with that for years, Rams. It's not going away."

"Yeah, but I haven't. It's not easy to sit back and hear someone you care about being called a name like that."

He opened his mouth, closed it, then took a drink of his beer. I couldn't help wondering what he'd almost said.

The waitress showed up with our food, breaking up the weird heaviness in the air. When she was gone, Garrett said, "You have mine."

My brows pulled together. "Your what?"

"Earlier you said you wondered what it was like to have a real family. You have mine—well, ours. Mine and Houston's. They love the shit out of you."

Yeah, I did have them.

We stared at each other, my chest feeling a little tight. Jesus, he really was so fucking sexy—his plump lips, the sweep of his hair over his forehead, his smile.

Garrett said, "We haven't fucked in the game room...or your home gym. We should give one of those a go next."

Part of me hated the change of subject, but the other part was thankful as fuck. This was stupid. It was a rookie move crushing on your friend's brother, on your teammate, but as we continued to eat, laugh, and talk, I wondered if that was exactly what I was doing.

16

GARRETT

"You got one more rep in you?" Ramsey asked as I pushed upright from the weighted squat and the bar rattled back into place.

"Nope." Sweat dripped down my face, but I kept my hands on the bar because I knew what was coming next. I was already regretting agreeing to work out with him in his home gym.

"Yeah ya do. Go again."

"Last one, fucking task master." My thighs and glutes were on fire. "I thought bye week was for relaxing," I groused as I set my shoulders and slid the bar out of its supports. Again. I lowered slowly, quads screaming every inch of the descent as Ramsey watched from behind me.

"Get that ass out farther."

"Your favorite words," I gritted, catching him grin in the mirror. "I see you shamelessly looking at it too."

"Just watching your form."

"Right."

"Now back up again."

Another bead of sweat rolled down my temple as I

strained to straighten. Ramsey was behind me in an instant, spotting me and helping me push the bar back into place.

"Fuck," I muttered, my head sagging forward as I panted. "What kind of prize do I get for that one?"

"Some sweet muscle gains? A shower?" Ramsey's fingertips drifted over my knuckles, and I lifted my gaze, locking eyes with him in the mirror as his hard cock pressed into my ass.

"Nope." I shook my head slowly. "Want something better."

Goose bumps prickled across the back of my neck as Ramsey brushed a kiss over my nape. His hands closed over the tops of mine on the bar. "Something like this?"

"I'm sweaty." That was just a warning, not a refusal.

He licked the side of my neck in response. "Don't care."

So weighted squats turned Ramsey on. I added that to my mental file and let out a soft groan, pulse spiking as he sucked gently on the other side.

"How about you keep those hands glued right where they are," he told me, skimming his fingers down my side, to my front, then sliding them inside the waistband of my shorts.

Ramsey inched my shorts lower, exposing my hardening cock to the cool air of his weight room as we both watched the mirror. My breathing went ragged as he cupped my balls, stroking a thumb over them while his hips rolled against my ass.

"How's this?" His other hand drifted lightly up and down my sternum, gliding over the sheen on my skin, teasing my nipples into tight buds while he wrapped a hand around my shaft and stroked me slowly.

"More in line with what I was thinking."

"You want this dick in your ass?"

"Yeah. *Shit.* Tighter." I arched into the friction. The fabric of his shorts was gonna chafe my ass, and I didn't even care at this point.

"Every time we're in the weight room, I think about doing this to you."

"Less thinking, more acting," I growled, and he chuckled as he glided a finger down my crease.

"No condoms or lube on me. I can go get—"

"Do we need them?" I interrupted, impatient as hell, as usual. "Neither of us has been with anyone else since our physicals. I mean, I haven't..."

Ramsey barked out a laugh. "You know I haven't. But...lube."

"Spit is nature's lube. Be resourceful, Ramsey, Jesus." I stared him down in the mirror until we both cracked up.

The touch of his fingertips over my entrance silenced me quickly enough, though, and I moaned as he pressed the pad against my entrance.

"Let me in."

I pressed back against him, and he worked me open with way more patience than I wanted him to have. By the time he shoved down his shorts, spread my cheeks, and rubbed the spit-slick head of his cock against my hole, I was whimpering with arousal, my dick throbbing in the air.

He breached me with the same patience, eyes glued to my ass, teeth clamping down on his lower lip with a satisfied hiss as I let him inside. "Goddamn this ass, Garrett."

I could've listened to him say that over and over, the need and desire in its rasp lighting up my core and making me drip. "Fuck, quit being so patient. Do it hard."

He glanced up then, a wild gleam dancing in his eyes as he smirked and jerked my hips back, sinking deeper inside me. The sting radiated outward, morphing into pleasure sliding up the base of my spine as he began moving, slower at first, bending his head to spit on his length, then faster, until he was slamming into me. My eyes rolled back in my head as the weights rattled in time with the smack of our bodies together.

I gripped my cock and let him fuck me into my fist, cursing with every thrust until pleasure crashed head-on into me with the force of a freight train. I gripped the bar again as my orgasm rocketed through me and I shot my wad all over the floor and the mirror in front of us.

"Fuck," Ramsey gasped out as I clenched around him. He closed his hands over mine, our fingers lacing, the power of his next thrust bowing me as he let go and came inside me with a cry.

Neither of us moved for long seconds, and then he wrapped an arm around my chest, dragging me down to the floor, where we both sprawled, shorts around our knees, chests heaving.

"Think anyone would say anything if we did this at our next team-training session?" I asked when I could manage a full string of words again.

"Probably no one would notice you yowling like a cat."

"Or you grunting out random shit like a caveman trying words for the first time." I grunted demonstratively, and Ramsey laughed and reached out, gently swiping a drip of sweat from my forehead.

My skin tingled where he touched it, and warmth spread through my chest, a far more dangerous sensation than the orgasm I'd just had. Because I fucking liked the tenderness in it, liked how his smile had become drowsy as he gazed at me.

"I..." Couldn't get enough of him, wanted to watch him make coffee in the mornings, and then follow him to the weight room, wanted the jokes and snide remarks, and busting each other's balls. I was in trouble. First rule of FWB club was you didn't admit feelings. Fuck it, no. The first rule of FWB club was you didn't catch them in the first place and, Jesus, had I come in hot on the front end with that one. When Ramsey lifted an expectant brow, I rerouted, blurting out, "I'm supposed to go look at a bunch of houses this afternoon with Houston. You should come. I mean, what else have you got to do?"

"Besides cleaning the mirror?" We both looked at it and busted up laughing. Ramsey rolled to a stand and extended a hand to pull me up. "Yeah, I'll come. Gotta make sure you don't drive the realtor crazy with dumb requests like secret passageways or a slide instead of stairs."

"Because I'm Scooby-Doo now?"

"If the shoe fits."

"Okay, Raggy." I rolled my eyes, then grinned. "Secret passageways would be cool, though. Don't even pretend otherwise."

"Get your ass in the shower. You stink."

"I didn't hear any complaints two minutes ago."

"You couldn't hear shit because you were yowling like a cat."

"You liked it."

Ramsey waggled his brows. "I did. Not gonna lie."

BY THE TIME WE'D SEEN TWO MCMANSIONS AND THREE ridiculously extravagant, ridiculously overpriced downtown lofts, I was starting to think gigantic and flashy wasn't exactly what I wanted like I thought I did. Houston's loft, while being spacious, in a great part of town, and nice, still managed to have a homey vibe. It felt like him.

Laura, our realtor, looked expectantly at me as we stood in the lobby of the most recent apartment, an ultramodern 3500 sq. ft. penthouse that had felt way too space-station sleek for me. Every appliance and electronic fed into a smart-home hub, and all of it talked. I hadn't known there was such a thing as too much tech, but there was.

"Do you have anything...smaller?"

Ramsey barked out a laugh behind me. "Guarantee you that's the first time he's ever said that."

"It is." I shot him a smirk as Houston groaned and rubbed his forehead. He'd chuckled and rolled his eyes when Ramsey showed up with me at the real estate agency, but four hours of the two of us was probably starting to get to him.

Laura laughed nervously, then looked at her phone. "I do have some other things... Give me five minutes. I'll make a few calls." She excused herself, stepping outside and leaving us in the lobby.

Houston leaned against a wall. "What was wrong with the first place? I liked it."

"Dunno, just wasn't feeling it." I glanced over at Ramsey. He was watching out the window as an older gentleman strolled down the street with his dog. Laura was running a hand through her hair as she spoke rapidly into the phone nearby. "Maybe she's saving the best for last. She did mention some stuff in Cedar Grove." That got Ramsey's attention. I grinned to myself. "House next to yours, actually," I lied. "Can you imagine how convenient that'd be?" Disappointingly, Ramsey didn't look as horrified as I'd imagined. I need to up the ante. "I could pop over for a cup of sugar anytime I needed."

He snorted as I waggled my brows.

Houston stared at us. "You two speaking in code right now?"

"I like baking."

"Bullshit." Ramsey laughed. "What's your specialty? Cherry pie?"

"You'd know, Cherry."

Houston pushed off the wall. "Damn, I thought you two pestering each other before was bad, but now that you're..." He gestured vaguely. "Whatever the fuck you two are doing, it's even worse. Jesus, now that I think about it, it's been, like, years of foreplay between you two."

"Definitely not the case." Antagonizing Ramsey had always been one of my favorite pastimes, a way to distract myself. I assumed him clapping back was just him playing along, but the way he met my eyes right then was so considering, it threw me.

"C'mon," Houston said, shattering my thoughts. "Let's go see what else she's come up with."

We followed him outside, tugging our coats tighter against the chill that nipped at our cheeks.

Laura waved her phone victoriously. "I've got a couple more things that could be promising, if you're up for a ride?"

"Always." The sidelong wink I shot at Ramsey earned another shake of his head.

"I've got a thing in an hour, so I'm going to bail." Houston managed to make his expression seem apologetic. "Pap at two o'clock, by the way."

We all followed his sightline, and sure enough, a guy halfway down the block was snapping photos. I was still getting used to the visibility that came with playing pro, so it caught me off guard sometimes. I waved to the guy as Laura fluffed her hair. "I've got an idea."

"No," Ramsey and Houston barked in scary unison.

"Let's all link elbows and skip toward him, *Wizard of Oz* style. Laura, you can be Dorothy. Houston's the Tin Man, I'm the Scarecrow, and Rams is obviously the Cowardly Lion."

"No," Ramsey and Houston repeated, again in scary unison. Typical party poopers.

I dropped it and turned to Laura. "So where are we heading?"

"Couple of things just came open in Cedar Grove. Not too big, not too small. They could be good contenders."

"Did you hear that? Cedar Grove." I clapped my hands to my cheeks and turned my head slowly in Ramsey's direction.

"Get the fuck in the car," he told me, then turning to Laura, said, "This new listing doesn't happen to be anywhere near, oh, Eagle Lane, does it?"

"It's a few miles away. I'm sorry if that wasn't the answer you were hoping for, but it's a nice place."

"Thank fuck." Houston pulled me into a neck hug and clapped my back. "I'm out, bro. See you at home later."

We followed Laura in my car out to the first house in Cedar Grove and, once again, it was an almost immediate no for me.

"How is it that you're this picky about houses?" Ramsey's voice echoed in the cavernous foyer with a chandelier the size of the Rock of Gibraltar hanging from the ceiling, and I shrugged.

"I wasn't aware I was."

"What's wrong with this one?"

"I dunno." I glanced around. There wasn't anything wrong with it. It wasn't over-the-top, aside from the chandelier. It was perfectly decent. "Just doesn't have the right vibe."

"Maybe vibes are best left in your dresser drawer."

I snorted and shoved him toward the door.

The next place Laura showed us was only a couple of miles away from the first but felt like a different world. As we wound up a long, gated driveway, I glimpsed a peaked roof in the distance. A few moments later we hopped out of the car in front of what looked like a tamer version of a mountain lodge.

Ramsey lifted a brow. "This is interesting."

"It needs a little work," Laura said. "But wait until you see the back. There's a pond and a huge deck."

Ramsey and I exchanged a smirk because apparently the more we fucked, the more juvenile we became in each other's presence.

"Right vibe?" Ramsey asked.

I studied the windows like I knew what the hell I was looking for. I didn't. "Maybe."

The interior was so far from the first mansion I'd ever envied, I couldn't believe I liked the place, but I did. Laura was right that it needed work, though. It was stuck in the '90s, with musty old carpet everywhere, but when Laura led us to a wall of windows overlooking a huge redwood deck that stretched out over the pond, isolated from the neighbors by thick blue spruce trees and scrub oaks, the view stopped us all in our tracks.

"All right, this is cool as shit," Ramsey murmured. "I've got a bunch of contractor names if you wanted to upgrade it."

Laura looked more excited than I'd seen her all day. "Do you think you might want to make an offer?"

"I need to sleep on it," I told her. But after we'd walked through the rest of the house again, I kept coming back to that deck. I could see it in the spring, a bunch of us hanging out there in the off-season. Grilling, drinking beer. Me, Houston, Cross, Ramsey...and goddamn, when had I gotten into family-style daydreams?

Once we said goodbye to Laura, Ramsey and I climbed back in my car so I could drop him off at home.

"It's a badass place," he said, gazing at the passing scenery.

I allowed myself five seconds to imagine Ramsey coming over, a late afternoon sunset, smoke from the grill mingling with a warm summer breeze that grew cooler as it passed over the water. The two of us sitting out there together, with a bucket of beers or, fuck it, even just glasses of water between us. "It could be really fucking nice," I said, hoping he'd assume I meant the house. But maybe some of the wistfulness in my chest seeped into my voice because his gaze shifted to me and lingered an extra beat before I snapped mine away and squashed the fantasy.

"I wouldn't hate having you as a neighbor, by the way."

"You should be so lucky."

"Especially with that deck. I'd be over all the time."

"Over *it* all the time."

"I said deck, not dick."

"Same thing."

Ramsey burst into a laugh, unbuckling his seat belt as I stopped in front of his house. "Goddamn, I don't know what to do with you sometimes."

"Shutting me up seems to be working out just fine for you so—" Before I could finish, Ramsey leaned over the seat, demonstrating how well that tactic worked by kissing me soundly on the lips before sliding from the car.

17

RAMSEY

The room was quiet except for the sound of our breathing. We were both naked, after I'd just come in Garrett's ass. There was nothing like fucking him, especially since we'd been going at it raw.

Garrett's head rested on my arm, which was around him, fingers drawing circles on his sweat-slicked skin. He'd spent every night of our bye week at my house. Even when we'd gone to look at places, he'd dropped me off, gone home for a bit or to see his parents, but then had ended up with me again.

It was...different. Not that I hadn't had women sleep over at my place—exhibit *A*: the stalker, sleeping photos—but not on the regular like G had been. It had always made me slightly uneasy with others, so I'd kept it to a minimum to avoid mixed messages. But I actually *liked* it when it came to Garrett. I wanted him here, liked cuddling with him, working out with him, feeling the bed shift because he couldn't stay still. He also did this cute thing right before he fell asleep where he'd sigh deeply, then almost whimper, before snuggling in like he was the most comfortable he'd ever been.

God, I was being all gross over this guy. I wasn't sure what to make of it.

"I can hear you thinking hard," he broke the silence.

"Just wondering how you got so lucky as to land me."

Garrett barked out a laugh. "First, it's the other way around. Second, I've landed you?"

He had a point, since we hadn't defined the relationship. "You know what I mean. You're lucky my dick lands in your ass."

He laughed again. "That one wasn't even good. You don't have to try so hard to be funny. I still like you even though your sense of humor sucks."

"Speaking of sucking...I know how you can put your mouth to better use," I teased, our quiet chuckles dancing together, before we playfully wrestled around in bed. I let Garrett get the best of me. That was my story, and I was sticking to it. He ended up on top, straddling me, holding my arms down.

"I win."

"I beg to differ." I jerked a hand free and reached up, gripped his nape, and pulled him down for a kiss. Kissing Garrett was hot. It made my pulse speed up, and not just in that wanna-fuck? way, but one that should make me a whole lot more nervous than it did.

We made out for a while, licking and touching, tasting and teasing, like we'd spent years doing this. When he settled in beside me again, he asked, "You okay? You seem a little off tonight."

I *felt* a little off, but I was still surprised he'd noticed. I was typically pretty good at hiding my shit. I looked up through the skylight above my bed. There was a remote to slide the blinds in place or to open them. The view was unobstructed tonight, dots of light spread out along the dark sky.

"My mom didn't want me to play football," I found myself saying.

Garrett rolled over, slid his arm around my waist, and kissed my chest, like he felt the heaviness of my statement. "Why not?"

"She was with my dad since college and into the pros. It took its toll on her. Plus, she blamed the game for my dad's issues, even though they were his fault. It was hard on her, though...the cheating, the drugs, his attitude; having to pick up and move when he'd get traded nearly every other year because he couldn't keep his shit together and ruined every opportunity he had. She used to tell me she wanted me to help people, but even though we're just playing a game, we do that, ya know? We bring people entertainment, make them happy. And our visit with Jared in the hospital...we fucking made his day. Not to mention, he made mine too when he gave you shit."

"Because of course he did," G replied.

"Anyway, at some point, no teams would sign him, and he got worse. He put all his energy into me, and I was still so fucking young. I remember one day, my parents were fighting about me playing, and I felt guilty because I didn't want to let my mom down, but I also fucking loved the game, ya know? And I knew I could do it, play and not be him. But then she got sick and died. It was fucking worse with him, of course. He went off the deep end. I wonder sometimes, though, if she'd be proud of me...that I'm doing this without being like him."

"Hell yeah, she would. You're Warner fucking Ramsey."

"Good point," I teased, then tugged him closer and

kissed his temple. "Ignore me. It's her birthday. I think that's why I've been all up in my feels this week."

"Shit, you should have said something. Is that why your phone was blowing up all day? Your dad?"

"Bingo." I hoped that didn't mean he was going to do one of his drop-in visits. I wasn't in the mood to see him.

"I really hate him."

"That makes two of us."

Garrett leaned down, nuzzled my neck, and whispered, "She's proud of you, Rams. How can she not be?"

I swiped at my eyes. "Thanks. Now talk to me about something else before I get embarrassed about how I acted."

"Um...what do you want to discuss?"

I wanted to know everything about him, but I settled on, "Hm...I don't know. When did you realize you're bi?" Since him teaching me the ropes had been how this whole thing with us started, I figured it made sense to wonder about it.

"Nope. Not going there." Garrett tried to pull away, but I wrapped my arms around him, holding his hard body to mine.

"Fuck that noise. Now you have to tell me."

"I won't do it, and you can't make me."

"Please?"

"No."

"Baby..." I begged—and we both froze. What the shit? "I have no idea what that was."

"Umm, you're in love with me. That's what that was."

"Ew. Gross. Now tell me." I swatted his ass.

"Ugh." I let him roll off me, pretty sure I was about to get my way.

"Once upon a time, there was this really gorgeous, intelligent, badass motherfucking wide receiver who thought he only liked girls."

"Pfft," I cut him off, but he ignored me and continued.

"When he was eighteen, he went to a party with his brother, who was in the NFL. He was looking for this really hot chick he'd seen earlier, when he ran into his brother's best friend."

That got my attention. My heart punched against my chest.

"He was annoying as shit. Cocky, loud, picked his nose..."

"Ha-ha."

"Stop interrupting. Anyway, despite the fact that he stank really bad, said badass motherfucking wide receiver thought, *Hm...maybe I should give this guy a chance. With a little work, he could be totally fucking hot...oh shit. I think I'm bi.* The end."

I laughed, an undeniable giddiness bursting in my chest. And fuck, I'd never used that word or felt giddy before, but I did right then. "First, I believe what you mean is, you spotted a guy who'd won the genetic lottery. And second, holy fuck, G. I was your bi-awakening." I guessed that explained his drunk-night rambling about how hot I was.

"Pretty sure it was the other way around. Who's been teaching whom the ropes?"

I ignored that. "So basically...you only liked girls, but then the most attractive man you'd ever seen showed you Ty's trophy room, and you couldn't help but want to bone him? You were like... *Damn, if dudes are this fucking hot, where do I sign up to join the bisexual club?* You're welcome."

"I hate you."

"Aw, come on, G, don't be like that. I'm irresistible. It's totally understandable." I laughed, rolled on top of him, felt the vibration of him chuckling too. "I'll tell you a secret."

"It better be a good one."

"I thought you were hot too." I gave him a loud, smacking, playful kiss, then rolled away. "Now let's go to bed. Tomorrow is our last day off before it's back to the grind. I might not let you out of my bed."

"I might not try," Garrett replied, then wrapped his arm around me, snuggled close to my back, sighed contentedly, and fell asleep.

When I woke up the next morning, my bed was empty. Garrett rarely got up before me. I was just tugging on some underwear when he came into the room with birthday cupcakes for my mom. That's when I acknowledged I'd done something incredibly stupid, that this was a little more than just a crush. I was legit falling for Garrett McRae.

OUR FIRST PRACTICE BACK WAS FUCKING BRUTAL. I'D MAYBE eaten too many cupcakes the day before and was feeling the sugar overload.

Garrett had stayed at my place last night too. We'd taken separate cars to the practice facility but arrived at the same time. I worried what the locker room would be like after the shit with Nance, but he kept his fucking mouth shut, so all was good.

We'd just finished getting dressed when Tucker asked, "What are you doing today? Want to watch some film for the next game?"

I glanced over at Garrett. We'd gotten to the point where we spent time together daily, so I assumed I'd be with him. It probably wouldn't kill us not to act like a married couple who were together twenty-four seven, though. As if reading my mind, Garrett shrugged, then turned to Cross. "What are you up to today?"

See, look at us speaking silently to each other and coming to an agreement.

"Yep, sounds good to me," I told Tucker.

"Bet," he replied.

We finished getting dressed. Garrett and Cross were done first, and Garrett sent a playful wink in my direction as the two of them walked out. Just as I was about to ask Tuck if he was ready, Coach said, "Ramsey. Get over here. We need to talk."

My heart dropped to my stomach. It was never good when Coach called for you in that serious, all-work voice.

"I'll wait." Tucker sat on the bench.

"Nah, it's cool. Wanna meet at your house in a bit?"

Tucker agreed and was on his way. Everyone filed out of the locker room while I headed to Coach's office.

He was sitting at his desk, playbooks and stat sheets spread out all over it.

"Something wrong?" I asked after closing the door.

"What's going on with you and McRae?"

Jesus, talk about cutting to the chase.

"I'm not sure I know what you mean," I replied, even though I knew exactly what he fucking meant.

"I've noticed the two of you getting close, spending a lot of time together, and I figured that's a good thing, just you taking him under your wing. But then your reaction to Nance last week—"

"He's a fucking homophobe."

"Which is disgusting, but you also nearly choked the guy in my locker room, Ramsey. Since when do you lose your head and let your emotions get the best of you? That's not you."

No, no it wasn't. Still, I asked, "Are you trying to say it's something my dad would do? Because that's different. He started fights because he's a hothead who can't handle anyone being better than him. I was defending someone I care—my friend."

He cocked a brow at me. I was fucked.

"Shit, Warner." He rubbed a hand over his face, elbows on the desk. He didn't need me to confirm G and I were a thing. All he had to do was look at me to know it. "Is this going to be a problem? I can't have fights on my team. Are we going to have to navigate dating, lover spats, and breakups in an NFL locker room?"

"Wow...way to have faith in our relationship. You already have us breaking up." His eyes narrowed, and I knew I shouldn't have said that. This apparently wasn't the time for a sense of humor. "It won't be a problem," I replied.

"We're here for football. This is...well, it's a PR nightmare waiting to happen is what it is. Plus, it's messy. I don't like messes. This isn't something the league has had to deal with. Honestly, I'm not sure it will end well for the two of you. Two men in a relationship on the same team? It's..."

"So trade me," I said. Coach's mouth dropped open, and not gonna lie, I had to keep myself from turning around to see if someone else had spoken those words using my voice. "If the issue isn't homophobia or us being on the same team, then let it go unless there's an issue. And if it becomes a problem, trade me." I had no idea what in the fuck I was doing. I didn't even know how Garrett felt about me, if he wanted this to be more than friends with benefits, but I sure as shit wasn't ready to walk away.

"Slow your roll there, Ramsey. Let's not go that far. We don't want to lose you. We built this team around you. No one knows about this. It was my coach's intuition. All I know is, we don't want a media circus."

"And you think I do?" I'd do just about anything to avoid it.

"This is off the record. I'm telling you this as a friend, your coach, and as someone who respects your game and how you handle yourself. You've never had a controversy. You don't cause trouble. You don't ever have the PR staff scrambling. I think it would be best if you and McRae kept this quiet. There are already pap photos of the two of you together all week, but that can be explained as just being buddies, especially if you have Houston with you more often. Let's keep this under wraps at least until the end of the season, and then we'll take it from there."

"And at the end of this season? If we're still..." Doing whatever the hell it was we were doing.

"We'll cross that bridge when we get to it. Unfortunately, I can't make you any promises."

That sounded really fucking bad. Still, I nodded. "Yeah, Coach. We'll be careful." We both wanted to keep this a secret anyway. How hard could it be?

18

GARRETT

After bye week, we headed to Kansas City, and while we didn't wipe the floor with the Crows, we came out with a respectable win, our defense keeping them at bay for the rest of the game after Nance scored a touchdown in the middle of the fourth quarter.

Cross had friends on the team and, since our flight didn't leave until early the next morning, a bunch of us decided to tag along with them downtown. I guilted-slash-goaded Ramsey into coming along.

"KC women are crazy hot," Tucker said as our group crammed into the hotel elevator.

"Las Vegas tops, though. All those performers," Ellis countered. "I hooked up with a contortionist from Cirque once. Jesussssss." He let out an appreciative sigh.

Tucker snorted. "She'd have to be able to find your dick."

A brief scuffle broke out amid the laughter, flattening Ramsey's back against my chest and me harder against the back wall. I lost track of the conversation as I let my hand roam up the back of his thigh and beneath his shirt.

Ramsey sucked in a quiet breath and froze when I

fanned my fingers over his lower back and then squeezed his hip, pulling him tighter against my burgeoning hard-on. I wanted this ass, wanted him. I suddenly couldn't remember why I'd wanted to go out in the first place.

"McRae!"

"Yeah?" Fuck, I'd missed something. Ramsey shifted, but I gripped his waistband and held him in place.

"Your cousin? In Vegas?"

"What about her?" Fuck, Ramsey's skin was so warm. I wanted to lick a stripe up his spine and spread him open, make him thrash on the sheets while I rimmed him.

"She hot? Does she have hot friends?"

"She's my cousin. Of course she's hot, and if any of you touch her, I'll..." I reconsidered, knowing better than to make it into a genuine challenge. Besides, Mya was the brainiac type and would probably turn her nose up at these guys. "If any of you ever hook up with her, don't fucking tell me about it because that's gross." I teased a finger over the top of Ramsey's crack, hoping we were done with that convo because there were way more interesting things demanding my attention as I inched my finger lower. Like the tension in Ramsey's jaw, the little flutter of the muscles there. How he shifted slightly, giving me more access.

A sharp burst of laughter from Cross interrupted my concentration again.

"The fuck are you laugh—aw, goddamn, dude. C'mon," Ellis groaned.

Fortunately the elevator doors slid open at that moment, and we all spilled out, hacking and sucking in the fresh air as Cross continued snickering, the nasty bastard so pleased with himself.

"I THINK I SHOULD TELL YOU SOMETHING." RAMSEY DROPPED onto the cushy bench seating next to me after returning from the bar. He plunked another beer on the low table in front of me. We'd been in the club for a couple of hours. Cross, Tucker, and several of the other guys had already found their prospects for the night. I had a nice beer buzz going, but I was keeping it tame, already envisioning the hundreds of ways Ramsey and I could put a happy ending on the night later. It was great motivation to keep from getting whiskey dick.

"That I'm the best you've ever had? I already know that," I teased.

"You're the *only* guy I've ever had." It was a fair quip, but a reminder that thunked like lead in my chest. My grin faltered as I circled back to what he'd just said about needing to tell me something. "What's up?"

"Coach called me in the other day. I was debating telling you, but I think I should." He blew out a breath that put me on the edge of my seat. "It's not a big deal, or it doesn't have to be, but he's got some idea we're hooking up."

"Shit. Really? How? The storage room?" Fuck, that really had been risky, and now I was running back through my memories, trying to pin down moments that could've given us away. Surely if Coach knew about the storage room, he would've said something sooner.

"No, thank fuck. That didn't come up. Though that was totally stupid."

"Stupidly hot. But risky, yeah. Bet you've never done anything like that in your life before. It's good to cut loose that way sometimes." I arched a brow at him, but his expression remained decidedly serious, which sent nerves jangling through my gut.

"I do that a lot around you," he said softly.

"And…" I frowned. "You don't want to mess around anymore? Wait, what did Coach say? Is he pissed? Fuck." My stomach flipped over on itself, knotted. "What if he sends me packing?" Not that I hadn't considered it before, but what I actually hadn't considered was that Ramsey and I would still be hooking up, and now I was in too deep to want to stop it. But the idea of being traded was sobering. Even scarier was that I wasn't sure I wouldn't choose being traded over stopping shit with Ramsey. "My contract—"

"No. Damn, McRae, slow down. You're not gonna get traded. He's not pissed. He's…cautious, I guess. He doesn't want a PR mess, just like you and I have talked about before. Doesn't want to fuck up the team dynamic. I told him that wouldn't happen."

"Because it won't," I gritted through my teeth. I didn't like the way he wouldn't look at me. "You know me better than that. You didn't answer my other question, though. Do you want to stop this?"

"Like I said, slow the fuck down. Jesus, you're so impatient sometimes." Ramsey met my eyes, finally, the focus in them sharp. "I don't want to stop. Do you?"

"Fuck no. In the elevator, all I could think about was laying you out on a bed when we got back, stripping those jeans off you, and eating your ass."

"Goddamn." Ramsey glanced around.

"No one's paying attention. I told you, I'm careful."

"Just like you were in the elevator with your hand down my pants?" The glint in his eyes said it wasn't entirely an admonishment, though.

"No one was paying attention then either. But I can cut that out too."

"I don't want you to. What I do want is for you to finish that fucking beer so we can get the fuck out of here."

"Where we going?"

"Back to the hotel so you can strip me and eat my ass."

WITH THE WARNING FROM COACH IN THE BACKS OF OUR minds, we left separately, Ramsey about twenty minutes before I made an excuse and bailed too, along with Ellis.

The TV volume was on low when I opened the door to our hotel room and stepped inside, Ramsey sitting on the end of the bed, elbows on his knees, hands dangled between them. The scent of soap was strong in the air, his hair still damp. He reached out and snapped the TV off as the door shut behind me.

"No one noticed anything, Rams. They were all wrapped up in their own shit. Ellis is gonna be sucking down Gatorades tomorrow. Probably shouldn't be telling the team captain that."

"Do you want to fuck me?"

I blinked. "Do cows moo? Do birds sing? Does Nance suck a fat dick? Does—"

"I want you to." Ramsey rested back on his palms and inclined his chin, a clear request.

I stepped between his thighs, nudging his knees with mine to widen them. "Are you sure? It's not like some step you have to take to have your bi card fully punched. It's not for everyone, and I'm totally cool with that. If you—"

"I want it," Ramsey interrupted me again, lifting his eyes to meet mine. No trace of his usual amusement within them, just an intent hunger that sent an answering thrum of electricity through me. "I want to know what it's like. With you." He took the hand I extended and let me pull him to standing. "What was your first time like? Actually, never mind, I don't want to know."

I skimmed my hands down his biceps, then worked his fly open as I brushed a kiss over his lips. Fuck, that I even got to kiss Warner Ramsey was still mind-blowing. His perfect mouth, how he turned into the kiss automatically now, familiarly. "Senior year of high school. Not long after that party at Ty's. Right into the deep end. It kinda sucked, to be honest. I was nervous."

"I'm not nervous."

I tipped his chin up and searched his eyes. He was nervous. "If you don't like it, we stop, simple as that."

"I'm not nervous," he repeated, adorably insistent, and nipped my lip when I grinned. "Quit looking so smug."

"It's not the kind of smug you think it is," I promised, shoving his pants down his hips and fisting his cock. He dropped his head to my shoulder with a groan, hips swaying as I stroked him.

"Fuck, that feels good."

I hummed, sucking the side of his neck as I worked the buttons of his shirt open with my free hand. "Lie on the bed, facedown." After pushing his shirt off his shoulders, I spun him around.

Ramsey hesitated for just a second, then crawled onto the bed and let me pull his pants the rest of the way off. I peeled my clothes off next as he watched me over his shoulder. "Okay, I'm a little nervous," he admitted, making me smile.

"I already knew that." I kicked out of my jeans and sank onto the mattress, catching myself on my palms inches above him and letting my naked cock glide along the crease of his ass as I kissed his shoulders, the nape of his neck, the side of his mouth until it opened for me and I found his tongue. He moaned with each roll of my hips, the precum that dripped onto his ass. "Don't worry," I rumbled the words low next to his ear. "I'm gonna have you moaning for my cock, just wait."

"You have no idea about the shit I had to think about to avoid getting hard in that elevator earlier."

"I didn't even try."

"You had me in front of you. That was cruel."

"We both liked it." I slid off the end of the bed and caught hold of his thighs, yanking him down as he yelped in surprise. Chuckling, I nipped his ass cheek, then spread him with my thumbs.

"Garrett!" he hissed, probably about to make some protest, so instead of answering him, I dived into his crease and flicked my tongue over his tight pink hole. "Oh God." His thighs quaked as his hole clenched and relaxed under the assault.

Protest gone, just like that. But my work wasn't done yet. My mouth moved over the tops of his thighs, the crease just beneath his ass, his firm glutes, pressing kisses and bites into his skin. I worked my way slowly toward his rim, softening his reflexes inch by inch. This time when I circled his hole with the tip of my tongue, he whispered out a curse but didn't flinch.

I guided him a little farther off the bed until I could reach between his legs and pull his dick back, keeping it in my hold as I worked him over, hole, balls, the head of his cock.

"Shit, Garrett, *shit*." That was the kind of praise I was looking for, and Ramsey's leaking cock was making my dick ache.

"I want this sexy ass." I kneaded his cheek and spread it wider. "This tight hole." Ramsey groaned as I licked it, then teased my thumb around the rim, pressing gently. "Gonna let me in?" Maybe he answered, but I couldn't tell what he said, just knew that when I flicked my tongue lightly next to my thumb and pressed more insistently, the muscles yielded as he hissed out a curse. "Fuck, you're tight, and you're gonna feel so fucking good on my cock." I worked him patiently and stroked his dripping crown with my other hand, soaking up the ragged sounds of his breathing. "Wish you could see how hard I am watching you drip all over my hand." I released his cock, still fucking his hole slowly with my thumb, and glided my slick hand down my shaft with a moan until my entire body vibrated with need. "Don't even need lube, you've got me so worked up."

"*Garrett.*"

"Uh-huh?" I bit back a smile as Ramsey twisted the sheets in one hand.

"I'm ready."

"You're *almost* ready," I corrected him.

19

RAMSEY

I'd been missing out.

I'd studied Garrett a lot when he was beneath me, took in the sounds he made, the way his body arched toward me, trembled, and melted when I fingered him, then pressed my cock in deep. But feeling it the other way? The initial burn and stretch, knowing I had another person inside me, and the pleasure jolting down my spine each time he brushed over my prostate...fuck, I didn't know how to explain it.

And he hadn't even given me what I really wanted yet—his cock.

"Fuck me," I begged. I'd be embarrassed by the need in my voice if I wasn't so turned on.

"I think I might end up with a hungry little bottom on my hands." I felt Garrett smile into my back before he pressed a kiss just above my ass cheek.

"What will you ever do?" I teased back, and he kissed me again.

"Give you what you need, Rams. Always." My heart sputtered, an engine that had needed a slight tune-up, but then rumbled to life again under Garrett's care. He meant sexually, obviously, but something about the rasp in his voice, about the low way he'd spoken, made me wonder if it could be more. But then he bit my ass, stroked my balls, and joked, "My very own bottom boy." It was so us, and in that moment, it overpowered any other thoughts.

"Oh my God. Shut up and fuck me before this night ends with me in your ass again."

I probably should have waited until we were home for this, but something about today—playing football with him, winning with him, the way he'd touched me in the elevator, and how his gaze lingered on me when he didn't think I was paying attention—got me all twisted up and needy for him.

Too needy. While I knew I'd do my best to hide what we had, verbalizing earlier tonight what Coach had said made it more real. It was why I'd done my best to avoid telling him before. I worried he would want to stop this, that he'd say it wasn't worth the risk.

It probably shouldn't be, but for me, it was.

And just in case it became that way, I damn sure was having him tonight.

My bag was beside the bed, up against the nightstand. Garrett leaned over, still managing to keep two spit-slick fingers in my hole while he fumbled to unzip and tug the lube out with one hand.

"Need some help?"

"I got this. There's nothing I can't do if your ass is the endgame."

I laughed. Cocky fucking G.

He did manage to get it, and poured some on his fingers before pushing a third inside. "Fuuuuuck." It was different. I couldn't pretend it wasn't, but each time his fingers slid over my prostate, pinpoints of pleasure exploded into fucking meteor showers inside me.

"You have no idea how hot this is, watching your tight little hole stretch around my fingers. Knowing you're giving this to me, that I'm the only man who's gotten to see you like this, the only man to take your ass."

"Yes to all that. Now start doing the taking."

"Of course you'd top from the bottom." His smile pressed against mine, and then his fingers slid out of my ass, leaving me feeling empty. He lubed up his erection, kneeling behind me. "How do you want to do this? Which way do you think you'll be more comfortable?"

"You choose." He was the experienced one, after all.

"Wow...can you say that again?"

"No, and don't get used to it."

Garrett didn't laugh, though, his voice serious and steady when he said, "Turn over. I want to see you while I fuck you." I wanted that too. I did as Garrett said, flipping to my back. He drizzled some lube onto my cock so I could stroke myself, then tossed it aside. "Legs up. Here, this will help." He grabbed a pillow and shoved it under my hips.

Our gazes held while I jacked myself. He was...fuck, he was gorgeous, so damned sexy that I didn't want to stop looking at him.

Garrett placed my legs over his shoulders, pressed forward, the head of his cock nudging at my rim. "Push out just a little. It'll help."

I nodded and did, Garrett easing in. It felt like it had with his fingers, only different too, thicker and hotter, the rush of blood beneath his skin radiating out and into me. I couldn't say it was perfect, that it didn't feel strange, but this was Garrett, and I wanted him.

"That's it...look at you taking my cock so well. You

should see how fucking hot this is, Rams. See your hole opening up for me. You're so goddamned tight."

He kept talking to me, and that helped, the journey slightly easier, my body relaxing to let him take possession of me. And when he did, when his dick was buried deep, his groin against my ass, we both breathed out together.

"Good?" he asked.

"I don't know. You haven't started the actual fucking yet." I winked, the gleam in his eyes saying challenge accepted.

Garrett pulled back, leaving only his crown inside me, before snapping his hips forward. The best kind of pleasure shot through me, making my whole body flush with need. "More."

"Fuck yes," Garrett replied, letting loose, railing my ass, his body slapping against mine. Each time it did, colors danced behind my eyelids. "Look at me," he ordered, and I did.

"So fucking bossy." But I liked it in this situation. All the time? No. But it was fun to give up control to him a little bit. I jerked myself, fucking my hand while he took me. Our gazes never left each other. He gave me a cocky smile that went straight to my balls. I was pretty sure everything he did had a direct line there.

"It's so hot seeing you like this. You gonna come for me, Ramsey? You gonna blow your load all over your chest before I fill your ass?"

Yes, yes I was.

I reached out, wrapped a hand around his nape, and tugged him toward me. My legs slipped off his shoulders, but I kept them wide and pulled back. Just like on the field, we read each other well, Garrett knowing what I wanted. He took my mouth, pressed his tongue in while he worked his cock in slow, deep, targeted thrusts.

My body trembled. With my free hand I stroked my cock. My balls drew up, and I arched toward him as I came apart beneath him, shooting rope after rope of my release between us.

Garrett thrust harder, his dick pulsing inside me, spilling his release deep.

He fell on top of me, our sweaty bodies stuck together with perspiration and cum. I caressed his back as he kissed my chest, and then he pushed up, his cheeks surprisingly pink. "Good?" The way he said that one word told me how much he needed it to be.

"Really fucking good."

"Yes I am," he answered, and we laughed and kissed.

This was so not turning out to be what I'd planned.

"HOW YOU BEEN, MAN?" TUCKER ASKED HOUSTON. IT WAS A Monday night. We'd had a home game earlier, which Houston and his family had come to. Tucker asked me to hang out since we had the following day off. I'd been with Garrett nearly every day and figured it would start looking suspicious if we were too glued to the hip, so we'd decided to do our own thing tonight.

"Good, just getting this knee stronger and trying to figure out what in the hell I want to do next."

We were in a private booth at an upscale Denver club, nursing beers, finger foods on the table between us. I wondered what Garrett and Cross were doing.

"Sucks, man," Tucker said. "We miss you out there. Baby G's doing good, but it's not the same as having you."

Houston took a drink, then set his bottle down. Tucker didn't seem to notice his discomfort, so I made an attempt to change the subject and asked Tucker, "Is your family flying out for the holidays?" He was from Florida. We didn't have a lot of time off, so Tucker's mom and three sisters often came to see him.

Thanksgiving was a couple of weeks away, and we didn't have a game on the holiday this year. I was expected at the McRaes' and couldn't help wondering how different it would be this time—you know, since their son now secretly put his dick in my ass and I did the same to him.

"They're hoping to." Tucker rambled on about his family for a while, then asked me what I was doing. "You know you're welcome with me," he said. It was shitty being the resident stray sometimes, but I was lucky to have friends who cared.

"I'll be with McRae...s. The McRaes, I mean."

His brows drew together slightly, I was sure because of how I'd fumbled my response, but he didn't call me on it. Houston, on the other hand, stifled a laugh.

Three women approached us then, all of them incredibly gorgeous, showing all sorts of leg and flashing us smiles.

"You're Houston McRae, aren't you?" the blonde asked. "And Warner Ramsey and Malik Tucker?"

"Yeah, we are," Tuck replied. "And who do we have the pleasure of speaking to?"

They gave their names.

Before Garrett had turned my life upside down, I would have been stoked, but now I was just trying to figure out how to get out of this situation.

"Do you guys want to dance?" Lydia, the woman with dark braids asked, gaze shooting to Tucker.

He stood and held his hand out for her. "I would love to dance with you." He turned to Houston and me. Neither of

us had moved. I didn't know what kept Houston from standing, but I had a man I was hoping would find his way to my
bed tonight. A man who was only supposed to be my friend
with benefits.

"Thank you for asking, but I'm going to have to pass
tonight." *Think, think, think.* It shouldn't have been this hard
for me to come up with a quick story. "I'm, um...seeing
someone," I stuttered.

Houston's head whipped my direction like he couldn't
believe I'd said it. He was right. I probably should have
come up with a lie. Now there would be speculation and
rumors about whom I was dating. People would look into
my life even more, unless I got lucky enough and the
women didn't talk.

"My knee is acting up," Houston said. Tucker's stare shot
between the two of us, but when all three women gave him
their attention, he was effectively distracted.

"Shall we, ladies?" Tucker said, and they seemed to be
down for all three of them to dance with him. They grabbed
him and tugged him to the dance floor.

"Ramsey."

"I know. I should have come up with a better excuse."

"You like him, don't you? *Like* him, like him."

"It's just sex," I lied because that was the easiest thing to
do. It was hard to admit I went and caught feelings, especially to Garrett's brother. Though I guessed that wasn't as
bad as talking about fucking him.

"Gross. Can we not?"

"What? Talk about how hot *you know who* is in the
sack?" I teased, and he gave me the finger.

"You like him," Houston said again, and I knew he
wouldn't let this go.

"It's fucked up, right? I can't believe this happened. I

don't know what he did to me, but it's a mess. *I'm* a mess. This shit doesn't happen to me, but now it has, and it's all his fault."

Houston was clearly trying to fight laughter...and failed when it burst through his lips.

"Shut up. I hate you."

"It's so weird to hear you talk about *anyone* like this, but this is *my little brother*. The world has gone mad."

"No, not the world. Just me." I ran a hand through my hair. "I'm freaking the fuck out. We're NFL players, on the same team, in a league where they pretend to be open but there's still plenty of homophobia. You know me, Houston. I don't want to deal with that shit. I don't want my career turned into gossip or anything other than how I play the game. I'm not ready, and now with Coach finding out—"

"Wait. What? You didn't tell me that. What happened?"

I relayed the conversation, and he sat there, staring at me with his mouth hanging open. "Are you broken or what?"

"You offered to be traded so you can keep being boyfriends with my brother?"

Oh...shit. I was usually better at this. "We're not boyfriends. And don't tell him that part. It'll piss him off I told Coach that. He'll feel guilty."

"Who are you, and what did you do with Warner Ramsey?"

"I've been asking myself that question for weeks." Catching feelings messed with a guy's head.

"Like before, I can't lie and pretend I'm not worried. You're not ready to come out, and you should never be pushed; plus, doing this is a risk for both of you..."

"I know that. You think I don't know that?" This whole situation was a fucking disaster waiting to happen, but the craziest part was, I'd keep doing it. As long as Garrett was game, I would keep it up, making sure I was the one who suffered the consequences.

"Wow...you're going to marry my baby brother."

"No I'm not."

"And have his babies."

"Ha-ha."

"You'll adopt a bunch of them, fill that big-ass house of yours, buy a minivan with stick figures on the back windshield."

"I hate you," I reiterated, but Houston just laughed.

"Sorry not sorry. I have to give you shit. What's family for?" We shared a laugh before I fell back against the booth and closed my eyes. "Whatever you need, Ramsey. I've always got your back. We'll figure it out."

I turned and looked at him. "Thank you. Please don't tell Garrett about any of this. I don't even know if he feels the same."

"I'm pretty sure Garrett's wanted a minivan and ten kids with you for years."

That shouldn't have made me smile—I didn't even want children—but it did.

We hung out for a bit longer, and when I was ready to head home, I sent a text to Tucker to let him know we were leaving. Houston bailed first, and I was outside waiting for my ride when Tucker sneaked up beside me, smelling like whiskey and putting an arm around me. With his mouth close to my ear, he whispered, "Don't worry. I won't tell anyone."

"Huh?"

"About you and McRae. I don't know how I didn't see it before. He's bi, and you guys have been close for years." *Wait...for years?* "I saw the way he looked at you in there when you admitted being in a relationship. I'm happy for you guys. You didn't have to hide being bi from me. No shame in the game. I fucked around with a few guys in college."

"Jesus." I dropped my head back. "I'm not—"

"Don't deny it. I won't believe you anyway. Your secret's safe with me. Now, if you'll excuse me, I have three women to satisfy." Tucker waggled his brows, then jogged over to the ladies waiting for him.

Great. Tucker had figured out my secret, only he had the wrong brother in mind.

20

GARRETT

Lately I found myself having to make a concerted effort not to pay too much attention to Ramsey, which was saying something since I'd already had years of practice.

But twice since arriving at my parents' house for Thanksgiving dinner, I'd had to bite back a comment that shaded too far into sexual territory for public consumption, and then I'd had to pull a last-minute quick change and punch Ramsey in the shoulder rather than the squeeze I'd intended for his big bicep as I passed him in the kitchen while he was getting out silverware to set the table.

Ramsey wore his usual supremely amused smile during all this, but Houston kept giving me the side-eye and finally caught me by the arm when I was heading to the bathroom, pulling me into his old room instead. "Is something going on with Tucker?"

Tucker's Thanksgiving plans had fallen through, and I'd taken pity on him and invited him to my parents'.

I blinked. I'd been expecting Houston to tell me I was being pitifully obvious around Ramsey. "With Tucker? What do you mean? Like *me* and Tucker?" I laughed.

"No, dumbass. I don't know. Tucker and Ramsey?"

I blinked again. "Fuck no." The very idea made me want to snarl.

"Tucker keeps looking at me."

"Looking at you how?" I asked cautiously.

"I dunno. Weirdly. Like he's watching for something. Waiting for something. Wait, does he know about you two? Does he think I'm pissed?"

"Oh. That. Um..." How to explain. Maybe simple was best. "It's possible he thinks you and Ramsey are in a secret relationship."

"He wha—"

Simple was not best. I slammed a hand over his mouth. "Jesus. Pipe down."

"Why the fuck does he think that?" His jaw tightened when I hedged. "Garrett, why does he think that?"

I cleared my throat. "Well, so, the last time you were all out, he saw you and Rams talking...closely. Or something. And he got this crazy idea that you two are together." Ramsey had told me about it the next day, and we'd shared a laugh. It seemed harmless enough, after all, and besides, that meant Tucker hadn't noticed anything between us, which I deduced meant the rest of the team didn't suspect anything either, and that was exactly according to plan, right? So, harmless.

Except maybe not, since he was now spending Thanksgiving with us.

"Ramsey didn't think to correct him?"

"He was caught off guard. Or he misunderstood at first, and then Tucker said he wasn't gonna say shit anyway, so he figured what did it matter? Took a little pressure off us, at least. Honestly, we both thought it was kinda funny. Tucker hasn't brought it up again. We figured he let it go. He was pretty drunk that night anyway."

Houston scrubbed his hands over his face and let out a laugh. "Jesus fuck, that's awkward."

"It wasn't until just now."

"Great, so I'm the straw man?"

"He's not going to do anything with that information, I told you. He and Rams are tight, and he'd never out anyone."

"And the two of you thought it was 'funny'?"

I didn't like the way Houston hung those air quotes. Looked a little too much like hooks. And then he smiled the smile I knew from growing up when he was about to lay down some big-brother fuckery.

"Houston." I let a warning creep into my voice as his smile grew.

"Well, if he's gonna keep staring, maybe I should give him something to watch."

"Wait a second. Houston!" I snapped, but he'd already skirted past me, cackling as he walked back down the hallway.

Fuck.

"Want a little more?" Houston held the serving bowl of mashed potatoes over Ramsey's plate, a solicitous smile on his face that Ramsey side-eyed before saying, "Sure, if you're offering. I can also do it myself?"

"Nah, I gotcha."

Ramsey had done a double take when Houston had pulled out a chair for him at the dining table when we'd sat down for dinner. Now he glanced over at me with growing suspicion in his expression. I hadn't had time to warn him before Mom had called us all to dinner.

I cut a sharp glance at Tucker who, sure enough, was paying shrewd attention to their exchange. I saw the realization dawn in Ramsey's eyes, and he hitched one shoulder and smiled. "Thank you."

Houston piled more mashed potatoes on Ramsey's plate and then shoved the bowl toward me and Tucker. "You two are on your own."

Damn, was I ever.

"You were on fire against KC, Warner," Dad said, cutting into a slice of turkey. "Think the Rush can hold Miami off next week?"

"Definitely. Our defense is doing great." He stumbled to a pause as Houston stretched his arm casually along the back of his chair, then cleared his throat. "We—"

A low growl rumbled up my throat as Houston rested his fingers lightly on Ramsey's shoulder. I pounded my chest and coughed loudly. Houston's fingers retreated, but his smile grew by a fucking mile.

"Sorry. Bone. Gristle," I gritted out, then grabbed my glass of water and chugged it.

"Give me your plate, I'll get you another piece." Mom reached out her hand. "There shouldn't be any gristle in there. Dale, I told you to make sure there wasn't any gristle."

"I did." Dad frowned.

I waved her off. "It's fine now. I got it."

"Mine's gristle-free." Houston smacked his lips. "G probably just forgot how to swallow again."

I wanted to disown him. Could you disown brothers? I was pretty sure you could. "Believe me, I know how to swallow."

"Not what I've heard," Ramsey chimed in.

Fucking Ramsey, he could fuck right off too. I glared at his smug smile.

"Boys." Mom gave us a pained look and then angled toward Tucker. "Hope you weren't expecting a classy Thanksgiving."

Tucker laughed. "Nah, you should see what it's like at my house. Shit-talk, I mean smack-talk, all the way. Feels just like home. This turkey is awesome, by the way."

Houston picked up the green beans, serving spoon piled high as it hovered over Ramsey's plate. "More beans?"

"I'd love some."

The fucker continued dancing right on the edge of obvious all through dinner until even my parents were looking between the two of them in bewilderment.

"I NEED TO GO CHECK ON SOME STUFF AT THE NEW PLACE," I said. "I'll be back later." We'd finished helping Mom wash the dishes. Tucker had left fifteen minutes ago, and the rest of us were sprawled half comatose in the living room, watching TV.

"I should probably get going too." Ramsey let out a jaw-cracking yawn and stretched, and I sneaked a look at his abs as his shirt lifted.

Houston snorted softly and muttered under his breath, "Very subtle."

Okay, it wasn't subtle, but I did fully intend on going to check out my new place. I'd put in an offer for the Cedar Grove fixer-upper three days after seeing it, and had closed on it a week ago.

"I'll deal with you later," I fired back, and he chuckled, completely unconcerned.

"Can I go with you?" Ramsey asked as we walked toward our cars. He checked something on his phone and frowned, then tucked it away.

"You really want to? It looks the same as last time." But inwardly, I was chuffed he'd asked. I loved the new place even in its retro state, loved that I had something to call my own. Look at me being a real adult.

Most of the time.

Out came Ramsey's phone again. He pressed the side button as my brows pinched together.

"You can get that, you know."

"No need."

"Your dad?"

"Yep. He's been blowing me up all afternoon, and I'm not dealing with him today." He stuffed the phone in his pocket. "Anyway, yeah, I wouldn't mind seeing your place again." His smile turned mischievous. "With you."

"You realize there's no furniture there yet. No bed."

"Since when do we need beds?"

He had a point, and not being able to mess with him all day had worked me into a strong craving.

We dropped Ramsey's car at his place and rode over to mine together. "This could be convenient," he said as we wound up the drive, and once again warmth flooded my chest. It wasn't a love declaration, but it told me he was at least into continuing our arrangement for the foreseeable future.

"Very."

We hopped out of the car, and I unlocked the door and let us in. The air had a musty, unused tinge, but I didn't even care. We walked through the house and stopped in front of the wall of windows overlooking the back deck.

"Damn, it really is a cool place," Ramsey murmured, one

hand sliding along my lower back. I wasn't even sure he was aware of the casual affection, but I certainly was.

"It's gonna be."

"Did you call any of those contractors I sent you?"

"Yeah, got a couple of meetings lined up soon." I leaned into the caress of his fingers. "I've come over here every day almost. I stand right here and look around and think about how amazing it is that I bought it outright with money I earned doing something I love, that I'm a fucking home-owner now. I wanted it, but there was always a little part of me that thought maybe I wouldn't get it. Maybe I wouldn't make the cut."

I wasn't one to emote aloud that much, and I felt kind of shy about the amount of pride I felt in a place that definitely wasn't the palace I'd thought I'd go for. But Ramsey's response made it worth it. His lips tipped up, the corners of his eyes crinkling with tiny lines. "You did earn it. Is it weird to say I'm proud of you too? Feels like I've been able to watch it happen from the start. It's a good feeling."

Our gazes locked, and the connection didn't crackle with the lustful electricity that usually preceded us ripping our clothes off, but with something softer, deeper, a simpatico feeling that hummed through my blood as he leaned over and brushed a lingering kiss over my lips.

"Fuck, all this being responsible is making me itch."

"That's probably just fleas in your carpet." We both peered at the shabby beige tufts underfoot. Then Ramsey arched a brow. "But just in case, want to do something irre-sponsible to make yourself feel better?"

This was different. "Are you actually proposing some-thing fun and reckless? I'm all ears."

Ramsey canted his head toward the windows. "How cold do you think that water is?"

"Fucking cold." The only reason the pond wasn't frozen yet was because the temps had been up and down lately.

"Last one in sucks the other one off first."

We both took off toward the door at the same time. Ramsey shoved me backward as he wrestled it open, but I managed to swing around him and pull ahead for two seconds before he caught up with me and shoved me again.

At the water's edge, we shucked our clothes at lightning speed. "This qualifies more as flat-out stupid than fun and reckless, but we'll baby-step you into it." My thumbnail snagged on my sock, and Ramsey tossed a wild grin back at me as he took two steps into the water, whooped, then dived under.

"Fuck, it's cold!"

"You were expecting a sauna?" I sucked in a breath and followed suit, barely letting the chill of the water register on my ankles before I dived in and came up gasping for air. "Holy shit."

We splashed and dunked each other a couple of times, and then Ramsey squinted down at the water before looking back up at me with a horrified expression. "There's a leech on my thigh."

"Fuck that." I had no recollection of exiting the water. I just knew one second I was waist deep and the next I was scrambling to shore, swiping at my body wildly and craning my head to check my back for bloodsuckers.

It took me a second to register Ramsey was cackling as he waded serenely toward the shoreline.

I glared at him. "You fucker. There are no leeches?"

There were no leeches.

But we quickly encountered a more pressing problem. It was fucking cold and, considering I hadn't moved in, there were no towels. "Told you that was stupid," I grumbled as we snatched up our clothes and hotfooted it inside.

"Hang on." Ramsey shut the door behind us, and while I stood in the middle of the empty great room shivering, he strolled over to the fireplace, fiddling with it for a second before the gas logs roared to life. He gestured grandly. "I give you fire. Get your freezing ass over here."

He wrapped his arms around me when I did, and we stood in front of the blissful heat until we both stopped shivering.

"I think my dick is still in the pond somewhere," I confessed. My balls were numb. "Probably fish food."

"Let me check."

Ramsey dropped to his knees, the heat of his mouth a balm on my cold skin, then an inferno as he licked up the side of my cock. "Think this is it. Could be your belly button, though. Not sure."

"Oh, fuck off." I broke into a laugh, then sank my fingers into the wet ends of his hair. "But don't stop. Aren't I supposed to be the one on my knees, technically?"

He grinned up at me. "Winner's choice."

I wasn't gonna argue with that.

We went from shivering to sweating over the next thirty minutes as Ramsey turned me inside out with his mouth, then turned me around and fucked me against the fireplace, the heat from the fire licking over my skin rivaled by the heat of Ramsey's body as he thrust into me until he cried out.

When we got back to his place, I stopped in to grab a quick shower before heading back to Houston's. At the door, he pulled me back for another kiss before I could get over the threshold. "Damn," I teased, nipping his lower lip. "We should jump in that pond more often."

"You growled at dinner when Houston touched me. That was...interesting."

"Told you, it was gristle."

"There wasn't any gristle in that turkey, and you know it."

"Gristle," I repeated, then peered at him, his hooded expression, lips damp from kissing me. "Did you like it? I mean, if it had been an actual growl? Which it wasn't."

He considered for a second. "I just made you fire, sucked your cock, then fucked you until you came a second time, so I guess I did." Then the smirky bastard winked.

I fisted his shirt and shoved him against the doorjamb, kissing him again.

I had one of those impromptu epiphanies as his lips moved over mine, the kind that smacked you upside the head. I'd had a schoolboy crush on Ramsey. The hot, cool football player, my older brother's best friend. And what I'd stupidly failed to realize was that once I'd gotten to know the below-the-surface Ramsey—the guy who simultaneously pumped me up, kept me in check, shared moments of vulnerability, and was apparently way more fun than I'd ever given him credit for—my old feelings for him now seemed like some superficial bullshit.

I'd been hoping the crush would fade with time and familiarity. Instead, it'd blown up into something dangerously...more. Something dangerously close to love.

We both froze at a noise, and I instinctively jumped back, putting distance between us as Ramsey cocked his head at something over my shoulder.

21

RAMSEY

My heart punched at my chest like a battering ram, my ears feeling slightly echoey. Christ, I hadn't even been thinking where I was, that we were in my open doorway, making out like I wasn't closeted and Coach hadn't warned me to keep this under wraps. Almost getting caught by one of the worst possible people who could catch us was *so* not being careful.

"What's wrong with you, Warner? Why are you standing there looking at me like an idiot?"

That was the dear ole dad I knew. His words shocked me out of my stupor. Not completely, because my palms were sweaty and I couldn't stop the question running laps in my brain: *had he seen us kissing?*

Somehow I managed a, "Happy Thanksgiving to you too."

Dad's gaze took Garrett in, then me again. Our hair was wet from the shower. His lips were swollen from the hard press of my mouth. Could my dad tell? Did he know what we'd been doing?

"Thanks for letting me hit your gym." Thankfully, Garrett had an excuse at the ready because I clearly didn't.

"No problem. See you at practice."

Garrett took me in, his gaze asking, *Do you need me to stay?* He lingered for just a second more before giving me a small nod and turning away.

As soon as he rounded the corner of the house for my driveway, Dad opened his big-ass mouth again. "He looks at you like he worships you. Ridiculous."

And there went my pulse, skyrocketing to the damn moon again. Logically, I knew he meant as a football player, but considering I'd had my tongue down Garrett's throat just before he'd showed up, I couldn't stop myself from wondering if it was possible he thought it was more.

I stepped back when Dad bulldozed his way into my living room.

Today had been damn near perfect. I always loved spending time with the McRaes. They made me see what it was like to have a normal family. One that loved each other, and even if they sometimes fought, they would always have one another's back. A family who also loved to tease the shit out of each other, like Houston had done with Garrett today.

I liked Jealous Garrett.

Maybe that made me an egotistical asshole, but I waited for a second to see if I cared, and nope, I had zero issues with being an egotistical asshole.

Now's not the time. Garrett could take over my thoughts in no time flat, but apparently, my good day was over, and instead, I got a dose of reality in the form of my father, who had a habit of bringing a shitstorm down on me just when I was getting used to the feeling of nothing but sunshine on my skin.

"Nice of you to want to spend time with your father on Thanksgiving."

"The father who only cares about me because of what I can give him? That's not a parent."

He ignored my comment, walking right over to my bar and pouring himself a whiskey.

"Make yourself at home, why don't you?"

"You spent your day with that kid?"

"Yeah. Correct me if I'm wrong, but we stopped having holidays together when I was just a kid. Once Mom died, you were done with it, even when I still lived at home with you."

Like he so conveniently did, he disregarded that statement too. "What's with you and him anyway? I thought you and Houston were tight."

"Houston and I are close."

"Now every time I see photos of you online, you're with him. Are you sure that's a good idea? He's one of the few queer players in the league. You don't want people to think you're like him."

"Fuck you," I gritted out. I was exactly like him, and there was nothing wrong with that.

Dad laughed, then took a swallow of his whiskey. "I'm just sayin'. I know how much you hate negative attention. Hanging out with gay guys probably isn't the best way to avoid rumors."

Was he trying to hint he'd seen us? That he knew what Garrett was to me? But then, that wasn't my dad's style. He was too impulsive to hold on to something like that. He liked to gloat too much not to directly hold it over my head, but hell, it had been close. It was a reminder of how easily it could have happened, with the worst person it could happen with, and at one of the worst times. A little over a month before the playoffs was *not* the moment this needed to get out.

"I know what I'm doing." I rubbed a hand over my face, worry eating away at me. "Why are you here, Dad? What do you want this time?"

He hesitated for a moment, watching me from across the room. "Been callin' ya all day. You're my son. It's Thanksgiving." His voice had a softer lilt that almost made me think he was sincere, but then he added, "I ran into some trouble... owe a few people some money."

"No." My jaw tightened. For a moment, I'd expected something else, something more, which was really fucking stupid. He'd never cared about me.

"Goddamn it, Warner."

"Goddamn it *you*! You don't get to do that. You don't get to call me all day on Thanksgiving just because you ran out of other options for cash. Maybe try not gambling your shit away, or whatever it is you do!" This wasn't how parents were supposed to be.

"There you go, thinking you're better than me again. Perfect fucking Warner Ramsey. One of these days you're gonna have your fall from grace."

That right there was the exact reason I feared what would have happened if he'd caught us today. Because he held his failures against me. He blamed me for making different choices than he did, and because of that, he would want to see me fail. Or hell, I could even see him selling us out for cash. "What happened to you? I can't wrap my head around treating your own son the way you do."

He flinched, a wave of what almost looked like sadness washing over his features. Then he said, "Your arm was weak in the fourth quarter of your last game." And just like always, hurricane Mike Ramsey stormed into my life, before walking out, leaving a wreck in his wake. I stared at the door he'd slammed closed.

"Fuck."

I waited a few minutes, giving him enough time to drive away, then grabbed my keys and phone and headed to Houston's. My fingers drummed against the steering wheel the whole drive.

Houston answered the door, took one look at me, and asked, "What's wrong?"

"Nothin'." Shit. Houston was going to kick my ass. He'd told me to be careful, that he didn't want his brother hurt. I'd promised we could keep this under wraps, but clearly, we couldn't.

"Liar."

"Is G here?" He'd only left my place an hour ago, but maybe he'd gone somewhere else.

Houston frowned. "Yeah, come in." He stepped out of the way. "He's in his room."

"Thanks, man. I'll talk to you soon. I just gotta..."

"You gotta talk to your boyfriend."

"He's not my boyfriend." We weren't complicating this even more with titles like that, despite my feelings for him, which kept growing, somehow beyond my control.

Concern furrowed Houston's brows, but I just shook my head and made my way to Garrett's temporary space. I knocked, and he shouted to come in, probably assuming it was his brother. I opened the door. Garrett was lying on his bed with his phone. He looked up, gaze colliding with mine, smiled, then sobered. "What did that motherfucker do?"

Okay, well, that was sweet. "You want to defend my honor again?" He'd wanted to do that the last time my dad had stopped by.

He sat up. "Yeah. I mean, that's how I do it. I'm badass

that way." Garrett stood and walked over, pushed the door closed, and slipped his arms around my waist. "What's wrong? Did he see something?"

A long pause stretched between us, one where a kaleidoscope of emotions crossed Garrett's face.

"I don't think so. He said I needed to be careful spending so much time with you because that's how rumors get started."

"I'm sorry. I should have been more careful. I shouldn't have kissed you."

"It's not your fault. Last I checked, we were kissing each other." I let go of him, paced the room. With each passing second, I got more and more pissed, more and more worried. "That was close, G. Really fucking close."

"I know. What do you think he would do? If he'd seen?" I looked at him, and he cursed, knowing the answer. "Hello, scandal. Sell the story to the highest bidder?"

I shrugged. "I would hope not, but you can't be sure. I should just come out."

"What would that do, though? It doesn't fix the fact that we're players on the same NFL team. That we don't know what management would do. That Coach specifically told you to keep this under wraps and not to let it get out. That we're heading into the end of the season and—"

"Not helping, G." I gave him a small smile, which he returned, almost sadly.

"What do we do? How do you want to move forward?"

Wasn't that just the question of the day.

22

GARRETT

"We can figure this out, Rams."

He gave me a long look, but I kept my gaze steady even as a slew of emotions stormed through me. I didn't know what it was like to have a parent like Ramsey's dad. I'd been fortunate to have the support and unconditional love of mine, and as I sat there and thought about it, I realized that maybe that was part of why a big flashy house and lots of expensive toys no longer mattered as much to me. What mattered were the people in my life who supported me. That included Ramsey. And I hated the stress I could see in his eyes and weighing down his shoulders.

"My college coach, my agent, Rush management, all of them have said at one point or another that I'll be fighting the stigma of my dad, that I had to be on my best behavior at all times. This...this could impact your career, Garrett. If we get outed unexpectedly and there's some kind of outcry about us being on the same team, who knows what would happen?"

Fuck, he wasn't wrong. There was no way to know how

shit would play out if we created a media circus. I'd honestly never thought we'd even get so far that it'd be an issue.

"You just bought a house," Ramsey continued.

"I don't care. If anyone gets traded, it'll probably be me. It *should* be me. The problem is, there's so much uncertainty with...everything." I didn't necessarily want to be traded, but I *really* didn't want Ramsey to be traded if Coach got pressured from higher up. "I know you're just trying to protect me."

"And you're doing the same, so..."

"Stalemate. Rock and a hard place. Catch-22. That's all I've got." I bit my lip. "We can't protect each other *and* keep going the way we have been. Something's gotta give, and I think we both know what the *responsible* thing to do would be." Ramsey gave me another hard stare, so I barreled on. "We're friends, right? And we're both capable of being adults in a shitty situation. I think. So...we go back to the friends part and nix the benefits part of that equation." I made it sound so simple, when it was anything but.

Ramsey frowned. "Is that what you want?"

I shrugged. "Not necessarily."

"Me neither."

Ugh, well, that threw a wrench in my gusto. I'd been expecting him to accept my statement on the basis of logic alone. "But what I want even less is to be the cause of a media circus around you. Or the team. Or have what we're doing cause you to feel like you need to come out."

"You've never pressured me."

"I know, but..." I gestured vaguely around. "The circumstances are, and I'm part of that."

"It's not the being outed that's necessarily the issue. I can handle that—"

"But you shouldn't have to."

"Let me finish," he said sternly. "It's that I don't want you in the spotlight for anything other than the badass rookie year you've been having." Ramsey rubbed his temples and flopped back on the bed. "So we're back to stalemate. Fuck you for making sense. You're right. Total rock and a hard place. I've never realized how much the responsible shit sucks sometimes."

"Welcome to the dark side. There's no welcome wagon, sadly. No one remembered to load it." I sprawled next to him, buoyed slightly when he smiled faintly at my dumb joke. "So we finish out the season as friends and teammates, and once the season is over, we'll talk. Agreed?"

Ramsey was silent for a long while. "Okay, yeah. Agreed."

"Good." I forced a smile that was reluctant to come. There was no guarantee Ramsey would still be into this once the season was over. "We can just focus on the playoffs."

"And getting a Super Bowl ring."

"Honestly, I was kind of getting sick of you sucking me off anyway. So sloppy."

Ramsey jerked his head in my direction, eyes flashing. "Seriously?"

"No. Not even close." I chuckled and was relieved to see his expression lighten. "The sloppiness is definitely a pro."

"Learned it from you, dipshit."

I shrugged. "Neatness is overrated."

"Like responsibility?"

"Touché."

I DROPPED HEAVILY ONTO A STOOL AT THE KITCHEN COUNTER after Ramsey left, watching Houston make one of his giant salads.

He eyed me as he picked up a bell pepper and started dicing it. "All right, lay it on me. What the hell is going on?"

"Ramsey and I are going to stop hooking up."

"Okay..." He set down the knife. "Feel like I'm not getting the full story here."

I slumped on the stool and filled him in on everything that'd transpired. When I was finished, his brows furrowed even deeper.

"So you really think you two can stop, just like that?"

"I mean, there was never a larger plan. We were just hooking up for kicks." I shrugged with a nonchalance I didn't feel. "And maybe this is the best thing anyway. Cut things off before it gets even more complicated, possibly with real, actual feelings."

Houston snorted. "You've had 'real, actual feelings' for Ramsey for a long time."

"No, I had a crush. That's different. Real feelings are..." More like everything I'd been feeling around Ramsey lately, but I wasn't about to say that to Houston. Didn't matter. The way he was looking at me said he already knew. "I figured we'd hook up for a while and then get tired of each other and move on. I'd...fulfill my crush and be done with it."

He shook his head with a sigh. "Yeah, because that always works out so well."

I narrowed my eyes at him. "Why'd you say that like you're speaking from experience?"

"Because I am." When I gave him a pressing look, Houston waved a hand and picked up his knife again. "It was a short thing in college. I had a long-standing crush on a dude. We finally hooked up. I figured that'd be the end of it. It wasn't."

"What? Who? Why haven't I heard about this?"

"Because I don't tell you every little thing about my sex life, Garrett, and"—he pointed his knife at me—"I appreciate it when you don't do the same. I cannot unsee or unhear some things where you and Ramsey are concerned, fuck you very much."

I latched on to the momentary distraction for what it was, a few minutes' reprieve from the shit I was currently dealing with. "Was it someone on the football team?"

"Yes," Houston said tight-lipped.

"Fucking A. Who?"

"I'm not saying. They weren't out either, so it's not my story to tell."

I got that, but still, I was all kinds of curious, especially since that muscle was fluttering along Houston's jaw, which definitely meant there was more to the story. "Okay, don't tell me who, but what happened with them?"

"Long-term? It was a nothingburger. We graduated and went our separate ways. But we're not talking about me right now."

"You brought it up."

"Yeah, as an example. And it's long in the past, so back to the present."

"It may not have worked for you, but sometimes it does. I had a fierce crush on Grady Holcomb sophomore year of college. We fooled around a couple of times and *poof*, it was gone, just like that." Never mind that Grady had turned out to be a jackass and a shitty kisser, while Ramsey was none of those things. "There were others too, so it's not like I could've predicted I'd get in deeper than I should."

Houston spun around, grabbed two beers from the

fridge, and came over to my side of the counter, plunking one down in front of me. "I know it sounds like I'm coming down on you, but I'm not. I just hate that you're both in exactly the position I was worried you'd be in, where one or both of you gets hurt."

I took a long swallow from my beer. "No one's getting hurt. We're good. We're friends. We'll keep being friends, sex or no sex." If I kept telling myself that, it'd be true, right?

Houston exhaled a skeptical chuckle. "Who are you, and what have you done with my brother?"

"This is Garrett 2.0. He comes with the responsibility expansion pack preloaded." I waggled my brows, and Houston shook his head, then dropped an arm around my shoulders.

"I'm always on your side, and I'll always support you. Just know that, even when I'm side-eyeing your choices."

"Humans have been making dumb choices since the dawn of time. Some more than others," I conceded. But I thought maybe for once I'd gotten it right. Ramsey and I could continue to kick ass on the field, keep our friendship on the sidelines, and in time, that niggling feeling in the pit of my stomach would fade. I hoped.

23

RAMSEY

"Stop checking out my ass," Garrett whispered, his voice low and just for me, but with that playful edge he always had. Just hearing that familiar teasing in his voice made me want to smile.

My eyes snapped away from his very tight, very round ass that I was totally checking out even though I shouldn't have. "I wasn't," I lied. Fuuuuuck, it was a great ass. I really missed having my dick inside it.

Garrett's loud laugh drew attention from a few of the other guys in the locker room. They all stared at us, expecting an explanation. "Private joke," Garrett hedged, as if unsure what else to say. When the guys stopped paying attention to us and resumed getting dressed, he added, "You eye-fuck me every time you see me."

"Yeah, well, I'm not the only one." This just-friends thing was harder than I'd thought it would be. Besides football, we didn't even hang out anymore, and I was pretty sure it was because we both knew that if we were alone together, we'd end up naked. The crazy part? The one I could never, ever let Garrett know? Or hell, even admit to myself outside of this one moment? It was spending time with Garrett I missed the most. He'd become such an integral part of my life—the person I wanted to talk to about things and laugh with and play video games or exercise with—that I felt really goddamned lonely. I saw him six days a week between practice and games, and yet I missed him. It was weird as shit.

"You're silently blaming me for this whole situation, aren't you?" he asked, and I couldn't stop myself from grinning, then forcing myself to frown. I shouldn't like that he knew me so well, but the truth was, I did like it. Garrett was just...different. Everything about him felt that way to me.

"No."

"Liar, liar, pants on fire."

Someone cleared their throat, and I looked up to see Tucker standing there. I didn't notice when he'd walked over, but it was evident he'd had enough time to hear some of what we'd said.

"I'm feeling confused," Tucker said. "I thought... You know what? Never mind."

"What's up?" I asked, but he didn't have time to reply before Coach's loud voice broke through the room.

"Hurry up, gentlemen. We've got a plane to catch."

We'd just finished a game in Baltimore, where we'd scraped out a win by the skin of our teeth. We'd gotten a *W* and lost two games since Thanksgiving, when all hell had broken loose. The playoffs started in less than a month. We really did need to keep our heads in the fucking game. Right now, that was more important than anything else. If Garrett and I wanted to have orgasms together again, we could after we got a motherfucking ring. Then maybe we could fuck our way through the off-season, before ending this shit for good.

Are you ever going to really want to end it? That thought had no business being in my head, so I told myself it wasn't.

We finished getting dressed, and then the bus took us to the airport, where we jumped on a plane for Denver.

Tucker sat beside me. The asshole had won rock, paper, scissors for the window seat. Cross and Garrett were two rows up on the opposite side. Most everyone was quiet, wiped out from the game. I knew Garrett would have bruises... Maybe he should come over and I could kiss them better? *No. Bad Ramsey!*

"Dude," Tucker said.

"Dude what?"

"You just groaned."

Shit. Had I? "My body hurts. Someone let me get sacked in the third."

Tucker laughed, but the sound was overtaken by Garrett doing the same while talking to Cross. My attention automatically shot to him. My brain completely malfunctioned all the time now because of G. He'd crisscrossed all my wires, and I didn't know how to untangle them.

"Shut up," Nance told them. "Some of us are trying to get some rest."

"Fuck off," I shot back, and Garrett whipped his head around and gave me a look that said I needed to be the one to fuck off when it came to opening my mouth with Nance. He didn't need me to defend him, but that shit came naturally. I'd do it with anyone I cared about.

Okay, so maybe I did it a little more with him. Sue me.

"Problem, gentlemen?" Coach asked, his gaze directed at me.

Fuck. Me and my big-ass mouth. Hopefully, I was the only one who heard the warning in his voice. "No, sir," I replied.

Garrett and Cross went back to chatting. I heard Cross ask him about hanging out and then mention some woman Cross fucked, liked Garrett knew who she was. My muscles were feeling a little twitchy. Was G fucking someone else? It'd been three weeks, after all. He had every right to, but the thought made me ragey. Like I was going to go all psycho on him and lock him in my basement because if I couldn't have him, no one could.

I didn't even have a basement.

I groaned again.

"Are you broken?" Tucker asked.

"Yes." He frowned, so clearly, honesty hadn't been the way I should have gone there. "I'm just giving you shit. I'm fine."

I stuck my earbuds in and tried to keep to myself the rest of the flight. Every once in a while, I'd find myself glancing at Garrett. A few times he was looking at me first. I winked. He gave me the finger. I wanted to tell him yes, we could fuck, but I was a good boy and didn't.

I kept my distance when we landed in Denver. Houston was picking Garrett up. He'd offered me a lift too, but I'd ridden in with Tuck and he'd left his car here. He was taking me home.

I risked a glance at Garrett. He was looking at me already, the right side of his mouth kicking up to half a smile, before he shrugged, his expression readable. He still wanted me too. This was way more complicated than it was supposed to have been.

I tried to turn away from him but couldn't. We were looking at each other like two puppies being separated, people moving around us while we just...stared.

God, the bastard really had broken me.

Garrett turned away first and got into Houston's car.

Houston said something to him, then looked at me, then at G again—and this was way too ridiculous, so I blew them both a playful kiss and was on my way.

It wasn't until we were in Tucker's ride that he punched me in the arm. "You fucking dumbass!"

"Um...I'm sorry?" I had no idea what I'd done. "What are you talking about? I mean, I'm a complete dumbass, but are you just figuring this out?"

"I'm such an idiot. I can't believe I thought you were boning Houston. Either some freaky shit is going down between the three of you and Houston and Garrett might end up arrested because of it, or I had the wrong fucking brother."

Shit...*shit*. Were we really that obvious? Clearly, we were, since my dad almost caught us sucking each other's faces off and now Tucker had figured it out. Still, I said, "I don't know what you're talking about."

"Yeah, okay, and I'm not the best center in the league. Garrett was staring at you with the mopiest damn look I've ever seen. I swear it was like watching a movie and the two of you were separated because your families are feuding or some shit, and you really just want to run off into the woods and maybe live with seven dwarves."

It wasn't the right time to laugh. The last thing we needed was someone else figuring this out, but I couldn't help it. "Yeah, well, we're gonna have to build a second house on the property because I'm not living with eight other people."

He cocked a dark brow. "That's all you have to say about this?"

I sighed, dropped my head against the back of the seat, and rubbed a hand over my face. "I don't know what you want me to say, Tuck. We had a friends-with-benefits thing going on. Coach found out. He specifically asked me to make sure we kept quiet about it and no one found out. Then my dad almost caught us, and we ended it. That's all. There's nothing more to it." The lie tasted bitter on my tongue.

"Nothing more except for the fact that you've been miserable for weeks, and now I know why. Also...what the shit? Coach knows? Why the hell am I just finding out? This is bad, Rams."

"You think?" I snapped. "Damn it. I'm sorry. That's why it's over. We need to focus on the team. On the playoffs. It was just temporary sex, and now it's becoming more difficult than we anticipated. Football is what's important, not a piece of ass."

He was quiet for a moment before he said, "Is it? Because looking at the two of you, it seems to me this is more than a FWB thing."

My pulse jumped, beat through my skin. "It's not." It couldn't be. There was no way. Yeah, I liked him, more than I'd planned. I'd even thought I was falling for him, but it was just a thing, and I'd get over it. *You offered to get traded for him. Doesn't that tell you something?* Denial's a powerful tool, my friends.

"That wasn't even partway believable."

"I'm not going to fuck up his career. He's a rookie. He still has to prove himself. Who the hell knows what would happen if this got out. He'd likely get traded, and while he wasn't happy about coming to the Rush at first, it's a good fit for him. You know how much harder it would be for him to get signed if people found out he was fucking a teammate. It would be a thing. You and I both know it would be, just like it'll be a thing here, and that doesn't even touch on the shit-show that would rain down on us because it's me. *Mike*

Ramsey fought with his teammates; Warner Ramsey fucks them."

"Well, I mean, it's only one teammate, unless there's more I don't know about."

I smiled. "There's not."

"This is big. I don't even know what the league would do if two players were caught sleeping together."

"I know."

"And then there's assholes like Nance."

"No shit."

"And I *do* think this will be an even bigger deal because it's you. In some ways, they've been waiting for you to fuck up and show them you're just like your pops."

A weird déjà vu wrapped around me. First Garrett had given me a rundown of why this was a mistake, and now Tucker. "Yes, I get it." He was just reminding me of all the reasons we'd made the right decision. It wasn't even about coming out. I hadn't planned on doing it now, but I could. It was more everything else that would fuck us, everything else that I worried about.

"Damn it. I'm sorry. I'm just trying to wrap my head around all this. You really are kind of screwed."

"Still not helping."

"I'm a shitty friend. If I were you, I wouldn't talk to me at all."

"I'm trying not to," I teased back.

I was quiet for a moment, and Tucker was too. I could feel his stare on me, could feel him dissecting me with his eyes. "You're crazy about him, aren't you?"

I hesitated. "Nah, it was just a thing." Maybe if I kept lying to myself, I'd eventually believe it.

24

GARRETT

There were plenty of things in life that sucked more than not hooking up with Ramsey anymore. Like spontaneous human combustion. Dying rain forests. Getting your toenails ripped out with tweezers. Global warming. Slamming your whole hand in a car door. Never mind that most of these things involved acts of bodily harm or global catastrophe. I mean, sometimes I *did* feel a physical pang. In my balls or, more troublesome, my chest, when I looked at him. I just reminded myself it could be worse. And most of the time it worked.

Worked-*ish*.

But we still had our friendship, even if now it sometimes felt like something was missing. Besides the obvious, it was the quieter moments too. The intimate ones where we collapsed in a sweaty heap together, the laughter or talking that followed while our fingers traced idle paths over each other's bodies. We didn't hang out together as much either, and I missed that too. Missed working out with him, our banter in the locker room after practices, our in-depth recaps of the games and, hell, talking about life in general.

We just needed to get to off-season. Pressure would ease for a while, and I could reassess. We both could.

The one thing that didn't change was the action on the field. We both threw ourselves into finishing the season strong, and no one, not even Coach, seemed to notice anything different. I had hits and misses, Ramsey too, but no more or less than before. Despite the mix of emotions I had about him, when I stepped on the field, I let it all go and focused on the game, just as I'd always tried to do. And when I'd catch Ramsey's eye, see the familiar determination in there I'd come to associate with him being in the zone, I knew he was doing the same.

Our last game of the season was against Minnesota, and we came out with a thirteen-point lead, but I'd taken a beating, as usual. One of their linebackers had slammed into me hard and taken me down just before I got into the end zone in the fourth quarter. My shoulder had hit the ground so hard, I was sure it'd made a crater in the turf. It hadn't, but the pain had radiated outward and settled into my upper back by the time we got back to the hotel that night.

To soothe it, I'd taken an extra-long shower after bailing early on the bar I'd gone to with the guys. When I came out of the bathroom, Ramsey was propped up in bed, arms folded over his bare chest, staring at the TV.

"Surprised you're back already," Ramsey said.

"I'm toast. I dunno, I wasn't feeling it, and our flight's early tomorrow anyway."

"How's the shoulder?"

"I had an extra gin and tonic. That helped."

Ramsey's lips curled. "Ahh, the miraculous anti-inflammatory properties of booze."

I dropped onto the end of my bed and grabbed the Tiger Balm from the nightstand, scooping out a big dollop and smearing it over the meat of my shoulder before working backward.

After a minute, Ramsey extended his hand. "Gimme that. It's like watching a toddler trying to figure out coordination."

"Really? I seemed to do all right with those two passes earlier. You know, the ones that helped clinch the game." But I handed him the balm and slid over onto the edge of his bed.

We hadn't touched in weeks. Back claps, sure, the usual teammate stuff, but he hadn't even smacked my ass the way we all sometimes did, and I'd be lying if I said I wasn't craving his touch in any form.

But fuck, I'd underestimated just how goddamn good his firm caress would feel. I bit back a moan and shifted, loosening the towel at my waist as he smoothed a hand along my shoulder.

Ramsey's fingers stilled. "Garrett?"

"Yes, I'm popping a boner. Don't flatter yourself, though. I haven't seen any action besides my own hand since you. Nance could probably spit in my face, and I'd get hard." Okay, exaggeration, but whatever.

"Are you into that?" Ramsey sounded amused.

"I could be." We were skirting dangerous territory, so I was glad when Ramsey mock-shuddered.

"Nance. Gross." He resumed rubbing the balm into my muscles.

"Exactly."

"So you really haven't hooked up with anyone else?"

I didn't dare look over my shoulder to see if his gaze was displaying anything more than mild curiosity, because if I saw any hint of a territorial spark in them, I didn't know if I had the self-restraint not to pounce him. It hadn't been my strong suit in the past.

"Nope. Focused on ball." That, and I honestly hadn't been able to muster up any interest in someone else, not even the hot hockey player who'd punched his number in my phone a couple of weeks prior when Cross and I were out. I'd eyed the number when I got home that night for a few minutes, debating, before deleting it from my phone. "You?" Why? Why did I ask that? What if he said yes?

"Nope. Same. And..." Ramsey paused, then laughed softly as he backtracked. "Same. No time."

"What were you about to say?"

"Nothing." Ramsey's hands stilled again, and I wiggled my shoulders to show he should please resume. I didn't care if he'd already coated me with the stuff, and I guess he didn't either, because he scooped out another dollop of cream and kept going. "I was just going to say that Alyssa texted me out of the blue last week. She wants to get back together."

"Yeah?" I asked carefully. I couldn't decide if Ramsey getting back together with a former flame was better or worse than him hooking up with another guy. Both sucked to imagine. "So are you gonna?"

"Fuck no." He barked out a laugh as relief drenched me. Crisis averted. "It just got me thinking..." Oh shit, nope, back to full alert. He hesitated again. "It just got me thinking that maybe I wasn't picky enough before, and maybe I let myself be that way, take what came easiest, because I never wanted to get too invested in something that could drag my focus too far from the game, too far from making sure I never went down the paths my dad did. I was always thinking of the game. Sometimes I regret that."

"I totally get it." I'd done my own version of the same.

"That's okay, though. It happens. And when something comes along that's right, you'll know it's right, you know?" God, what the fuck was I even saying? Because as I threw out words meant to reassure him, they rang true through my gut with a bittersweet ache.

"Maybe." Ramsey's knuckles pressed against my back, loosening the tension there. "I didn't say any of that looking for reassurance or something. That's not info you're supposed to do anything with. It was just on my mind. Everything was...easy with you."

Fuck my life. "But came with its own set of complications."

"It did, yeah. I guess I just wanted you to know that despite everything or how it might all play out, I don't regret anything you and I did."

"I don't either." Double fuck my life, because I did look over my shoulder then, to find Ramsey's blue gaze. Our eyes locked, and I'd been right; I definitely wanted to pounce him.

"Garrett," Ramsey's voice was a quiet command.

"Yeah?"

"You have to get the fuck off my bed now."

I nodded and hopped back over to mine, too afraid to make one of my usual quips until there was more space between us. He'd been hard too. I'd seen it as I moved. Now my mouth was dry, my dick aching. I scrambled for a distraction and reached to put the top back on the balm. "Jesus," I said, glancing into the little pot to find it near empty. I was gonna smell like this stuff for days, get it all over the sheets. "How much of this shit did you put on me?"

"Exactly the amount you wanted me to." Ramsey smirked and flipped off the TV. "You know me. Concerned teammate and all, just wanted to make sure your muscles were properly soothed."

"Yeah, you're very dedicated that way." Damn, the images just saying something like that conjured. Ramsey's hand smoothing down my back, his fingers patiently working me open... I thrust the memory from my mind and pulled the covers around me.

Ramsey reached out and switched off the light.

"Have you ever jacked off with this stuff?" I asked into the darkness.

"The fuck? No!"

"Good. I do not recommend it."

"If you start jerking off over there and give yourself third-degree burns, you can suffer alone."

"But I thought you were my concerned teammate. You wouldn't soothe my dick? Sounds like dereliction of duty."

"Night, G."

I grinned. "Night, Rams."

25

RAMSEY

Los Angeles was one of my favorite cities to play in. Yeah, I fucking hated the team, and Whitt was a dickhead of epic proportions, but I loved playing here. There was something electric about it, an extra current of energy zipping through the air, all coming from the fans that loved their team so much.

That made the win even sweeter when we kicked our rivals' asses.

And we would tonight. I'd make damn sure of it.

I wanted that for G. Wanted him to claim the *W* from the team I was pretty sure he already felt plagued him.

Even though there was no reason to, he blamed himself for our loss the first time we went against them earlier this season. The second time hadn't been his fault, but they'd beaten us a-fucking-gain, and there was no way I was accepting that shit this time. Not in the first game of the playoffs. They wouldn't be the reason our season ended early.

I caught Garrett's gaze. He'd just finished getting his uniform on. As if feeling my eyes on him, he glanced my way, and I winked. Fuck, I missed him. It had taken every-thing in me the other night not to strip him bare and bury myself in his ass until I fucked away all the want inside me, want that should have been extinguished by now, but it hadn't been. All it did was grow, multiplying at an even faster rate now that I couldn't have him anymore.

I hadn't watched even one single episode of *The Good Place* without him because it wasn't as enjoyable without Garrett teasing and saying, "What the fork," along with Kristen Bell.

He was supposed to be an itch I'd scratched, then moved on, but somehow he had burrowed beneath my skin, sank down, and rooted himself in the marrow of my bones, and yeah, that was some poetic fucking shit, but it was how I felt. He'd somehow become a part of me, this extension of myself that lived inside me.

And it definitely wasn't beneficial when we were about to go play the biggest game of Garrett's career so far.

This fucking guy had totally ruined me and— "*Ouch. Shit.*" I rubbed my side where Tucker elbowed me.

He cocked a brow that said, *You dumbass. You look like you're about to jump his bones in the middle of the locker room.*

My dick was on board with that idea, so I figured it was smart to look away. "Thanks, man."

"I can't believe this," he said in a low voice. He'd muttered those words countless times since finding out about Garrett and me, so I ignored him. Mouth close to my ear, he added, "Focus on football tonight."

Now wasn't the time to get lost in thoughts about Garrett. It was the time to win a fucking football game and rub it in Whitt's face when we did. I was a vindictive moth-erfucker. So sue me. And if I planned to pummel them, I should probably get my head in the game. "We're gonna go out there and show these motherfuckers who we are!" I said loud enough for the whole team to hear.

Everyone but Nance cheered. He'd decided he hated both Garrett and me. Good thing the feeling was mutual.

"Hell yeah!" Cross concurred.

"Let's fucking do this!" Garrett chimed in.

Coach gave us one of his speeches about playing as a team and being smart with the football, all the shit we'd heard before, before telling us it was time to show them what the Rush were all about.

Everyone broke away after that. I approached Garrett before we made our way out of the locker room. This game meant a lot to him. He didn't have to tell me that for me to know because...well, fuck, because I knew Garrett. He could hide his nerves with everyone else, but he couldn't with me. "You okay, G?"

His gaze darted away. "Yeah, I'm good."

"You don't have to hide with me."

He sighed, then shrugged. "Guess I couldn't even if I tried. I want this win, Rams. I fucking need it."

I'd held myself back from doing it since we put the brakes on this thing between us, but I didn't now. I smacked his ass. "Then we're gonna do it. I promise."

We both knew that wasn't something I could guarantee, but instead of calling me on it, he smiled and agreed.

I WAS FUCKING FLYING.

It was a bit ridiculous that one playoff game could make me feel like I was on top of the world, but as Garrett got the first down halfway through the third, the Rush up by fourteen points, a damn fireworks display went off in my chest.

Playing with him was almost like foreplay, edging me and making me want more from him.

"Motherfucker," Benson, one of LA's defensive men, gritted out, before heading back to the line.

Coach mumbled a play in my earpiece, which I relayed to the guys in the huddle. We broke into position. I winked at G, who smiled around his mouthpiece at me. I could see the light in his eyes, damn near feel it radiating off him. This game was ours, and it was great to share it with him.

"White 80! White 80! White 80. Set hut!" I called out just before Tuck snapped the ball to me. I caught it, eyes darting around the field for Cross, who Coach had called this play for. He was covered, and so were Nance and Garrett. Just before I settled on a short play to at least gain a couple of yards, Garrett broke free of Whitt. I swear a fucking trail of fire shot out from his heels, he was running so fast, zipping around players so perfectly that part of me just wanted to sit back and watch him shine. He was so fucking beautiful when he played that I knew beyond doubt this was where Garrett belonged—on the field.

I cocked my arm back and threw a pass for him. It was as if the ball was as magnetized by him as I was, like it couldn't stay away and fell right into his arms. Garrett caught the pigskin and kept going, sidestepping two guys, shooting around another, and heading right for the end zone. The crowd went quiet, knowing what I did—that Garrett was about to make his first touchdown in his first playoff game in the NFL, putting us up by twenty points and likely adding a nail in LA's playoff hopes.

It felt like someone had hit the slow-motion button, decelerating everyone's movements as Garrett jumped through the air and crossed the line, securing the points. Right after his feet hit the ground, two LA players rammed into him, one helmet to helmet. Like a ragdoll, he flew a few feet, colliding with another player and then dropping to the turf.

Garrett was on his back, arms splayed out. He didn't move. Why the fuck wasn't he moving?

My heart stopped beating. I was pretty sure I left it behind when I ran for Garrett on weak legs.

Fuck, please make him okay. He had to be okay.

He was still laid out when I slid to a stop beside him and the people already crowded there. My chest was tight. I couldn't breathe. Holy fuck, I couldn't breathe. I'd never hyperventilated before, but I was heading that direction now.

"He was out for a second," Cross said, "but he's coming to now."

All sorts of penalties were called. It was clear it had been an accident, but I didn't care about that or the outcome of the game, just about G.

"Is he okay?" I asked, my voice broken with fear. The medics were trying to talk to him, asking if he knew his name and where he was, and fuck...why wouldn't he know that? He had to, right? Logically I knew they were concerned about a head injury, a concussion, but everything was all tangled with worry in my brain.

They ignored me, paying attention to Garrett. "G?" fumbled from my lips, but Garrett didn't respond. A hand moved to my arm, and I knew it was Tucker, offering me his silent support.

They slid the board under Garrett, making sure not to jostle him because fuck, they were worried about a spine injury too, weren't they?

"G?" I asked again, though how I expected him to respond, I didn't know. They had his head and neck stabilized, his body strapped down, and began to lift him with the board. I followed, which I had no fucking business doing. Tucker tried to hold on to me, but I pulled out of his grip as anger at the hit and worry battled inside me.

I saw acknowledgment when Garrett looked at me, like he was trying to say something. My heart jump-started again. "Win for me, Rams. Come find me afterward, but win this motherfucking game for me." His voice was low and choppy, like he was struggling to get the words out, but I got what he was saying. My place was on this field. I wanted to be with him, but damned if I wasn't going to get this *W*, if for no other reason than because Garrett asked me to do it. I wasn't sure there was anything I wouldn't do for him. I... Jesus, I needed him, didn't I? My whole life I'd tried not to need anyone, but I did when it came to Garrett McRae.

"I will," I replied, then, "And I expect a reward when I see you next."

Surprise flared in his eyes before they took him off the field. At that moment, I didn't give a shit who heard me or what conclusions they'd draw. Garrett was hurt, and he was mine. I took care of what was mine.

We sorted through the penalties, and while hurting Garrett had been an accident, we were out to avenge our teammate.

LA didn't make it easy on us. Garrett's injury had taken the wind out of our sails a bit, and they'd come back and scored two unanswered touchdowns. We couldn't seem to get our shit together. We needed our wide receiver back.

We squeaked out the victory. Sure, we saw a twenty-one-point lead whittle down to seven, but I'd thrown a long-bomb to Ward at the end of the game, and gotten one last touchdown to redeem myself. They were out of the playoffs, and we were heading to the second round. None of that mattered as much as the fact that I'd kept my promise to Garrett.

My heart punched against my chest the whole time I got dressed. Tuck tried to talk me down, but I couldn't see past the all-consuming need clawing at my insides. I needed to see Garrett, to make sure everything was fine. Once I knew he was okay, I'd sort through the rest of it.

"Where's he at?" I asked Coach, who sighed.

"Cedars-Sinai."

"Thanks." I turned and headed for the door. I should have waited until they let us know how he was doing, stay with the team. It wasn't like I could do anything, but this was Garrett, and rules didn't apply when it came to him. My insides felt like they were being gnawed away at, this strange emptiness in my chest that I was still trying to work through. I'd felt like that since we called it off, hadn't I? Kind of empty.

"Warner," Coach said.

"I'm going. I don't care what that means for my career." And I didn't. Not when he was hurt and I didn't know if he was okay. Garrett was...fuck, he meant too much to me for anything else to compare.

"I was just going to say good game. Given the circumstances, you kept your head in it, and that counts for something."

I breathed out a sigh of relief. "Thanks, Coach."

I ordered a car, and thankfully, they were only two minutes out. My leg bounced up and down the whole ride. I forced myself not to check my phone. I figured Houston would have messaged to let me know what was going on. I was sure he and his family would have gone to the hospital since they were in town for the game, but if it was bad news,

I couldn't handle hearing it yet. I had to see him, be close to him first.

"I need to see Garrett McRae," I said when I got to the hospital.

"Are you family?"

Fuck. Fuck, fuck, fuck. "Yeah, I'm his...partner," I replied. Someone might hear, but whatever got me in the room with him.

Partner...hmm... The word hadn't even felt weird on my tongue. I kinda liked it.

"Warner?" the receptionist asked. When I nodded, she added that Mr. McRae's brother said I could be let back. She didn't seem to recognize me, but this was also Los Angeles, so they were used to celebrities coming in. She gave me a visitor's pass and a room number. He wasn't in the regular emergency room. I wasn't sure if that was because of who he was or because he was already doing okay.

I followed the signs to his room, hands shaking, thoughts spinning because I'd just told that woman I was Garrett's partner and I wasn't freaking out. Everything else seemed so...small, so insignificant all of a sudden. All I was worried about was him.

The door was closed. I knocked and pushed it open. Houston and Dale stood close, their heads together as they talked. Connie was beside the bed, holding Garrett's hand. I couldn't imagine what she was going through. First Houston's knee and now this.

Four sets of eyes shot toward me. I took them all in before landing on Garrett. He wasn't in the neck brace anymore, thank God. He did have an IV, and he looked out of it, sort of loopy and perfect and beautiful. Fuck, he was so goddamned beautiful. The emptiness in my chest started to disappear, and I was suddenly filled with nothing but him.

Holy shit...*holy shit*. My heart was racing, my breath coming out too quickly. Everything inside me clicked into place. The confusing thoughts, being willing to get traded. Wanting what was best for him, how it felt when he talked to me and held me and—

"Did we win?" Garrett asked.

"I love you," slipped out of my mouth and...what the fuck was that? Why had I said that now, in front of all these people? And how much would they hate me if I turned around and ran out? Claimed temporary insanity?

Houston laughed. Connie smiled. Dale looked puzzled as fuck—welcome to my world, buddy. I was still coming to terms with being in love too, and the ferocity with which it had hit me. I'd known I liked him, had known I was falling for him, but falling for someone and knowing you were in love with them? Fuck, that felt bigger. It felt like more.

"I'm sorry. I shouldn't have said that right now. I mean, I meant it, but I shouldn't have said it in front of—hi, Mr. and Ms. McRae. How's the head, G? Are you—"

"I love you too," he cut me off.

"You do?" I couldn't have stopped the question if I wanted to, but when I realized how needy it sounded, I added, "Clearly."

"I think we need to leave them alone," Houston said, taking a bewildered Connie and Dale by the elbow and steering them toward the door. "I'll explain in the hallway."

I went to Garrett's bedside, kissed his forehead, his temple, before my lips found their home on his.

"Did you mean it?" he asked.

"Yeah."

"We're fucked."

"You're telling me." I kissed him again, just needing to know he was there and was okay. "Seeing you get hurt like that...nothing else mattered. I don't give a shit what the league says or if the media freaks the fuck out. You make me feel..." *Happy. Loved. Worthy. Important.* All those things and more were true, but I settled on, "Everything. You make me feel everything."

Garrett's smile was so bright, it lit up my insides.

When he didn't reply, just lay there staring at me, nerves trickled in. Maybe he'd changed his mind? Maybe this was too much, too fast? Hell, maybe his head injury was to blame for his initial return of affection, and now he was trying to figure out how to let me down easily.

I pulled back, stomach in knots, and waited.

26

GARRETT

R amsey's expectant look said I was supposed to be doing something, saying something, but coherency was a bit of a challenge at the moment. My head wasn't on fire anymore, thanks to the meds I'd been given, but there was a persistent throb in the base of my skull and a fuzzy warmth cocooning my body that could've been meds, but could have also been everything Ramsey had just said. *"You make me feel everything."*

"Everything?" I repeated slowly. "But, the good part of everything, right? Not the annoying, shitty parts of everything?"

Ramsey chuckled. "A lot of the annoying parts are actually my favorite parts of everything." He frowned. "Now you're getting me all jumbled up."

"Welcome to my current headspace." I shifted in the bed and winced, and Ramsey's brow immediately creased with concern.

"Need me to call the nurse or—"

"No, I'm fine. Promise. Can you say the part about everything again, though? Or maybe all of it?" I circled a finger around my temple. "Kinda taking longer than usual for things to process." That was mostly true. I also just wanted to hear him say it again. The shock of him blurting it out earlier had completely discombobulated me.

"You mean all the stuff about me being in love with you?"

I nodded. "And that part where you don't care what the league says, and then the part about how I make you feel."

Ramsey's eyes narrowed with realization, but instead of calling me out, he bent low, fingers dusting lightly over my jaw as his lips brushed the shell of my ear, the words soft and intimate. "I love you, Garrett McRae, and I don't give a fuck who knows."

Words I never thought I'd hear. Never expected to. They swooped through me and settled in my chest, a spark of warmth burning through the pain.

Ramsey pulled back. "You never thought you'd hear them? But you wanted to?"

"Fuck, is my head inside out again?" But clearly, that was the case, given Ramsey's expression. "I wanted to, yeah. I think...fuck, I'm not sure I should tell you how long I've been in love with you."

"I think you should."

"At least a day. Maybe a week. Possibly more like...months?" Not years. That would be too much. That could be...stalker-y?

"Years?" Ramsey's brows flickered up, a smile playing over his face.

"Goddammit, I know I didn't say that out loud." Fuck me, had I?

Ramsey's eyes twinkled with humor. "You didn't say it out loud, but now I know you were thinking it."

I barked out a hoarse laugh. "Can I take back my 'I love

you' now? Because fucking with a man in a hospital bed like that is cruel."

Ramsey caught my hand and pressed a kiss to my lips. "No more so than pretending you didn't hear what I said in the first place."

"Fair point, but I'll also warn you right now I'll be milking this for all it's worth, and you'll take it if you really love me."

"I really do."

"And I really love you, Warner Ramsey. I don't care who knows it either." I yanked him close again and accidentally slammed his elbow into the railing. This hospital bed was already cock-blocking me. "I know there's a lot of shit that's got to get figured out and sorted—"

"Starting with getting you healed up, back on your feet, and back on the field. I'm not gonna let anything come down on you, Garrett. I don't care what happens to my career anymore."

We could go around and around trying to protect each other, but one thing I knew for sure. "We'll figure it out together. For right now, can you just stay here?"

Ramsey's eyes softened with warmth. "I'm not going anywhere. I promise."

And for whatever reason, it was that sentence that hit me square in the gut, blooming outward, erasing the anxiety and tension that had lingered inside me for months. I drew in a shuddery breath, and then coughed to cover it up, but I was pretty sure Ramsey saw right through it, the way he took my hand again and squeezed it. There was understanding in it, and love, and I knew exactly what he'd meant when he'd said *everything*.

He pulled one of the chairs closer to the bed and

dropped into it, raking a hand through his hair with a long sigh. "Fuck, today feels like a lifetime."

"I hardly remember the game."

"Do you remember getting hit?"

"Sort of, not really. All that's fuzzy."

"It was a great play, though. You caught that bullet like a fucking champ."

"'Course I did."

He snorted softly. "Good to see your ego's still intact despite that blow."

"Are you offering?" I tried for seductive, but considering my current state with an IV in my arm and propped in a hospital bed, it was dicey. It all felt like overkill for a concussion, but no one had wanted to take any chances.

Ramsey's amused gaze traveled the length of my body, lingering at the sheet pulled over my lap. "Pretty sure all the monitors and IVs you're hooked up to would make that difficult."

"If you really loved me, you'd figure it out."

He chuckled. "Patience. We've got many blowjobs ahead of us, I hope. And besides, it's much more fun when you can actually get hard."

A knock on the door cut off my gasp of mock offense. Houston poked his head inside. "Hey, sorry to interrupt, but the nurse needs to check your vitals and go over some notes."

"She can come in," I told him.

His gaze moved between me and Ramsey before settling on our intertwined fingers. "All good here?"

"All good," Ramsey answered just as I said, "Extremely good."

"Jesus. Holidays are about to get even more annoying."

Houston shook his head, but I didn't miss his smile as he turned away, shutting the door.

"I told the person at the front desk you were my partner," Ramsey said.

"Really?" Damn, that made me smile.

"Yeah, I was panicking, thinking they wouldn't let me in and, well, I was hoping I wouldn't end up being wrong."

"Did it freak you out to say it aloud?"

Ramsey considered. "Nope. It felt good. The kind of good that makes me look forward to saying it more."

"You can say it as often as you want from now on."

"I plan on it."

The nurse swept inside after a short rap on the door, an iPad in her hand.

"Can I go yet? Say yes, or this guy's gonna jailbreak me."

She chuckled. "Not quite yet, but almost."

I WAS OUT OF THE HOSPITAL AND CLEARED FOR FLYING THREE days later, and despite Ramsey's promise to stay by my side, I'd all but shoved him out the door the next morning so he could get back to Denver for practice before the second round of playoffs, which I'd be watching from the sidelines since I was in concussion protocol. I hoped I'd be able to keep playing for the Rush, but word from Coach that we'd be meeting with the Rush management the Thursday before the next game had me on edge.

Today was the day, and we were ushered into one of the stadium's conference rooms in the early evening, the peaceful swirl of snow outside the windows at odds with my pounding heart.

"It'll be okay." Ramsey spoke low, fingertips brushing the

back of my arm as we filed in, along with our agents. But I wasn't so sure.

Across the long table sat Coach Baker, Jack Terrapin, the Rush's general manager, and Paul Marsh, from the Rush's PR and media department.

I swiped at the sweat beading my brow as Coach gestured for us to sit. "How you feeling McRae?"

"Antsy to play."

Their muted laughter sounded polite, which didn't help the anxiety jittering through my veins.

Ramsey sat down beside me, our agents flanking us, and Coach considered us for a long moment before rubbing a hand over his forehead and exhaling a sigh. "Not in all my years of coaching have I been in a situation like this."

From the corner of my eye, I saw Ramsey's jaw clench as he looked over the trio. "I told you before, if it's an issue, you can trade me."

I shot a look sideways. "You told him what? Are you crazy?"

"Maybe." Ramsey smiled and offered a helpless shrug that made me want to grab his face and kiss him right there.

"Don't trade him." I turned back to them. "That would be a dumb move. Trade me if you have to."

My agent, Bowling, put a staying hand up. "Hold on now. Everyone here is aware of the situation, yes?"

"Well aware," Terrapin said. I couldn't get a read on his expression. It was too carefully neutral, which wasn't exactly reassuring. But fuck it, I knew now what mattered most to me. There was no going back. The press of Ramsey's leg against mine said it was mutual.

Allen, Ramsey's agent, said, "And it's also safe to assume that everyone is well aware there's no official language in the rules forbidding teammates from being in a relationship."

"Not technically, no." Terrapin leaned forward, folding his arms over the table. "That doesn't mean it's not an issue."

Fuck. My heart sank even as Ramsey's knee nudged mine reassuringly again. I hadn't even wanted the Rush at first, I reminded myself. I could get used to playing somewhere else. Ramsey and I could... I didn't even know, but we'd figure it out. Still, the idea of not practicing with him, not seeing him every day, gutted me. I forced an understanding nod, though, because I knew we'd put them in a tough position.

Bowling said, "The league has made it a point to stress how inclusive they are—or try to be. We have a handful of queer players. Garrett and Ramsey are some of the best players in the game. The only reason they would get traded right now is because they're together, which doesn't seem real inclusive to me." He eyed Coach and management. "I don't think it would reflect kindly on the Rush organization to let them go because they're in love with each other."

Terrapin and Coach exchanged a glance, and then Coach said, "You've both earned your spots on this team, no matter what your personal relationship is. What we've gotta figure out is how to get a little ahead of how this plays out."

My brows hiked to my forehead. "Wait, you're saying you're keeping both of us?"

"How hard did you get hit, son?" Coach squinted at me. "Isn't that what I just said?" I decided it wouldn't be wise to point out he hadn't said that exactly, but some of the tension drained from my body.

Marsh stood and started pacing in front of the windows. "From a PR point of view, here's what we're thinking: We need to get through the rest of this season without distracting from the game. We need everyone's head in it, not on what's happening within the team. So we need you two to keep lying low and get through it."

Terrapin added, "We called this meeting before the next game because we wanted your focus to be solely on it and not what might happen in this room." He gave Ramsey a pointed look.

"Understood." Ramsey nodded. "And thank you."

"After the season ends," Coach said, "I'll lead a team meeting to bring everyone up to speed."

I grimaced, thinking of Nance. Probably a few other guys too. "That might cause some problems."

"It's definitely gonna cause some rumblings, yeah. Problems? We'll see." Coach put up his hands placatingly. "But we'll deal with it, take it as it comes. I've been doing this for twenty years. Part of my job is negotiating team dynamics, even when two knuckleheads go throwing a wrench in everything. You just keep doing your job and let management do ours."

I glanced at Ramsey to find him already watching me, the relief in his eyes evident, and stretching all the way to the smile that followed.

"What about the media?" I asked.

"We'll handle that too." Marsh inclined his chin toward Ramsey. "We can set up a conference if you want to make an announcement. Come out publicly and whatnot. Showing people that the Rush is inclusive wouldn't be a bad thing."

"What if..." I interrupted.

"Oh God." Ramsey chuckled, but I put up a hand so he'd let me continue.

"Nah, just listen. Why do you have to make some big announcement? It's not the sixties anymore. If we want to normalize loving whoever the fuck we want, then do we even need a spotlight on it? Why can't we just continue on as normal, minus the hiding part, and if the media comes to us, fine, we can deal with it or talk about it then."

All eyes moved to Marsh, who considered a moment and then shrugged. "We could play it like that. It's not the worst idea."

I beamed.

"I wouldn't say teammates in a relationship is 'normal,'" Terrapin said.

Bowling straightened beside me, and I thanked my lucky stars I'd chosen him as my agent. He'd always gone to bat for me. "Okay, true. But, no way it never happened before in the history of all sports."

"I'll bet it happens far more often than people are aware. Warner and Garrett are just sick of hiding it," Allen said.

"The league has barely gotten used to players being out, much less an open relationship between teammates." Coach rubbed his jaw, then shrugged. "But, like we said, however you two want to play that part, we'll support it at this point, provided you both keep playing the way you have this season." He gave us a meaningful look. "And I have faith that you both will."

"Yes, sir." Ramsey nodded, and I did as well.

"Thank you," I said simply, then clamped my lips together so the rush of gratitude I felt wouldn't come barreling out.

Once our agents were gone and we were in the parking lot alone, Ramsey sank against his car and blew out a long breath. "That went better than expected." His gaze flickered to me. "You okay?"

"I'm good." I leaned next to him, my shoulder brushing his, soaking in the warmth of his body. "Relieved I'm not getting traded. Yet. I really like my shitty house. And being near you isn't bad either." It was tempting to lean in and kiss the smile that followed, but I held back. Management had asked for discretion for the time being, and we could both do that. "What'd you think about not having a formal conference?"

Ramsey's forehead crinkled. "I see your point, but I want to think on it some more."

"I'm game for however it goes down. I just wanted you to feel like you have options. You get to make the decision."

"I know." Ramsey winked. "Part of what gets me all hot over you."

"Hold on." I narrowed my eyes. "That was specifically meant for the whole coming-out thing. You don't get to make *all* the decisions forever."

"I know. Which also gets me all hot."

I cracked up. "Okay, so it's a win-win."

"Yep." He pushed off the car and spun to face me. "Forever. I like the sound of that, regardless of who's making the decisions."

"Hnnnn." I shoved him back lightly. "Don't say shit like that when I can't kiss you." Because, God, I'd thought I wanted to kiss him back in the conference room. Now it was tenfold. Forever with Ramsey? I could definitely handle that. "Distract me STAT, before I do something stupid."

He laughed and canted his head toward the car door. "Wanna go pick up some food, take it to Houston's, and annoy the ever-loving shit out of him?"

"Hell yes."

"And then we'll go take a look at your house, and you can kiss the fuck out of me. Maybe more."

"Double hell yes."

27

RAMSEY

The next two weeks were crazy as hell. We lost to Houston in the second round of the playoffs. It fucking sucked, and I still wasn't over it. Partly, at least, I'd wanted to win it all with Garrett on the field with me, to share that experience with him. That would be something to look forward to, I kept reminding myself.

I couldn't pretend we weren't both a little nervous, even after the meeting with the Rush management, but they seemed to be behind us. They knew Garrett and I made this team better, so as long as we kept playing at this level and football came first—at least in their eyes—I had to believe we'd be okay.

"We ready for today?" G asked, turning toward me in bed and nuzzling my chest.

"Not sure. I was thinking we should probably blow each other first."

"You're the horniest motherfucker I've never known."

"Are you complaining?" I rolled on top of him, bent like I was going to kiss him, but licked the length of his cheek instead.

"Gross."

"Aw, you like my tongue on you. Doesn't matter where I'm tasting you, does it?"

"No." He thrust his erection against mine. "And no, I'm not complaining. I too happen to be a horny motherfucker."

"So you wanna fool around?" I waggled my eyebrows playfully.

"Fuck yes. But you also know it's okay to be nervous about today, right?"

Sometimes it sucked that Garrett knew me so well. I wasn't sure how that had happened so quickly, but it had. While I'd decided I didn't want to make a big deal about coming out and being in a relationship with Garrett, we knew we had to make an announcement to the team, at least. It was one thing to let the world figure out on their own and hope there wasn't too much fallout, but another to lie to our teammates. Especially because I didn't plan on hiding how I felt about him.

"Nervous? Who's nervous?" I kissed him.

"Rams..."

I kissed him again.

"Stop trying to distract me with your mouth."

"Should I distract you with my dick instead?"

"I mean, maybe." Garrett winked. "We don't have to do this. If you wanna keep quiet for a while, we can. We can just be roommates or whatever."

"Um...do you live here?" I teased.

"Oh...I didn't mean to insinuate... Why did I..."

"I'm kidding. You stay here almost every night, already. It sucks sleeping without you. Who am I supposed to cuddle with? My body pillow doesn't compare to Garrett fucking McRae." He laughed, but I was serious. "You'll be having renovations done on your house anyway. Might as well stay with your boyfriend until they're done."

Garrett looked at me like I'd lit up his whole damn world. "You wanna?"

"I wanna." Another kiss. "I also wanna tell the team because I'm not hiding you. I told you that already. You're it for me. Fuck keeping that quiet."

"Just for that, I'll lick your hole the way you like."

"That the only reason?"

"No. I just like my tongue in your ass."

Garrett ate me out as promised, then sucked my cock down his throat and fingered me until my dick erupted like a volcano in his mouth. After that, I gave him the best blowjob in history, and we showered together and got dressed. We'd just made it downstairs when a familiar pounding sound came from my front door. "Fuck my life."

I hadn't seen my dad since Thanksgiving, when he'd almost caught me and Garrett together. He must have found some money, so he hadn't tried to get some from me for a while, but he always came back.

"That who I think it is?" G asked.

"I'm pretty sure. Well, unless the paparazzi found out about us already and they're breaking down my door."

"Can I get it?"

I signaled for him to go for it.

Garrett walked over with a self-satisfied grin and opened the door. "Can I help you?"

I chuckled.

"I'd like to see my son." He shoved his way into the house, and Garrett let him.

"What do you want, Dad? My boyfriend and I are heading out." I might as well start the *not hiding* right now. We were on our way to tell the team anyway. Eventually, it would leak. I'd meant it when I said I was done keeping quiet, and I wasn't going to tiptoe around my dad either. If he turned out to be homophobic, it was another reason he didn't belong in my life unless he made changes.

"Your...the two of you...Jesus fucking Christ. Are you an idiot? The both of you! It's going to get one of you traded and maybe the two of you thrown out of the league!"

"No," Garrett said, "it won't, but even if it did, Ramsey would be worth it. That's what it means to love someone. I'd do anything for him."

My heart stumbled before doing a fifty-yard dash in my chest. I'd never known what it was like to be loved that way. My dad had never put me first, not once in my life, but I had no doubt Garrett would. "He's worth it for me too. I love him."

Dad looked back and forth between us like he didn't understand, as if the concept was completely foreign to him, and I guessed it was. He'd only ever loved himself. "Dumbass kid," he said. "I didn't teach you nothin'."

"Nothing good. Is there something we can do for you?"

Again, his eyes darted from Garrett to me, then back to Garrett. "Nah. Just came over to say hi." We all knew that wasn't true, but he didn't want to ask for money in front of Garrett, and he knew I wasn't going to talk to him in private.

"As I said, we're heading out soon, but if you want, you can come over sometime. Maybe have dinner with us." I was surprised by my own words, but when Garrett reached out and threaded his fingers through mine, I wasn't so much anymore. Because even though I resented my dad, I knew what it was like to feel alone. I wasn't alone anymore, but I figured Dad was. Dad's was more his choice than mine, but now I had family because of the McRaes, and a super-hot boyfriend who was my ride or die, so I was willing to extend an olive branch. "We can start there." I hoped he understood what I was saying. I couldn't make promises, and I wasn't going to be his ATM, but if he wanted to, we could try.

"We'll see. I got a lot of shit going on."

Well, that was that, then. He knew the offer was there, and he'd take me up on it if he wanted.

He made it all the way to the door before I said, "And next time, text first. If I don't answer, wait until I do to come by."

Dad grunted out a reply and left.

The second he did, Garrett hugged me. "It was cool of you to invite him over. So totally blowing you again the second we get back home."

"Why do you think I said it?" I teased. We both knew I was lying, but I wasn't turning down some head either.

Coach finished up his discussion before tossing a glance my way. We were at the practice facility, in one of the rooms where we went over film. I gave him a simple nod. "Before we're done, Warner and Garrett have something to tell everyone. I want it to be known that they have the full support of the Rush organization."

A few people grumbled, the loudest of them being Nance, but most just gave us their attention. I figured they knew what was going down anyway, and honestly, I didn't think most of them would care. I stood up. "I'll make this short and sweet. I'm bisexual, in a relationship with Garrett, and—"

"Fuck that," Nance spit out. "There has to be some kind of rule against that. We can't have teammates going around fucking each other."

Coach cut in. "There isn't a rule, and we don't discriminate on this team."

"How can we guarantee Ramsey will be fair? He's our fucking quarterback. How do we know he won't set McRae up for more plays, try to help his little boyfriend get ahead?"

I rolled my eyes. "Do you hear yourself? Are you twelve? I'm out here to play ball and win. That's what I care about. Garrett doesn't need my help to outplay you anyway."

"Ooooh," Tucker said.

"Fuck you, Ramsey." Nance turned to Garrett. "And fuck you."

"Nah, I'm good. Ramsey is enough for me." Nance sputtered like he wasn't sure how to respond, and Garrett sighed. "Look, man. You're a homophobe. We all fucking get it. But, we're teammates. All I want to do is win football games. Do we really gotta do this all the time? Can't we just play football and leave our personal lives out of it?"

Well, shit. Look at G being all mature about it when I just wanted to punch Nance in his stupid, ugly face. We had a bit of a role reversal sometimes.

Nance ignored him and turned to Coach. "So this is it? We're just gonna have teammates fucking each other now? And the league doesn't have a problem with that?"

"Jesus Christ, man. Let it go," Tucker told him, and damn, did I appreciate my friend's support.

"Yeah, why the fuck do you care so much?" Cross chimed in next. "I want to win a motherfucking Super Bowl, and we can do that with McRae and Ramsey. Why does it matter if they bone?"

"This is the way it is," Coach said, his tone brooking no further argument. "Unless it turns out that the Rush organization is better off without one or both of them, Ramsey and McRae will stay on the team just like the rest of you. The only time you're not all equally safe is if you do something wrong or if a trade is the natural part of the game. Ramsey and McRae have already proven football comes first. I can't imagine it was easy for Ramsey to play after McRae's injury, but he did, and that's what I care about. Now, this conversation is done. If anyone has a problem, they can talk to me privately. Have a good off-season, guys, and get ready to get us a motherfucking ring next season."

Everyone except Nance and one or two other guys cheered. Nance grabbed his shit and walked out, slamming the door behind him. It sucked, but I wasn't surprised. I just hoped we could all find a way to play together next season.

Coach eyed Nance as he left, then turned to us. "I'll talk to him in private," he assured us, then lingered, arms crossed, as a few people came up to talk to us and offer their support.

And when G and I headed out, we headed out together and proud.

"You know we gotta win next season, right? Shut all the haters up?" Garrett asked.

"Fuck yeah. I'm not accepting any other possibility."

"If Ramsey wills it so, then it will be."

I looked at him and laughed. "What the fuck was that?"

"I don't know."

"Aww. My boyfriend is such a dork." I grabbed him right there in the middle of the practice facility parking lot, pulled him into a hug, and kissed him. If someone saw, well, I hoped they enjoyed the show. We were hot as fuck together.

"You like doing that—calling me your boyfriend."

"Eh, it's all right."

"Yeah, right. All I did was give you the look one time,

and then I threw out the line, reeled you in, and now you're in love with me. I'm even better than I thought."

"Wait...didn't you say you loved me for years or some shit?"

Garrett pushed me, and we laughed before hugging again. Goddamn, I was so happy. "I love you, G," I told him, mouth close to his ear.

"I love you too."

EPILOGUE
GARRETT

"Damn, that's a lot of meat," Houston said, then reached out and preemptively covered my mouth with one hand as he tossed the lighter onto the island, where Ramsey and I were in the midst of slathering sauce and seasonings onto trays of chicken, burgers, and ribs.

"I wasn't going to say anything."

Houston must have understood my garbled response well enough because he relented, starting to lower his hand only to smack it over my mouth again when I opened it.

Ramsey and I both cracked up, and I shoved Houston's hand away. "See, this is me not making a dumb meat joke."

Ramsey eyed me sidelong, a smile playing over his lips. "It's killing you, though, isn't it?" He glanced over at Houston. "It's killing him."

I pressed my lips firmly together and shook my head.

"It's definitely killing him." Houston chuckled. "Your face is turning red from how hard you're trying to hold back, G."

My cheeks did feel a little hot. "Nope." I poured some more barbecue sauce over my tray of chicken. "Just enjoying the simple domestic bliss of grilling for my friends." I picked up the tray and carried it out to the deck.

Outside, a balmy breeze rushed over the back of my neck, carrying a lush green scent mixed with the tang of the pond below.

Renovations had been completed two weeks before training camp, the dingy carpet gone, everything repainted in the muted hues I loved at Ramsey's place, new fixtures installed, the kitchen gutted and redone. But the deck was still my favorite spot, and I knew without a doubt I'd made the right decision. I'd been making a lot of those lately, and it felt good.

I set the tray down on the table beside the grill and glanced at Ramsey as he set another beside mine before holding out his phone. "Check it out. They got your good side."

I studied the images on the screen of me and Ramsey at Lake Havasu. It'd been the last trip we'd taken before camp started. "This is a close-up of your hand on my ass."

Ramsey grinned. "Like I said, your good side."

I flipped him off with a laugh and scrolled through the rest of the photos. There were a couple more of us on the boat we'd rented, then of other celeb couples on various vacations. "Huh. We're in pretty good company here."

Ramsey shrugged. "I can't help it that I'm such a badass QB."

"Yeah, but whose ass did they zoom in on?" I smirked and handed his phone back, then grabbed the tongs and threw some chicken on the grill.

"Because *my* hand is on it."

Laughter bubbled out of me, and I didn't bother to jab back because I loved how, over the past months, he'd gotten more relaxed about us being out together. We'd never made a formal announcement, but we'd been papped hot and heavy in a club one night, and the reporters had come running. The Rush's PR team had issued a statement of support, and the initial frenzy had died down after a couple of weeks. I imagined there'd be more to come once the season officially started, but I didn't think it would be anything we couldn't handle together.

Inside the house, I could hear some of the other guys arriving. Tucker's booming voice, Houston's laugh, Ellis bitching about something.

Ramsey nudged me as I closed the top on the grill. "What was the meat joke you were gonna make? I'll listen to it." He looked pointedly at the kielbasas. "It was gonna be a sausage joke, wasn't it?"

"I'll never tell." I motioned with my tongs at the tray. "But I'd definitely prefer my sausage stuffing your mouth than lying sideways on a plate."

He squeezed my side and brushed a quick kiss along my jaw. "I'll get to that later, promise. C'mon."

We headed inside and greeted everyone. After showing them around, we ended up back on the deck. I'd had a projector installed on the covered portion, and we hung out and ate and watched an NFL preseason special.

"Goddamn Whitt," Tucker groaned as the LA cornerback's face flashed on the screen. He had a nice smile, I'd give him that. "I don't get the obsession."

Cross laughed. "You're just saying that because he's faster than every one of us out here."

I swallowed a bite of burger. "He's not faster than me."

Houston sniffed. "He runs, like, a 50.45. You're what, 51?"

"50.73. Kiss my ass. It's all the muscle packed into my thighs that slows me down."

Ramsey put his mouth close to my ear. "Could be the meat in your pants."

I grinned, then barked out a, "Hey!" as something hit the screen in front of us and slid down, leaving an orange smear trekking down the side of Whitt's cheek.

Tucker cackled. "I fixed him."

"Your messy ass better wipe that down."

"Yeah, yeah." He stood, grabbed a napkin, and loped over to the screen, cleaning it off before plopping back down. "I just think he's overhyped, is all."

Ellis snorted. "You mean you think you should be up there instead."

"Centers get no love lately. And look at this smile." Tucker flashed a gleaming grin and clucked his tongue. "Way more pleasing to TV audiences."

"How did I never notice how cocky all you mother-fuckers are?" Houston thwapped Tucker.

It was true, though.

A couple of hours and cases of beer later, everyone headed out. Ramsey and I picked up the trash, gathered dishes, and reassembled the kitchen, which looked like a barbecue-sauce-loving tornado had blown through.

"How is there sauce on top of this cabinet door?" Ramsey groaned, rolling onto his toes to swipe at the smear.

"Cross threw a chicken wing at Ellis."

"Idiots."

"Yep."

We finished cleaning, got two bottles of water from the fridge, and went back to the deck, where we dropped into two loungers set alongside each other. I threw a leg over Ramsey's thigh as I cracked open my water.

"Just can't get enough of me, can you, G?"

"Nope." I didn't even try to deny it. Even months into our

relationship, we still went at it every chance we got, and now that we were in the open, we'd had endless adventures and dates. All the time together that we wanted, and it still never seemed like enough. I'd never been so into someone in my life.

Ramsey dropped a hand on my thigh and stroked it idly. "Same."

We sprawled in contented silence, listening to the *buzz* of crickets in the background, until Ramsey groaned and pulled out his phone. "My dad," he said, glancing at the screen. He fired off a quick text back, then set the phone facedown on the deck. "I told him I'm busy and I'll call him tomorrow."

"Think he wants money?"

"Who knows? Probably." Ramsey's relationship with his dad was a work in progress. He'd come to Ramsey's place for dinner with us exactly once and, as Ramsey had predicted, it was awkward as hell, but we both noticed his dad was less aggressive. And Ramsey had gotten a month's reprieve before he asked for money again. "The intervals are stretching out, at least."

"I know he's probably never gonna be the dad you deserve. I'm glad you have us as your...surrogate family? Something like that." My parents had always welcomed him with open arms, but now that we were together, my mom seemed to have taken that as license to dote on him like her own son, constantly haranguing him until Houston and I would crack up and tell her to lay off. He loved it, though, found comfort in it, I could tell.

Ramsey laughed softly. "Yeah, they're great, thank fuck."

"You realize we can't ever break up, right?" I mused a few seconds later, considering Ramsey's dad, as well as how we'd both been working on anticipating potential media frenzies.

"What? Have you been thinking about us breaking up?" Ramsey's brows shot up as he jerked his head toward me, and I laughed.

"No. Jesus. Not like that. I mean, imagine the media meltdown it would create."

Ramsey rolled his eyes with a laugh, and I caught his hand in mine, threading our fingers.

"I also meant, I've been thinking about us and how much time we spend together, and..." God, the words were suddenly thick on my tongue, but I took a deep breath and pressed forward. "What do you think about moving in here?" I'd stayed at Ramsey's place during the renovations, but we'd both known that was temporary. This was different. This was permanent.

The momentary pause before he spoke was unnerving. "Put my house on the market and move in, huh?"

"Yup. You've been around for all the renovations. We've spent a lot of time here. I dunno, kinda already feels like you're a part of it."

He cast a glance out over the deck and the pond, a smile spreading slowly over his face. "I know I usually harp on you and your bad ideas, but I think this one's right on point."

"Is that a yes?"

Ramsey stood and extended a hand, then yanked me up and pulled me close, his lips brushing mine. "It's a hell yes."

I caught him by the chin, drawing out the kiss for a few seconds longer. "Good. Where are we going now? Celebratory jump in the pond?"

"Fuck no. I'm gonna take you inside and turn you inside out."

I was already hard, but that heated promise sent electricity snapping up my spine. "Way better idea."

Ramsey laughed as I pulled him toward the door, my body already on fire at what the next few hours held for us, along with the softer comfort of knowing I'd wake up next to him tomorrow. And all the tomorrows after that.

—END—

MORE BY NEVE WILDER

Rhythm of Love Series

(Contemporary Romance, audiobooks available)

Dedicated

Bend (Novella)

Resonance

Extracurricular Activities Series

(new adult/college, audiobooks available)

Want Me

Try Me

Show Me

Nook Island Series

(Contemporary Romance)

Center of Gravity

Sightlines (Novella)

Ace's Wild Series

(multi author series)

Reunion (Novella)

Wages of Sin Series

(Romantic action adventure and suspense, co-written with Only
James, audiobooks available)

Bad Habits

Play Dirty

Head Games

MORE BY RILEY HART

Series by Riley Hart

Secrets Kept

Briar County

Atlanta Lightning

Blackcreek

Boys In Makeup with Christina Lee

Broken Pieces

Crossroads

Fever Falls with Devon McCormack

Finding

Forbidden Love with Christina Lee

Havenwood

Jared and Kieran

Last Chance

Metropolis with Devon McCormack

Rock Solid Construction

Saint and Lucky

Stumbling Into Love

Wild side

Standalone books:

Strings Attached

Beautiful & Terrible Things

Love Always

ABOUT RILEY HART

Riley Hart is the girl who wears her heart on her sleeve. Although she primarily focuses on male/male romance, under her various pen names, she's written a little bit of everything. Regardless of the sub-genre, there's always one common theme and that's...romance! No surprise seeing as she's a hopeless romantic herself. Riley's a lover of character-driven plots, flawed characters, and always tries to write stories and characters people can relate to. She believes everyone deserves to see themselves in the books they read. When she's not writing, you'll find her reading, traveling or dreaming about traveling. She has two perfectly sarcastic kids and a husband who still makes her swoon.

Riley Hart is represented by Jane Dystel at Dystel, Goderich & Bourret Literary Management. She's a 2019 Lambda Literary Award Finalist for *Of Sunlight and Stardust*. Under her pen name, her young adult novel, *The History of Us* is an ALA Rainbow Booklist Recommended Read and *Turn the World Upside Down* is a Florida Authors and Publishers President's Book Award Winner.

ABOUT NEVE WILDER

Neve Wilder lives in the South, where the summers are hot and the winters are...sometimes cold.

She reads promiscuously, across multiple genres, but her favorite stories always contain an element of romance. Incidentally, this is also what she likes to write. Slow-burners with delicious tension? Yes. Whiplash-inducing page-turners, also yes. Down and dirty scorchers? Yes. And every flavor in between.

She believes David Bowie was the sexiest musician to ever live, and she's always game to nerd out on anything from music to writing.

And finally, she believes that love conquers all. Except the heat index in July. Nothing can conquer that bastard.

Join her for daily shenanigans in her FB group:
Wilder's Wild Ones

facebook.com/nevewilderwrites

instagram.com/nevewilder

bookbub.com/authors/neve-wilder

amazon.com/author/nevewilder